Lucky Penny

Lucky Penny

Courter P. Donnelly

Peoh Point Press
Seattle, WA

Peoh Point Press
Seattle, WA 98109

Print and electronic versions of *Lucky Penny* by Courter P.
Donnelly are available at amazon.com

Cover design by Greg Hollobaugh

ISBN: 9781796682311

For the Washington Trails Association volunteers and other trail maintenance crews who do the tricky work of keeping the wilderness both wild and accessible.

PROLOGUE

August 27

It doesn't matter what he wants, it matters what I want. And what I want is more than a ride in his exclusive sports car— "exclusive," that's what he called it—because I'm not the kind who just goes along for a ride. I'm the kind who drives. Not that he knows it. Yet.

"Well, Joshua," he says when I show up from the station on my crap bike. "You decided to come after all." Big white teeth. Posh aftershave. Jeans that cost a month's rent; two months if a person isn't choosy about the neighborhood, which I'm not.

"Yeah, hi," I say, cool not cold. "Not easy getting by your security dickhead there at the gate, but here I am." I give him just a trace of a smile for encouragement. "Thought I'd see if this car of yours really does exist."

"You know she's real," he says, boastful like always. "Just arrived from the factory a day ago." He sweeps his arm in the direction of the sports car sitting in his swank courtyard, all "tada, here it is," right? He's going on about how he had to wire the charge station himself. A technical wizard, he is. But he's nervous, which is good for me, and the car's low to the ground and curvy, which they all are. Flaming red, of course, because he's got no imagination. Still, it's a pretty thing and I decide I would like to have it.

"Is it ready now?" I say. I walk past him close enough to brush against his thighs and belly and slow enough to give him a good look at my ass. I bend over just a little and lean my bike on one of the metal posts at the top of the parking pad.

"You know she's ready," he says, stepping over the thick red power cord plugged into the car's grill and squeezing past me to the passenger's side. The door opens with a quiet electronic click. "Get in. You'll be on the maiden voyage, lucky boy."

I turn slowly, smile slowly. "I'll drive," I say.

He's surprised, of course. I keep one hand on my bike's handlebars, like I might just get on and ride away. I can see he doesn't want to lose me.

"Well, Joshua," he says again, "it's just that it's the first time."

"First time's worth something, right?"

He looks at me hard, not entirely friendly. Puts me off a bit, but I keep my eyes steady on his and my half-smile on my lips. We stand that way for what seems like a lifetime, and I can see him decide.

"I suppose you're right about that," he finally says. "I suppose you only have one first time." He nudges the door and it closes with a solid thump. Then he walks around the front of the car to the driver's side, and that door opens all on its own without his even touching it. He leans in, puts something on the console between the seats. "You're old enough to have a valid license, correct?"

"You know how old I am." I give him a full smile this time. I'm not quite 17 and unlicensed, but that isn't my concern, right? I let go of the bike. Walk forward slow, bend low, and get behind the wheel of the car. He closes the door, smiles at me from outside the open window. I stare at the controls.

"How do I start it?"

"Push the button," he says.

* * * * *

Massive Blast Rattles Queen's China

Teen dies when exotic sports car explodes at tech titan's London penthouse

Screams "loud at first," says witness, but "got quiet fast"

by Nigel Turner
Informant Staff

London: A 16-year-old boy was killed last night when the experimental sports car in which he was sitting exploded, causing a massive fireball to roar through the courtyard in front of billionaire businessman Winston Drummond's London penthouse.

Drummond, who apparently was standing near the car at the time of the explosion, is hospitalized with burns and abrasions described as non-life threatening. No others were injured in the early evening blast that blew out neighbouring windows and rattled the Queen's china in nearby Buckingham Palace. No damage to the palace has been reported.

The dead boy was identified as Joshua Fielding, the son of Harry Fielding and Nanette Jones Fielding, a married couple employed on Drummond's Cotswold country estate. The boy was apparently sitting in the driver's seat of the car, a prototype vehicle not yet available to the public. The cause of the explosion is under investigation.

Passersby said they saw the car in flames and Drummond unconscious on the ground about 50 feet away, presumably blown clear of the vehicle while the boy remained trapped inside.

"There was a massive blast, like a bomb going off, and then I could hear him screaming," said Benjamin Brantley, 23, who was passing the front gate of the St. James's district mansion when the car blew up. "It was loud at first, but it got quiet fast. There was a terrible smell, like burnt plastic."

In an exclusive interview with the *Informant*, Joshua Fielding's grieving parents declined to explain their young son's presence at Drummond's home in Shakleton House Terrace. Drummond, founder and CEO of Rational EvoAg, a biotech company that develops seeds and farm animals using genetic modification, purchased the mansion's penthouse last year for a record £35 million.

The wealthy gene tweaker has been a frequent presence on the London social scene. In recent months, he has been inseparable from Emma Turnstone, leggy daughter of American billionaire investor Curtis Turnstone.

"Sweet Emma," as her friends call her, has her own explosive background. The statuesque blonde enrolled at London University last spring after prosecutors declined to bring charges against her in the botched bombing of a research facility in her hometown of Seattle, Washington. Two members of a

terrorist animal rights group calling itself
the FreeThinkers remain in custody in the
United States as they await appeal of
convictions in the bombing.

Since Turnstone's appearance in the city,
London society has openly wondered which
excites stronger passions in the tall, cool
blonde: gene tweaker Drummond or the animals
he experiments upon?

Sweet Emma was unavailable for comment.
London University registrars confirmed that
she has withdrawn from the institution. She is
believed to be on her way to the western
United States.

Stick with the *Informant Online* for on-the-
spot updates.

–end

My editor turned away from the words on her screen, a frown
puckering her youthful forehead. "Is she really known as Sweet
Emma, Nigel?"

I shoved the travel voucher under her nose and waited for her
signature. "She is now."

Chapter 1

MARY BETH DRAKE

September 29

"It's worse than substandard," said the man walking behind me. "I don't know what to call it. Maybe 'appalling?'"

"Ghastly?" I tried. "Abysmal?"

"Inferior," he said with grim satisfaction.

With that, we settled back into silence, one boot in front of the other down the trail after another long day of site visits. But if I knew my husband Nathan, the subject of the truly inferior outhouse we'd just seen wasn't closed. I heard his footsteps behind me quicken.

"The worst part," he fumed, "is the placement." I knew without looking at him that the vertical crease between his green eyes was deepening and he'd stopped to remove his baseball cap so he could vigorously rub his head. I leaned into a chunk of granite to get the weight of my backpack off my hips while I waited for him to work through his dismay.

It was true that time had not been kind to the toilet. The step to the wooden box that served as its pedestal was reduced to broken slats and the lid on top was missing, exposing its contents. There was evidence of animal visitations and the whole apparatus listed drunkenly downhill. The only thing that saved a visit to the Peggy's Pond privy from being a thoroughly disheartening experience was the view. If you managed to balance on it just right, you got a face full of Mt. Daniel, snow-covered, glistening, and so close it seemed you could reach out and touch its icy contours while you did your business.

"I mean, let me ask you, Beth," Nathan said, although 22 years of marriage had taught me he wasn't looking for an answer, "why would they put a toilet so close to the pond? God knows what it's doing to the bacteria count."

I mumbled "hell if I know" and resumed walking. It was late in the season and I was tired of toilets and trails. The ground was so dry now that the few remaining huckleberries had wizened to raisins on their stems, and the sun was playing peekaboo with the clouds, burning through every so often with the last-gasp ferocity of September in the Pacific Northwest. I was hot, then cold, then broiling again, although that just might have been oncoming hot flashes.

We rounded another switchback and looking down the zig-zagging trail below us I saw the top of a huge orange backpack. A blonde head bobbed beneath it. "Great," I said under my breath. "Just what we need. Another HiWI." Nathan and I had come up with the term on our last maintenance trip. It's short for "Hikers with Issues" and describes a certain subset of Pacific Crest Trail "thru-hikers," those deranged individuals who attempt to complete the entire 2,600-mile hike from Mexico to Canada in one season. Unlike other thru-hikers, though, HiWIs aren't out to see the country, or take on a physical challenge, or even become one with nature. HiWIs are out to fix whatever's wrong within their own heads.

This one, I saw as she inched closer, was a long-legged girl, maybe a couple of years younger than our niece Lacey, which would put her somewhere around 20, maybe 23. Her fair hair was plaited in two fat braids that stuck to her flushed cheeks. An old-fashioned key on a silver chain bumped rhythmically against her chest with a persistence that would have driven me crazy within the first mile of walking, and she wore an odd combination of tight, thigh-high yoga shorts and a dirty goose down jacket that looked remarkably like the one I'd favored at her age 25 years ago. In fact, all her gear looked like the stuff I had well back in the last century: the bulky synthetic sleeping bag, the clanging tin cup hanging from the ancient pack frame, even a Frisbee flying disc tucked into the pack's back pocket. But the most notable thing about her was the sling that held her left arm close against her chest. It was bloody.

I moved to the uphill side of the trail to let her pass. When she was nearly on top of my toes, I let loose with a cheery, "Hello there!" The girl's head snapped up, her blue eyes went wide, and her mouth formed a perfect "O," all of which made me wonder just what she saw when she looked at me. Woman of her mother's era, just the other side of slender, uncommonly sweaty, with a bad case of hat hair? Muddy knees, I reminded myself uneasily. Pockets stuffed with granola bar wrappers and a dirty handkerchief. A nasty rip in the right shirtsleeve held together with duct tape, the skin beneath scraped off by a privy hinge. If she sniffed at me, I knew the girl would detect a smell, and it wouldn't be a pleasant one. I clamped my arms to my sides just as the girl's foot met with a tree root in the trail. She stumbled, and for a moment I feared she'd end up squashed beneath her clanking heap of gear. That's when I noticed the skinny, copper-colored puppy trailing behind her.

"I'm sorry," I said. "I didn't mean to scare you." That, I admit, wasn't entirely true.

When she recovered her balance, she glanced at my face and then stared intently at Nathan, who'd stopped a few feet up the trail from us. "No, that's OK," she said slowly. "I think it's my bad. I mean, because I didn't see you."

Having no kids myself, I'm not the most maternal of women, but something about the girl invited sympathy, even from me. Maybe it was the puppy. Maybe it was the bloody sling.

"You didn't do anything wrong," I said with a gentleness that surprised me. "It's hard to see people above you when you're concentrating on walking uphill, especially if you've got the brim of a hat in your way. That's why downhill hikers should always yield to uphill traffic." It was a pet peeve of mine that they didn't, and, as Nathan often pointed out to me, I never missed a chance to educate the next generation on the matter.

The girl looked at me as if astounded to find I still stood in front of her. "I'm Beth Drake," I told her. "That's my husband Nathan up there."

"Where are you and your little friend headed?" Nathan called, gesturing with his hiking pole in the direction of the puppy, who was nosing around the girl's uninjured hand, maybe looking for a treat. "That's a sweet little dog you've got, but she looks about done for the day. Is she a Viszla?"

The girl looked down at the puppy and frowned. "Yeah, she is." For a moment, we all stared silently at the puppy, who flopped in the dust of the trail. The dog's long pink tongue dangled from her mouth, and I wondered if the girl carried a water bowl for her pet. If she did, she made no move to retrieve it. Nathan broke the silence.

"So, where to tonight for you guys?"

The girl gazed back at him, then dropped her eyes to the dog again. "Up this trail to the Pacific Crest junction," she said, gesturing vaguely with her good arm. We waited, but it seemed she was finished talking.

I'm usually not one to intervene, no matter what Nathan will tell you. He says I'm too quick to jump in when it's not clear that I'm wanted, but I say how do you know if you're not wanted before you jump in? I took a breath and let it out slowly. "So, we're headed out today," I said. "We've got some extra food that's just weighing down our packs for no good reason." I looked up into her blank blue eyes. "What I mean is, do you need anything?" She didn't answer, so I kept going. "Any help with your injured arm? Or with your puppy? We have some extra water too, and Nathan there carries the most complete first aid kit you've ever seen. He could probably amputate if necessary."

I was surprised to see tears start in her eyes. This one truly did have issues. "I was just kidding about amputating," I mumbled as the dog whined in sympathy. The girl nodded, shaking loose a few tears from her thick lashes. They made sad little tracks down her dusty cheeks. As I so often do, I regretted my attempt at humor.

"Look, let's all just take a minute and see what we can do about …" I searched for the right word. "Things." It annoyed me that was the best I could come up with, but I shook it off and called up to Nathan, "Hon, can you bring the first aid kit and grab a few energy bars?"

"No, it's OK," the girl said, although she didn't move. "I have to get going." The dog whimpered again at the sound of her voice and, in a tangle of puppy paws and floppy ears, began to rise from the dust. The girl suddenly turned and went to her knees next to the exhausted animal. "Oh, Penny," she wailed, gathering the dog in her arms. "I shouldn't have brought you. None of this is your fault."

At this, Nathan seemed to make a decision in favor of action. He chucked his pack and moved down the trail to join us, dodging around me to get to the girl's side. Once there, he began flapping his hands about her pack uncertainly. He looked at me as if for guidance. I shrugged. Who knows if it's OK to touch a Millennial's backpack without permission? Not me.

"So," Nathan finally said, "OK if I help you get this thing off?" The girl slipped out of the shoulder straps before Nathan got his grip right, and with a faint grunt he stumbled into me.

"Ow," I said.

"Sorry, Beth," he tossed over his shoulder before continuing to address the girl in an affable manner that struck me as a marked contrast to the complaints he'd been directing my way not five minutes earlier. "Now, *that*," he marveled, "*that* is quite a load. Better with it off, I bet?" The girl nodded and placed the dog on the trail in front of her. "Now," Nathan continued, "what was your name again?"

"Mm," the girl hummed, as if the answer required thought. "Bella."

"All right, Bella," Nathan said happily. He handed her an energy bar and she gobbled it while we tried not to stare. It seemed as if we were going to be stuck with the girl for a while, so I took off my pack too and fished out one of the heavy-duty plastic canisters we store our food in, the better to keep the bears out. I began searching it for our extra cashews and the plastic bowl we use to stir up powdered hummus mix at lunchtime. Once I found the cashews I stuffed them into the side pocket of the girl's pack.

The girl accepted another energy bar from Nathan and broke off a piece for the dog, who ate it with gusto. I filled our bowl with water and set it down in front of the puppy. She was a pretty little thing with a short, reddish-gold coat and expressive golden eyes. Her oversized ears hung forward, framing her face and giving her a quizzical look. She gazed up at me and wrinkled her forehead, as if considering whether I was trustworthy. Against my better judgment, I smiled, and when I did, the puppy put her nose to the bowl and lapped up the water. I filled the bowl again.

"We're just coming down from the Pacific Crest Trail at Peggy's Pond," Nathan said. "Are you going up there?" The girl shrugged, red-rimmed eyes on her running shoes. "Well, if you do," he began, "just wait till you see the latrine."

"Are you hiking the Pacific Crest Trail, Bella?" I interrupted, heading Nathan away from the subject of sanitation. For a basically quiet guy, he can get a little too enthusiastic on the topic of backcountry toilets, which, after all, are the focus of his work. I'm used to his passion for poop, but most people? It freaks them out. I handed the girl my extra bandana, the one with Smokey Bear on it, and she wiped her face.

"Yeah, I'm going up to the Pacific Crest Trail," she said as she accepted a third energy bar, this one heavy on nuts and seeds. Chia hulls. Quinoa grit. No wonder the toilets were taking a hard hit this season. "At least," the girl said, "I was going to hike the PCT. It's pretty hard."

"It is that," said Nathan as he methodically dug through his enormous first aid kit. "But you don't have to hike the whole thing, right? I mean, you probably know that already since you're starting in an unusual spot." His voice trailed off to a murmur, as if he were talking to himself. "Starting in the middle part of Section J. If you were a thru-hiker, this time of year you'd probably be somewhere north of us."

She looked up at him, her eyes wide and dry once more. "Look," she said, "you guys have been great, but I really have to get moving."

"I didn't mean you have to rush," Nathan said as he located his tube of antibacterial cream. "You've got plenty of light left and you're almost to the PCT junction." He smiled at the tube, set it aside, and resumed excavation. "I'm just trying to find the right-sized bandage, here." He located a small bundle swaddled in a zipper-lock plastic bag and double-secured with a rubber band. "We don't want butterflies," he murmured, rejecting the packet. "Not a deep gash, is it?" He didn't seem to notice that the girl didn't answer. "And not gauze. Gauze would probably work, but it gets dirty fast."

"Oh, for crying out loud, Nathan," I said. "We're not at the Mayo Clinic here." I advanced on him, grabbed the kit, and tore through it until I found a tidy pack of fabric adhesive strips. I handed them to my husband. "Use these and that gauze."

Nathan accepted the bandages in dignified silence and reached toward the girl's injured arm. "If you want to stop soon," he told her, "we know a great little campsite off the trail, not more than two miles from here." He motioned for Bella to remove her sling, but she remained still. "Once you get to the PCT, go north for about a half mile, and at a sharp switchback near the creek, look for a little stack of dark rocks on the left side of the trail. When you see that, you'll notice a faint trail-of-use. It takes you about a quarter of a mile uphill to a sweet flat spot tucked in the boulders right underneath the Mt. Daniel glacier. There's good water there."

The girl listened carefully but made no move to offer her bloody arm for Nathan's doctoring. "OK, that sounds good," she said. "But I've got to go, like right now, OK?"

"At least stay and let Nathan take a look at your arm," I said. "He knows something about public health—mostly water quality, but still. Better than nothing."

"Nope, I've got to go now." She looked at each of us in turn. "Listen, though. I do need a favor. Or two favors." Nathan and I silently exchanged glances.

"Please," she said, "don't tell anyone you saw me."

"What?" we asked in unison.

"I wouldn't ask if it wasn't really important." She put her hand on Nathan's, the one that held the antibacterial cream, and squeezed. "Promise you won't tell anyone about me. They'll kill me if you tell."

Kill? I'd usually assume this was just a young woman's hyperbole, but in this case, I wasn't so sure. I began to hum very quietly, a nervous habit I have when I'm warming up to ask a few questions, but Bella had her blue eyes on Nathan and he answered her for both of us.

"Well, all right. If it's a matter of life and death, we won't tell a soul. But you should at least take this antibacterial cream. Use it twice daily." He glanced at me. "And the bandages. Take whichever ones you like."

The girl nodded and pocketed the cream and the bandages. "And the other thing is," she paused, and this time she addressed me, "will you take Penny with you? My puppy?"

"Your puppy?" I asked. "You want us to take your puppy?"

"She's not mine," the girl said. "I just found her." She took the briefest of pauses. "This morning," she resumed. "Lost. In the trailhead parking lot. Look at her, poor little fuzzball. She can't make this trip. She can't even make it up to the trail junction."

"But, if you don't mind my asking, why bring her up the trail at all?"

"I couldn't just leave her in the parking lot, could I? Someone's got to take her, and you're headed out to the trailhead, right? You like her, right? You gave her water and everything."

"Right," I said uncertainly.

"Look, just take her. Say you found her in the parking lot. In fact, why don't you keep her?"

"I don't know about keeping her." I looked over at Nathan, who was offering the puppy a piece of lint-covered jerky he'd fished from his pocket. "But we'll take her out for you. We'll try to find her owners."

"No. Don't try to find her owners. They're bad people. I mean, they've got to be bad people if they dumped her in a wilderness parking lot, right?" The girl must have noticed the dubious look on my face because she took a long, ragged breath and added, "Well, OK. But she's a really good puppy. She doesn't deserve to be stuck with the guys who lost her." She picked up the dog and snuggled it against her chest, and her voice went high and babyish, the way people's do when they talk to animals.

"They don't deserve you, Penny. You're such a good dog. Yes, you are. Little good luck charm. Yes, you are." She put her tear-streaked cheek against the top of the dog's furry head. "You go with these nice people. They'll take care of you." She set the puppy down at my feet, turned, and took the Frisbee out of her pack. "This is Penny's." She offered me the disc, along with my bandana, now moist with snot and tears.

"Keep it," I said.

"That's so nice. I love Smokey the Bear." She stuffed the bandana in her coat pocket, struggled into her pack, and began moving up the trail. The dog barked and started to follow, but I held her fast by the collar looped around her neck. "Bye-bye, Penny," the girl called raggedly over her shoulder. I couldn't see her face, but I heard mucus-muffled sniffles and assumed she was crying again. "Be a good dog."

Chapter 2

NATHAN DRAKE

September 29

She was a very pretty young woman, and I couldn't believe how nice Beth was being. I love my wife, but she does have some pet peeves. One is people who get their spelling and grammar and basic cultural facts wrong. I think that comes from having been a newspaper reporter for so many years. Another peeve? Hikers with Issues. Like Bella.

"It's Smokey Bear," Beth corrected once the girl was out of sight. "Not Smokey *the* Bear."

"I guess so," I answered, but my mind was on the girl and her chances of making the Canadian border before the first snows. For thru-hiking HiWIs, the Pacific Crest Trail is no pleasant walk in the woods. It's a test of self. You can see it in their eyes, boring into you as they stride by in the middle of another 25-mile day. Or maybe that intense stare just means they're starving. Or high. Hard to say. Not many stop to talk.

The girl didn't quite fit the classic HiWI mold. Yes, she was the hot demographic on the trail these days: the solo female spurred on by a bestseller from a screwed-up hiker who didn't even have to complete the entire trip before she turned her life around. And Bella certainly had issues. But something was off. Wrong gear. Wrong place. Unfocused. That's probably why Beth, usually not one to converse at length with HiWIs, had quickly become protective of this one. Of course, there was also her injury. And the dog.

Before we met Bella and the dog, we'd been trucking along, talking about the inferior latrine we'd just checked out on behalf of my nonprofit, the Drake Water Quality Project, also known as "High Country Crapper." That's what the thru-hikers call us, despite my best efforts. At any rate, we were just beginning to think about getting back to town for a beer and a burger, but now we were stuck. You can't just walk away from a lost puppy.

"Somebody's looking for a nice dog like this," I told Beth. "Chances are they'll come by."

We both looked down at the dog; she aimed a look at me, then Beth. She was one of those dogs who makes serious eye contact. Probably smart. A little bit skittish. We regarded each other for a long moment, then we all looked off into the trailside thicket of Douglas firs.

By the time a quintet of 30-something male backpackers marched noisily up the trail, Penny had displaced most of my thoughts of bad toilets and good food. I was still anxious about our sudden forced adoption, but I must've already been feeling a connection because when the hiker with the bushiest beard reported that they hadn't seen anybody searching for a lost dog, I was secretly glad. Maybe Bella had a point: What kind of owner would lose a puppy up here?

The group lingered just long enough to register concern and cast cursory glances into the woods, but we all knew the score. They were just starting their hike and we were going out. Etiquette dictated that we take responsibility for the lost dog.

* * * * *

That's how, two hours later, I found myself on a lightly used fisherman's trail, pushing aside willow and chokecherry branches and trying to get closer to what sounded like a whole bunch of barking dogs.

Beth and Penny were back at the car. We'd hung around the trailhead parking lot for a half hour, but none of the dozen or so hikers coming or going knew anything about a lost dog. Penny seemed to find comfort in standing alertly in the back of our Subaru. So, I left the two girls in the parking lot and walked down the dirt road to the tree-darkened campground that stretched alongside the La Likt River.

I was a man with a purpose, or at least a man with a good excuse to walk up to campers and start asking questions. I did the whole campground loop, knocking on flimsy trailer doors and yelling enthusiastic "hellos" at zippered tent flaps. For a moment I thought I caused simultaneous cardiac arrests in one senior couple scrunched low in folding chairs with their paperback thrillers. I rousted the camp host from his nap. I checked the bulletin board. I flagged down the guy in the sagging Ford Ranger who had the toilet cleaning concession. No lost dog.

It's only when I crossed the one-lane bridge to the other side of the river that I heard the yips and yaps. The noises got louder as I made my way through dense brush away from the swish of the main river channel. I began creeping up a small drainage—Fortune Creek, if I remembered correctly—and in a clearing ahead the yipping finally synced up to an image. A copper-colored puppy that looked a lot like Penny barked excitedly and chased a stick into—this surprised me—a large pond. The stick had no doubt just been thrown by the skinny guy in jeans, dark blue T-shirt, and black baseball hat who now stomped to the pond's shore.

Was this guy Penny's owner? I began mentally rehearsing how I'd step forward and ask if anyone had lost a dog. But I stayed put. I guess another wrinkle of my cortex was already assessing this guy's worthiness for dog ownership.

Over by the pond, the dog climbed out of the water, dropped the stick, and licked furiously at its right haunch. Hat Guy grabbed the dog by the collar and yelled, "Hey, hey, hey! What'd I tell you?" He swatted at the dog's nose with his palm and it broke free of his grasp, ran along the shoreline, and started rolling crazily in the grass.

Hat Guy straightened up slowly and looked at the dog. He wiped his hands on his jeans. It was quiet, just a background buzz of insects. I could see the gauzy specks of blue darner dragonflies patrolling horizontally along the edge of the pond. Hat Guy turned and looked in my direction. I reflexively hunkered down as he reared his head back, cupped his hands around his mouth, and bellowed, "TOMMY!" He waited a second, then issued a three-syllable variation: "TOMMM—MMEEEE—EEEEE."

A pause. Then, erupting from the brush just to my left, making my heart jump like a flushed grouse, came the booming response, "YO! What?"

After some thrashing, a heavy figure wearing canvas Carhartt shorts and a long-sleeve T-shirt in camo print—Tommy, I figured—broke out of the willows and stood with his back to me, just a few yards in front of my hiding spot. He was one of those stubby guys with massive calves and a splotchy tattoo on each, just to direct your gaze there in case you'd missed all that meat. His head, covered in a thick tangle of hair, looked pretty massive too. Hat Guy was moving toward Tommy and me. At half-volume, he said, "Dude, come on back. You're not gonna find her."

"Hey, she's worth seven-fifty," said Tommy. "Maybe a thousand in Seattle."

"I know that, man. She'll come back like the others."

"Maybe I should go up to the campground."

"She knows where the food is."

"C'mon Cody. Maybe she'll get ate by a cougar," Tommy said impatiently. "Maybe something like that."

They moved away from me to the far corner of the pond and went silent, looking out over the murky water. Hands in pockets, side-by-side. They were different sizes—one skinny, the other stocky—but something about their pose and their comfort with silence told me they could be brothers. Thin and thick versions. Two hands dealt from the same grimy deck.

Again, it went all quiet and buzzy. And again, I took a breath and prepared myself to step forward and pronounce the good news about their lost pup. But I didn't move.

They turned their heads in unison to the dog, still on the pond's edge, but now yelping and struggling to stand. The dog's back legs weren't working at all, just dragging through the grass. The poor pup stopped in an awkward sideways pose on its flank, then flopped heavily to the ground, exhausted, panting.

The brothers walked to the dog—definitely brothers, that odd identical arm swinging—and Tommy gently scooped up the dog and carried it as they disappeared through a cluster of trees. A minute later, I followed.

The men walked toward a cottage that squatted in the shade of mature pines and firs. The wood siding and trim of the cottage were painted a shade of Mistake Blue, a color that once no doubt aspired to subtle spruce but in execution has gone hideously awry into the turquoise range. The vivid cottage was surrounded by broken-down cars and snowmobiles, old tailgates and spent batteries—the classic display of transportation-based hoarding that signifies rural homeownership in upper Sahaptin County.

An army-green Jeep Wrangler was parked by the front door. Next to it, in a carport with a high aluminum roof sat an impressively large black motorhome. I saw the model name stenciled in script above the rear window: "Intruder." Beth would get a kick out of that. An orange dirt bike with hard-shell saddlebags was gripped in a rack mounted above the RV's back bumper.

Across the wide gravel drive sat an older, barn-like structure. As I moved in to get a better view, I heard dogs yelping, whining, and occasionally giving up a high-pitched yip. Through the open door, I saw Hat Guy—Cody, his brother had called him—struggling to outfit a dog with one of those plastic cones-of-shame that prevent scratching and nipping. Angling in closer, I saw a row of ten or more small metal cages filled with

Hungarian Viszlas of different sizes. There may have been more on the other side of the barn. About half of the dogs wore cones. This would be the time, I thought again, to call out something like "Hey, anyone here?" But the impulse was now even weaker than before. I just stood there thinking that, even on such a warm afternoon, it was probably awfully cold inside that barn. I was also thinking about how the dog had collapsed by the pond.

That's when I saw a different kind of dog charging out of the barn. My first thought: pit bull. I had just enough time to brace for the speeding ball of muscle before the dog's bony head lunged for my throat. Instinctively, I raised my knee and blocked the dog so that it fell back, snarling and rearing on its haunches, ready for another thrust.

"Monty, no!"

The dog froze in its crouch, mottled white skin shivering with excitement. Up close it looked like a mixed breed. Maybe Rottweiler and pit bull. Or who knows, maybe some boxer or schnauzer too. I'm no dog expert. All I knew is it looked like something bred to bite. Snarling, it slunk around me toward the voice. I pivoted slowly to follow the bigheaded dog and came face-to-face with the bigheaded brother, Tommy. Crooked teeth, wild hair, a patchwork beard covering chin and cheeks afflicted with some sort of rash. His eyes, lava black, latched onto mine. The crazy stare intensified as he screwed his big head in close. I remember sneaking a look at the incoming forehead to check for a little tattoo swastika, like the one Charles Manson wore. I felt silly for thinking this. Then I looked down and saw the heavy black pistol in his right hand.

"What're you doing here?" he hissed. "Where you from?"

"I just came down from the trailhead," I heard myself say. The dog began growling in earnest. Its skull was wider than it was long, if that was even possible. I kept an eye on it as I continued. "We just finished a backpack trip, my wife and I, and I was looking for a place to wash off. That's when I saw your pond. I was just curious. I'm in water quality and I . . . ."

"Oh, is that right?" he interrupted in a disgusted tone, his black eyes once again boring in on mine. He waved the gun low and slow, like he was peeing at my feet. "So, where are you really from?"

"I have a place in La Likt."

"Well, I'm from right here," he snarled, stepping even closer. "My grandfather built this place and we still own 480 acres up this creek. Lease it for cattle grazing, not that it's any of your business. I live right here, so I want to know: what are you really doing here? On my private property."

"I'm just," I began to back away from the man and the dog. Apparently my hands were up in the air, so I started to bring them down as I turned toward the pond. "I'm just going to go back to my car and . . ."

"You ain't going nowhere."

A sharp blow to the back of my head sent me stumbling forward. My hat fell to the ground, and I waited, stooped over, for the blow to translate into a level of pain. These things can go either way. This particular head crack was not, it turned out, too bad. I was, after all, still standing. The pain registered more like a standard head-wham on the corner of the poorly designed Subaru rear hatch door. In short, it hurt like hell, but no trip to the ER required.

I guess Tommy and I were both surprised that I hadn't crumpled to the ground like in the movies when a guy gets cold-cocked. I turned to him, still slightly bent over, palming my head. We eyed each other. He looked a bit sheepish and then grinned crookedly. Either he was covering his embarrassment at the failed takedown or this was the Merry Prankster side of Manson now twinkling in Tommy's black eyes.

As I reached down for my hat, the dog took the opportunity to again spring for my face. I managed a quick half-turn to protect my throat, but the slobbering beast gashed my right arm.

"Monty, down! Down! No!"

The dog dropped to the ground, eyes once more downcast. Beyond Tommy, I could see that brother Cody was running from the barn, two Vizslas prancing wildly at his heels. When he reached us, Cody tried to snap a chain to the big dog's collar as he turned to his brother.

"What the hell, Tommy?" And then to me, "Who the hell are you?"

Before I could answer, the big dog broke free and lunged at the smaller of the copper pups. In a moment, the pit—or whatever the hell it was—had the Viszla pinned in the gravel, trying to set its teeth into the poor pup's neck as the Viszla's eyes went wide with terror. The second Viszla tore off toward the pond.

"No!" said Cody, kicking the dog in the ribs and yanking him off the puppy. "Damn it!" The big dog dropped heavily to the gravel, panting, eyes never leaving its victim, who lay on its side, panting heavily. Cody finally managed to get the leash attached to the choke chain. Both he and the big dog backed away a few feet from the ravaged pup, which struggled to its feet and set off after its litter mate toward the door of the barn, dripping blood all the way. Inside the barn, all the caged dogs went off. Howling cries. Moaning.

Eventually, the three of us turned away from the attack dog and took a moment to size each other up. My brown fleece pullover was torn and the pain in my arm momentarily overrode the pain in my head. I gingerly felt around my elbow, hoping the carnage we'd just seen might distract the brothers from my trespassing. But an injured dog apparently was just the cost of doing business around here.

"This guy was snooping around the motorhome and the barn," said Tommy, suddenly matter-of-fact. He tucked his gun into the back of his waistband. "Says he's just out hiking. Been out overnight with a wife he's got somewhere."

Cody gave me a once over, from my Italian-made hiking boots and Eddie Bauer trekking pants to my bloodied polar fleece jacket. His eyes lingered on my hand, which still held my khaki ball cap with the foreign legion sun flaps.

"Where'd you camp at up there?" he asked.

"Came up from Snoqualmie Pass," I said. "Camped at Park Lakes. Spectacle Lake. Waptus. Near Mount Daniel."

"What're you doing here now, huh? How you gonna get back? You got a car?"

"We dropped the car at the trailhead last week. Rode our bikes back to La Likt. Got a lift to Snoqualmie Pass with our packs to start the hike."

"Show me your license. You're trespassing, you know that? You see the signs?"

I eased my wallet out of my back pocket and offered him my driver's license. He studied it briefly, looked at Tommy, shrugged. Then he took a phone out of his back pocket, held my license in his left palm, and took a picture of it. The throbbing in the back of my head and my elbow seemed to alternate, like a tennis match, back and forth, with each heartbeat.

Cody handed my license to Tommy, who sneered at it.

"Yeah, I thought so. You ain't in Seattle anymore, Nathan Drake," he said, once again locking on to my eyes and pushing his shaggy head close to mine. "I live here. This is my home. You can't just come in here."

He was holding out my license.

As I reached for it, he delivered a round-house slap to my left cheek and ear. More surprising than painful. The dog snarled and yanked against the chain, pulling Cody's arm out toward me. "Drop it," Cody said to the dog, which reluctantly settled on its haunches. The three of us looked at each other, unsure of what came next.

"Well, hell. Right there, Tommy, what'd we talk about hitting?" Cody said to his brother. He sighed and turned to me. "OK, Nathan Drake," he said, a trace of all-is-forgiven in his voice. "That sounds like a nice hike you and the wife took. You got to forgive my brother. We had a break-in last week and so we're extra careful. Lost a couple dogs now. Tommy just clipped you, there. A warning, right?" His lips curled upward in a meager show of politeness. "You understand. You're all right."

It seemed more a conclusion than a question. And I was ready to conclude. "Sure," I said.

"Hey." Tommy pointed to the skinny Viszla, the one with the intact neck, which now cowered over by the fire pit. "You see a little dog on the trail? Looks like that one?"

I looked at the dog, which had begun rolling on its back. She was coated in ash and dirt and shivered as if she had just gotten out of an ice bath. I cradled my elbow.

"Nope."

* * * * *

My elbow throbbed, but now that the Subaru was finally off the pot-holed forest road and onto the smooth pavement along Lake La Likt, I didn't want to stop to get the ibuprofen. Beth was nodding off in the passenger seat. Penny, in Beth's lap, was finally closing her eyes, too.

Beth, of course, had been concerned when I told her I'd fallen on some rocks by the river after failing in my search for the dog's owner. I didn't make a big deal out of it. I kept my hat on, and the gash on my elbow was mostly hidden under the torn fleece jacket.

There was no way I was going to tell her the truth: that I'd found Penny's home. Not with those losers in charge of what sure looked like a puppy mill. Who benefits from knowing about that? The whole thing was embarrassing, too, being slapped around like a kid in the schoolyard.

I glanced over at Beth. "I'm awake," she said, but soon her eyes closed again. The smooth road rolled on toward La Likt. In the passenger seat, Beth began to snore quietly. Except for the warm puppy on her lap, this soothing car ride out of the wilderness was like a hundred others we had taken together.

The first time I saw Beth, she was standing by a Sierra stream in an old pair of cutoffs and a ratty T-shirt, a blonde ponytail hanging halfway down her back. Her hair is now shoulder-length with a few intrusions of gray and her blue eyes stare back at me through a pair of stylish dark-framed glasses, but otherwise she's remarkably the same now as she was then, with a trim athletic build and legs that can out-hike most men half her age.

In fact, hiking is still what we both like best. Beth's actually the one who announced last year that she wanted to take a buyout from the newspaper so we'd have more time to get outdoors. That's why I licensed the patent for the water filter I'd invented during off-hours from my main job at the county department of health. As it turned out, my little side hustle netted us a nice nest egg, and some pretty steady royalties.

Now, though, Beth has trouble saying the "R" word—retired—when people ask the inevitable question, "What do you do?" I can fall back on my work with High Country Crapper. Beth, I think, has a harder time of it.

"You know," Beth said suddenly, awake and contemplating the cottonwoods flashing past her window, "we'll never make it to the animal shelter by closing time."

"True," I said. "Why don't we just take Penny back to the townhouse in Seattle, keep her tonight. See what happens."

Beth didn't answer. I saw her give Penny a rub behind her big ears.

We came down the grade into the town of Vincent, and I turned the radio on low to the Mariner's game. As the commercial break ended, the play-by-play guy finally got around to informing us that it was the bottom of seventh at T-Mobile Park and the M's were two down. I've tuned in to worse scenarios for our hapless team. I turned the volume up slightly.

Penny stood bolt upright in Beth's lap, suddenly alert and vibrating. She yipped, jumped into the back seat, and started an eerie howling.

In a panic, Beth flicked off the radio and I pulled over. Almost immediately, Penny quieted. She licked her lips and eyed us over the headrests.

"Wow," I said. "Look who else can't stand that smarmy announcer."

Chapter 3

Charlie Johnson-Medra

Facebook

Charlie Johnson-Medra

Intro

Hiking the Pacific Crest Trail (PCT)
Graduate Student in EnviroGeo Program
  at University of Washington
Lives in Seattle, WA

Timeline

Charlie Johnson-Medra
September 18   Above Cascade Locks
Continuing north on PCT, just crossed into Washington
State. Perched above Bridge of the Gods and watching all my
PCT thru-hiker brethren—Rambler, Cedar, Sweet Pea,
ChloroPhil, Conehead, et al—climbing up from the Columbia
River. Observations + questions on homo cresttrailian:
    1. Observation: All the seekers of wisdom-within, I can see,
are now earbuds in, seeking distraction with music, podcasts,

trail apps, and blogs. Question: What would happen if, God forbid, we were truly alone with our thoughts?

2. Observation: All the loners who started north in the California desert are now traveling and camping together in noisy groups. Question: Do we exist without an audience?

3. Observation: All the job-ditching morning meditators have found new ways to keep score: First on Trail in Morning, Longest Day, Fastest Day, Coolest Photo of Yoga Pose on Rock. Question: Can we ever stop comparing?

Stella Johnson-Medra
Life is a trail... and you are a true wanderer, Charlie.

Signe Arrat
We can't escape ourselves...

Jack Scanlon
Geez, take a selfie, Charlie boy! Ask yourself what you see? And then post another soulful update.

Bella
You finally did it, Charlie. Keep going. See U soon maybe?

Charlie Johnson-Medra
September 21 Mt. Adams
Can't believe the packs of humans climbing Mt. Adams then glissading back down like children on sleds. As if "bagging the peak" or an adrenalin rush was the goal. The Yakama tribe had it right: respect the mountain, live on the flanks, accept the bounty given. Glad to be moving north. Old Snowy Mountain in the distance.

Stella Johnson-Medra
You are soooo right, Charlie. Stay safe.

JoAnn McNanty

Beautiful photos! Wish I was there!

Jack Scanlon
Oh, c'mon. I've seen you bombing down the slopes at Whistler.
Stay high, Charlie!

Charlie Johnson-Medra
September 24   Above Tieton River
Really cool stretch of PCT here. Dropped the pack and spent the day scrambling down the North Fork Basin. O Mighty Tieton! Saw three mama bears with cubs, not a single person. Tumac Mtn. is a sea of rhyolites. Serpentine and olivine intrusions. So nice to get off the PCT freeway. I could spend a month here.

Stella Johnson-Medra
Those rock pics are like Pollock paintings! So cool!!

Jack Scanlon
What's your average miles per day? You got to get going, boy. BTW, Emma says hi.

Bella
Call me

Charlie Johnson-Medra
September 29   Snoqualmie Pass
Hey Facebook friends. I've decided to finish this summer's PCT hike unplugged. All is well, and don't worry. Not sure where I'll end up. See you all in October!

* * * * *

Excerpt from the journal of Charlie Johnson-Medra

Sept 29

So today I start writing for myself like humanity has done for centuries—with a Blackwing pencil in my waterproof notebook. I got a cell signal yesterday up near Stampede Pass (epic mushrooms up there!) so I called Emma like she asked and found out she's going to start hiking with me! We'll meet at Peggy's Pond later this week. She said to stop posting on FB for a while because the FreeThinkers are back in the news and it's best if nobody knows where she is. Nobody but me, that is. She checked in with Jack in Seattle and he told her he got rid of the recording of her and the boys from Eugene, which is a relief, but I don't really know if Em should trust him.

Fine with me quitting Facebook, anyway. Who needs more photo brags from the trail? Kind of neat with the humble pencil and notepad. No revisions. No audience. Messy, like life. Probably more me, more truth, than anything I post online. I can be myself here. I won't miss the snarky comments from Jack, that's for sure.

Hope Em has gotten over her parent issues. Who knows, maybe she'll even let go of the whole FreeThinkers thing. She talks so much, is so smart. She inspires people. Like on that recording. Classic Em. Lure those boys in, tell them what you want them to do, then clear the hell out. Without that lawyer her dad got, she'd be doing time in the supermax down in West Virginia. So Em, maybe lighten up with all that talk about your Daddy's blood money?

Not sure why she had to leave London, either. Seemed like a sweet setup. Or why "Bella" said she needed a place to hide out for a while. Maybe she left London just so she could meet up with Jack and they could bang each other for three days straight. Whatever, now she suddenly wants to meet me on the PCT and go to Canada. OK Em, that'll be fun for me, but WTF? Canada? Perfect sense, Em!

Chapter 4

MARY BETH DRAKE

September 29-October 1

Nathan thought I hadn't noticed the gash in his arm, but of course I saw it. He was dripping blood all the way across the dusty parking lot. "It must have been an awfully sharp river rock," I said, trying to move in for a closer look. He skittered away from me. "River rocks are usually smooth. Talk about unlucky." I tried to look less skeptical and more sympathetic. "Why don't you let me drive home?"

"I'll drive," he answered, grabbing the handle on the car door as if possession was 9/10ths of deciding who gets behind the wheel.

"I was just thinking you might like to take care of your arm. Looks painful."

"It's fine. You get sleepy in the afternoons. I'll drive."

End of discussion.

The man can be rather succinct, but then, his whole family is that way. I thought big, Irish-Catholic clans were supposed to be loquacious, but after a few years of observation, I concluded that all nine members of the Drake family harbored a secretive streak. They said only what needed to be said, and sometimes not even that. At holiday dinners, Drakes by birth let the brothers- and sisters-in-law carry the conversation, often to our disadvantage. I remember the Thanksgiving Day I caught a brother's new girlfriend in the kitchen, sneaking an extra glass of wine. "That's it," she told me. "You've now heard every one of my stories, including how I got expelled from St. Teresa's in my sophomore year." I never saw her again.

It was dark when we got to Seattle with our bewildered Penny, who didn't seem like such a good luck charm to me despite what the girl on the trail had said. Nathan was still insisting that he hadn't been hurt at all, even though he'd been driving one-handed for the last 60 miles and blood had long since seeped through his brown fleece jacket. I practically had to dial the number for the health care advice line and hold the phone up to his ear, but Nathan, guarded as usual, waved me off when a nurse picked up the call. He turned his back and walked out of the room so I wouldn't hear the conversation. Truth was, I was antsy to get back down to the mud room anyway. That's where Penny was pacing back and forth, alternately nipping at her balding haunches and wolfing the cat food I'd begged from our next-door neighbor.

"I don't like the way she's scratching," I told Nathan when he came downstairs to see how Penny and I were doing. "Maybe we should take her to the emergency vet."

"Funny thing," he replied. "The advice nurse says I have to go to the ER too."

So, Nathan headed southbound toward the county hospital while Penny and I started northward to the 24-hour vet's office. The puppy and I pulled into the parking lot just as a sobbing middle-aged man lashed an empty cat carrier to his Dutch Bike and slowly pedaled away. Penny twitched her floppy ears forward so that the skin above her eyes wrinkled, giving her an eerily human expression of concern. I had to admit, she was a charmer. I scooped her up and carried her inside.

Five patients and their people grimly occupied the waiting room's straight-backed chairs: two yowling cats outraged to find themselves imprisoned in their carriers, a golden retriever possessed of one bloody paw, a French bulldog with a breathing issue, and a red and blue parrot the size of a fire hydrant who was attached to its owner by a thin leather strap looped around its horny leg. The bird turned its beaky head and eyed Penny like prey. I did my best to stare it down as we waited for our names to be called.

The wait gave me time to think about all the fishy stuff I'd encountered that day: a pretty young woman who cried too much. A sweet puppy she claimed to have just found, even though she had time to give the dog a name. A husband who returned from a stroll through a campground closed-mouthed and bleeding. I reached for my phone and found my friend Muriel's name among the recent calls. Muriel headed up the local Forest Service office in La Likt. If anyone had reported a missing hiker, she'd know about it. She picked up on the fifth ring.

"Hey," she said. "Where are you? Want to go get a beer at The Corner? It's acoustic music night."

"Wish I could, but I'm in Seattle, waiting at the animal ER with a dog we picked up on the Cathedral Rock trail today."

"That's new for you," Muriel replied. "A dog."

"Yeah, that's why I'm calling. The dog came along with a girl—20-ish, blonde, a thru-hiker maybe. She headed up the Cathedral Rock trail and left her puppy with us. I was wondering if you'd heard of anyone looking for her, or someone maybe thinking she was missing."

The vet's assistant appeared at the door leading to the exam room. "Paco Swengaard?" she asked. The parrot and its owner rose from their chair.

"No," said Muriel slowly. "I haven't heard about anybody looking for a hiker. Something not right with this one?"

"Well, apart from her bleeding arm . . ." A furious squawking interrupted my answer.

"Where the hell are you?" Muriel asked.

"I told you, emergency veterinarian getting the new dog checked out. There's some kind of troubled bird here with us. Anyway, Muriel, that reminds me: Is anybody looking for a puppy, smallish, short-hair, kind of a red color?"

"No missing dog reports either, as far as I know."

"OK, thanks," I said. "Next time, I buy beers."

Penny shifted in my lap and stuck the tip of her russet nose under her outsized puppy paws. Her skinny sides expanded and contracted all at once as she heaved a sigh that reminded me of my mother during my teenaged years. It was warm in the waiting room and the dog and I both closed our eyes.

Our naps ended when the door to the exam room flew open with such force that it banged violently against the wall. The bird and its escort appeared. The man had a bandage stuck to his right cheek. The bird had a band around its beak. Both seemed irritated.

The vet's assistant peeked around the rebounding door. "Penny Drake?" she asked.

Two hours later I returned to our townhome with a dipped and shampooed Penny, a tube of ointment, a fabric cone to be placed around the puppy's head should haunch nipping persist, twenty pounds of pricey, highly nutritious dog food, and instructions to watch for signs of mites among the human members of the pack.

"And what about you?" I asked Nathan after we'd settled our exhausted Penny into a nest of never-to-be-used-again blankets.

"Got a tetanus shot. It hurt, but at least I don't need to wear a cone on my head."

"Which reminds me," I said, "when are we going back to La Likt to look for Penny's real owners?"

My husband grimaced. "Maybe Penny's better off without them."

* * * * *

A couple of days passed before Nathan and I got organized enough to return to La Likt, and by then, Penny had nosed her way into our routines. She was a puppy of regular habits who, it seemed to me, could size you up, decide where you most needed improvement, and then gently nudge you toward better behavior. Take, for example, Penny's morning routine, which quickly became ours.

Since we quit our jobs, our sleep patterns have become slovenly, I admit. Where once, proclaiming he felt like "getting a jump on the day," Nathan regularly rose before daybreak to tinker with his water filters before work, now there seemed to be little reason to bound from bed into the bright day ahead. What, after all, was the hurry?

Penny, it seemed, didn't take such a languid view of things. The puppy still slept in her nest of blankets in the mudroom, leaving the upper floors of the townhouse to Nathan and me in the evening. Come first light, however, we'd hear her paws against the bamboo flooring on the stairs: one flight, then a pause to look out of the window next to the front door. If there was a squirrel sighting, we'd hear a faint yip, more questioning than threatening. Next, we'd hear the sound of paws climbing one more flight, and five noisy laps at her water bowl.

"No," Nathan would moan. "Too early."

"Be quiet," I'd whisper. "Maybe she'll stay where she is."

The next sound, however, was inevitable: puppy paws on the final ascent to the bedroom level. I always took the side of the bed closest to the door, but Penny walked right past me, around the bed, to Nathan's side. There she'd sigh meaningfully, place her front feet on the mattress next to Nathan's head, and press her wet nose to his forehead. If that didn't get him moving, a few swipes with her pink tongue usually did.

"Well," Nathan would sigh, "might as well get a jump on the day, right, Penny?"

I suppose I should have been annoyed, but Penny's persistent efforts won me over, enough so that I wasn't looking forward to returning the puppy to her owners. I suppose I felt it was nice to have someone take an interest, even if she was just a puppy with abandonment issues.

But even while I dreaded the day we'd have to give her up, I was dying to find out why Penny was dumped on us in the first place, and to learn what had become of our HiWI, Bella. I hadn't felt such an intense curiosity, bordering on a physical craving for information, since I quit my job at the newspaper. That's why, once we were finally headed back to the cabin, I was against stopping at Technical Mountaineering Supply in Seattle. Nathan, though, was certain we needed a better map of the Alpine Lakes Wilderness.

"We already have at least two Alpine Lakes maps," I pointed out as he aimed the Subaru toward the outdoors store's labyrinthine parking garage. Penny was settled on my lap, but I didn't know how long she'd be happy there and it was a 90-minute trip over the pass to our cabin, traffic permitting, which it usually wasn't.

"A good map is never a bad investment," said Nathan, squeezing the Subaru into a space labeled "compact." I held my breath as we came within millimeters of the Mercedes SUV on my side. "I'll only be a minute."

I watched Nathan wander toward the store's entrance. Viewed from behind, he could pass for a 20-year-old—wiry, with long legs that gave him the distinctive loping stride I fell in love with the summer I was 19. When Nathan reached the store's entrance, he turned and waved at me. His short beard is gray now, and there are laugh lines at the corners of his eyes and across his broad forehead. His smile, though, is still irresistibly crooked. I lifted my hand from Penny's nape and waved back.

The puppy had her eyes on Nathan too, and as he disappeared, she whined and pressed herself against the passenger-side door. I ran my hand down her smooth back to the spot where the scabby rash was clearing nicely. I'd noticed how Penny became anxious when our little pack separated. That was normal, the vet told me during a follow-up visit, especially given how we'd found her wandering and alone.

When I heard that, I'd had to bite the inside of my cheeks to stop myself from telling the vet a more accurate version of Penny's story. Nathan, however, was adamant that we honor our promise not to give away Bella's location. He shot warning glances my direction whenever anyone asked too many questions about how we'd acquired a puppy. I, meanwhile, wasn't so sure that our trailside promise was binding, and

Nathan and I had bickered over the last few days about the wisdom of keeping quiet.

"Bella's probably got a family, you know," I told Nathan one afternoon as I watched him prepare a dog food recipe he'd found on the internet, a stir-fried mixture of ground turkey, spinach, carrots, peas, and brown rice. His hand hovered briefly in front of our collection of vinegars and spices before he chose the good Italian olive oil and doused the wok with a large splash. Penny stood, tail up and attentive, at his feet.

"Think back to when you were her age, Beth," Nathan said. "There comes a time when you have to separate." He slipped Penny a small nugget of the turkey and smiled as her tail whipped against his pant leg. "You have to become your own person. Before I rat Bella out, I need proof somebody's looking for her."

Nathan must have realized that I'd think of my sister then, because he put down his spatula and took my hand. "I didn't mean," he began, then retreated into silence.

"It's OK." I tried to say it lightly, but my voice came out in a quavering quack. It's been 40 years, but it'll never be easy for me to talk about what I need to say next. I guess it's best just to spit it out, like I was writing it on deadline for the paper.

Something bad happened to my family when I was 8 years old. My big sister Laura disappeared. She was 16 and the family favorite, a girl so winning that it never occurred to my brothers and me to put ourselves in the competition for our parents' affection. She had us beat and we knew it.

It was early spring when she left us. I remember the scent of wet earth and plum blossoms as I stood in front of my elementary school in Sacramento, waiting for Laura to run across from the high school next door so we could walk home together as usual. I remember watching the boys' track team lope across the parking lot toward practice, and the sun slowly sliding behind the gym. I remember wondering if it would be OK to sit down on the damp grass while I waited, and that I was still standing when my eldest brother showed up in the family station wagon and waved me inside.

My parents tried to protect me from news of the investigation into Laura's disappearance. But it was the late 1970s, a time when serial rapists and axe murderers dominated the local newscasts—the East Area Rapist, the Trailside Killer, and the I-5 Killer, who always called his victims' families to let them know exactly what had become of their girls. Back then, I had my own ideas about where she might be, but to this day I don't know what really happened to Laura. All I know is we never found her.

There. I guess I buried the lead to that story, didn't I?

I don't like to use Laura as an excuse, either for winning an argument or assuming the worst. So that dog food afternoon, I gave Nathan's hand a squeeze, and in my choking duck voice I repeated, "It's OK. Really, it's OK. But you might not be so happy you've kept her secret if something happens to that girl."

Back in the parking garage, my phone buzzed me out of my reverie. I flinched in surprise, and Penny scrambled from my lap into the vacant driver's seat. "It's OK, doggie-dog," I told her as I rummaged in the daypack at my feet for the impatient little device. Muriel's name shined at the top of the screen and I swiped to answer. "Hi," I said. "What's new?"

"That girl you met on the trail up to Cathedral Rock last week," she said, "I've got some intel."

"Good," I replied, locating a pen and a pad of sticky notes in the car's door pocket. "Fire away."

"I was over at Buster's Hardware, looking at the bulletin board they've got there, you know?"

"The one with the notices of snow machines for sale and fundraising drives for cancer patients?"

"Right. Well, there was a missing persons notice." She paused. "Kind of a missing persons notice, anyway. It looks handmade and it's pretty short on details, but somebody's looking for a girl and she sounds a lot like your hiker."

The phone's audio turned hollow as Muriel switched to speaker. "It says, 'Missing: Tall, blonde girl, early 20s. Answers to Bella. Last seen September 28, Fortune Creek area. Reward." Muriel took a deep breath. "Then there's a phone number. It says to keep trying. Under that, there's a blurry picture of a girl. Blonde. Pretty. She looks like she just lost her last friend."

"That sounds like our girl, all right. Any mention of a dog?"

"Nope, that's all there is. If you want, I can text you the picture I took of the notice."

Moments later the photo came through. The hand-printed lettering on the flier was messy and, to my annoyance, a couple of words were misspelled. The picture, as Muriel said, was blurry. But it was Bella.

I looked over at Penny. "You'll recall," I said, "before Nathan consents to contacting the authorities, he needs proof that somebody's looking for that girl." Penny thumped her tail twice on the upholstered driver's seat. "I would say this is proof."

I like to be right. I spent almost 25 years as a newspaper reporter, 15 of them covering the police beat back when newspapers had police beats. Hell, it was back when newspapers had reporters, not loose coalitions of unpaid bloggers, neighborhood busybodies, and anonymous malcontents, all of whom ought to be denied access to the local library's broken-down copier, let alone a general-circulation publication. I've been right, and I've been wrong, and right is so much better. I couldn't wait to tell Nathan that, despite taking early retirement, my instincts hadn't completely atrophied.

"You stay here, Penny," I told the puppy, who thrust her ears forward and wrinkled her brow in what was becoming a familiar expression of doubt tinged with concern. "I'm just going to be a minute." I cracked the window, eased the door open slowly and, cursing the Mercedes in the next slot over, baby-stepped between the cars. Once free, I gave Penny the thumbs up sign and trotted toward the entrance.

The downtown Technical Mountaineering Supply is the chain's flagship store: three floors filled with diorama-like displays of extremely well-outfitted adventures. The place is known by its acronym, of course. TMS. Old-timers around here are only half-kidding when they say it stands for Too Much Stuff. I race-walked past the three-story climbing wall, zigzagged across the mountain bike testing trail, and stopped dead in front of the acre devoted to tent display. Spread before me was a significant swath of the male population of Seattle, all dressed in jeans more comfortable than stylish, organic cotton T-shirts, and polar fleece jackets. The only variation in their plumage was the logo on their baseball caps. Fortunately for me, not many of them were stoic Mariners fans like Nathan. I darted around the store peering up at their headwear. Nathan wasn't in maps and he wasn't mooning around in his favorite section, water filters, either. Finally, I found him in the pet section, comparing the nutrition labels on vegan dog treats.

"I thought you were only going to be a minute," I said.

"Oh, hey, Beth. Which do you think Penny needs more: omega three fatty acids for healthy coat and skin or extra calcium for strong bones and teeth?" He glanced up at me over his reading glasses. "Maybe both."

"Look," I responded, shoving my phone in front of his face. "Look what Muriel found. A wanted poster for Bella."

He took the phone from my hand and turned it so the image grew larger. "Huh," he said.

"'Huh' is right. Someone's looking for Bella, just like I said. We should call."

"If they've waited this long to post a notice, they can wait till we get to La Likt and look at the original ourselves." Nathan moved toward the check-out line. "How did Muriel know about Bella, anyway?" I didn't answer. Instead, I shifted my weight from right foot to left and shot imaginary death beams from my eyes toward the customers in front of us. "Calm down," Nathan murmured. "It's going to take as long as it takes."

Finally, Nathan's maps and Penny's dog treats were scanned and stowed inside one of our reusable bags from Trader Joe's, and we headed toward the parking garage. "Let's take the stairs," I told Nathan. "It'll be faster." He nodded and reached for my hand.

* * * * *

If you asked me, I'd say that Nathan and I are well-suited to each other, despite all appearances to the contrary. We agree on the big, philosophical issues that govern our lives. It's the smaller stuff that gets us in trouble. Take our getaway cabin above the tiny mountain town of La Likt, a windy outpost just off the interstate where the population once depended on the railroad and coal, two economic engines that stalled decades ago. Nathan loves the cabin. I'm less certain.

Holding my phone in one hand and a print-out of the wanted poster for Bella in the other, I looked around our 900 square feet of old-growth timber and similarly long-established mold. I like the charm that comes with a classic 1902 miner's bungalow as much as the next person—well, OK, maybe I don't, but is it too much to ask for a few modern conveniences, like maybe functioning indoor plumbing? I sighed, gave our three rooms another once-over, and settled onto the camp cot to call the number listed on Bella's poster.

Outside, Nathan was discussing remodeling plans with our design/build guy while Penny happily danced around his feet. I could hear snippets of their conversation through the open window: "maximize light but maintain architectural integrity," "match old-growth quality with recycled equivalents," "remain within the existing footprint for natural water filtration." As I watched, they walked down the gravel drive and gazed at the spot where my husband was planning to construct his dream outbuilding: a 1,000 square-foot freestanding garage that would house everything from our backpacking gear to his beer-making equipment. Nathan's father was coming up from his home in Sacramento in a couple weeks to check out the plans. Out there on the corner of our lot, the two men and the dog looked like they were enjoying themselves. I closed the window, took a deep breath, and opened my phone's recording app.

All my life I've wanted to be a hard-boiled reporter, and I suppose I did achieve some success before the newspaper industry collapsed around me and I took the buyout. I had a good reputation locally, and I was proud of it. I got a crooked sheriff removed from office, even shared a Pulitzer for uncovering scumbags who smuggled unsuspecting women into the country for the sex trade. The truth, though, is I've always been a nervous reporter. Even now, perched on the flimsy cot with a notebook balancing on my knees, I could feel butterflies shifting aimlessly in my belly. I tried to slow my thudding heart with controlled breathing—eight counts in, eight counts out—and tapped in the number written on the poster.

The phone trilled six times before a man picked up. "Yeah?" he said.

"Oh, hello!" I babbled, as if shocked to discover I was on the phone. "I'm calling about the missing girl?"

"You seen her?"

"Well, yes. Or maybe. I'm not sure. Can you tell me a little more about her?"

"It's on the poster, man," he said. "Really tall chick. Blonde hair. Got a red dog with her." A red dog? That wasn't on the poster. I heard the cabin's front door open and close. Nathan and Penny crowded into our little sleeping alcove, and I waved at them distractedly. "You hear me?" the man on the phone was saying. He paused, then spoke his next words in a louder voice, cleaning up his enunciation as he went, "Have you seen the girl?"

With a jolt, I realized he thought he was dealing with some tiresome old dear who was likely borrowing the phone down at the senior center. I stared at Nathan, not really seeing him, while I figured out my next move.

"Hello?" the man yelled. "You there?"

"Now, I think I did see a young lady like that, and I'd like to help you find the poor girl," I finally said. "But I'm just not sure. It might help if you could tell me a little more about her."

He sighed noisily, and in the background, I heard the snarl of a motorcycle starting up. "OK," he said once the engine noise had crested and faded to a macho pop and growl, "this tall, blonde chick. Her name is Bella. She's probably got a little red-colored puppy with her. She's probably carrying a big backpack, and she's probably headed somewhere like the backcountry. Or Seattle."

"Seattle," I repeated. "That's a long way from here, isn't it?"

"Not that far." He was becoming impatient. "We need to find her. She's in trouble, so you better tell me if you've seen her."

"There's no need to be rude just because I need a little help remembering." I decided to sneak in another question. "What's your name, dear?"

"Cody."

"Now, Cody, tell me again, why do you need to find this girl?"

Exasperated, he yelled, "Because she's got our dog and our product, and we want it back!"

There was a pause while I took in this new information. "All right, then," I said. "I see. Those are good reasons, Cody. What kind of product do you young men make?"

"Who is this? Are you a cop?" His voice lowered. "Or are you just messin' with me, whoever the hell you are? You better not be, because when I find out who you are, it won't be fun for you."

With a trembling hand, I scribbled "Cody" in my notebook, regretting that I'd used my own phone for the call, which meant he now had my number. "I'm just trying to help you, Cody, and I think I did see your missing girl in town, so if only I had a little more to go on . . ."

My phone beeped three times in rapid succession. He'd ended the call.

Chapter 5

Money, Mystery and ... Murder?

Sexy heiress flees London in wake of deadly explosion

"Sweet Emma" Turnstone seen hiding out at Daddy's frontier mansion

by Nigel Turner
Informant Staff

Medina, Washington: In the impenetrable woods that rise just beyond the boomtown of Seattle, towering beauty Emma Turnstone is hiding behind Jackie O. sunglasses, though the days are unrelentingly overcast.

Mists envelop the majestic evergreens shrouding her wealthy parents' estate, obscuring the construction cranes that crowd the rising city skyline just to the west. For a girl like Sweet Emma, used to enjoying the glamour of London on the arm of billionaire gene tweaker Winston Drummond, the rapid transition from glitter to gloom must be dispiriting.

Imagine the poor rich girl, heiress to storied American investor Curtis Turnstone's fortune, moping about the grand lawn that leads to the high-tech homestead in which she so spectacularly grew up . . . and up . . . and up some more. That's where the *Informant* spotted her, not long after her hasty departure from London following the explosion of her boyfriend's experimental sports car. The blast, described by witnesses as sounding like a bomb going off, killed a 16-year-old boy who sat inside the car and injured Drummond. Its cause is under investigation.

Why Sweet Emma fled instead of rushing to her boyfriend's side is the latest hot question among those who wondered what the cool blonde from an outpost only recently risen from insignificance was doing with the debonair Drummond in the first place. The British billionaire made his money through manipulating the genes of animals, while the Turnstone family is famously antivivisectionist, giving away millions of pounds each year to animal rights groups.

Sweet Emma herself has admitted to being a former leader of one of the most radical of those groups, the FreeThinkers, or FT. She disavowed FT earlier this year after members were implicated in the terrorist bombing of a University of Washington research laboratory. The botched bombing, meant to free research animals, killed 16 chimpanzees and ruined decades of scientific study. Two members of FT were convicted in the bombing and are in U.S. custody while awaiting appeal.

"She'd be with them if it wasn't for her daddy," said a former FT comrade in Seattle, one of several who asked for anonymity fearing the Turnstones would use their wealth and influence to harm them should they speak their truth. "She picked the target. She planned the mission. And she messed it up."

She also was the only FT member to give court-sealed evidence against the two imprisoned 28-year-old men who, our sources say, were formerly her very special friends. That, sources say, has made her a target for revenge-minded FT hardliners.

"Our guys go to jail and Emma goes to London," said one. "We won't forget that."

As for the Drummond sports car explosion, Sweet Emma's former friends say the gene tweaker might have got off easy, even while his young guest paid the ultimate price.

"She's screwed up bombings before," mused one former comrade familiar with Sweet Emma's skills. "I've got complete confidence she could do it again."

Stick with the *Informant Online* for the latest revelations.

--end

As soon as I sent the story, the Childe Editor was back at me with one of her instant messages.

"Cut by half," she'd typed. "Send video."

Chapter 6

NATHAN DRAKE

October 3

"What's up with the red eye and the scratches?" asked my friend Dave.

"Long story," I told him. "Attacked by a bush, basically."

I'd known Dave Schmidell for only a few months, but we saw each other several times a week when Beth and I were in La Likt.

Dave was a reliably low-key guy. Plus, he made really good beer. Good enough that he'd taken the money he'd saved from working construction and opened his own brewpub on the main drag in La Likt. Truth be told, watching his stainless-steel tanks come off the truck was a tipping point in our decision to purchase our cabin above town. My decision, anyway. Maybe the economy was finally turning here. Could a vegan bakery be far behind? After sampling Dave's ales, I was doubly anxious for his one-man operation, called Cenozoic, to survive. That's why I occasionally jumped behind the bar to pull pints while he tended to the vats in back.

"Geez," he said, "Just as your arm was getting better."

"Always some damn thing," I said.

I took a long sip on my pint of IPA, redolent of local hops, while Dave rolled a keg into position beneath the bar. He stood, scratched his neck, and glanced over at Penny, who was curled up behind the bar on a blanket. She seemed to sense the attention, raised her head, and sent us both a disappointed look before tucking herself into an even tighter ball.

One of Dave's many exemplary traits is sensing and sidestepping topics his patrons want to avoid. Kind of basic for a bartender, I guess. At any rate, he quit questioning me about my eye. Instead, he said, "You mind watching the bar for a while?"

After he went out back and started unloading cases of empty 22-ounce bottles off his old Toyota truck, I let my fingertips explore the fresh scratches on the side of my face. I closed my sore right eye and pressed gently on the lid. Damn elk.

The morning had started with me sitting on a hunk of granite, elbows braced on knees, binoculars pointed toward the puppy mill in the pines a half-mile down the slope. Even with the binoculars, the only features of the wooded property I could distinguish were the reddish pond and the shiny metal roof of the RV carport. Also, a wisp of smoke, presumably from the blue cottage beyond the dogs' barn. But the key thing, the reason I was perched on this particular rock outcrop, was the unobstructed view I had of the brothers' gravel driveway as it emerged from the thicket of trees to meet Forest Road 41.

Yesterday it had taken only 15 minutes of online futzing to discover who owned the property I'd stumbled upon last week. County tax records named the deed holders as Thomas and Cody DeRoux. Four hours of internet sleuthing, though, yielded no good information on Tommy and Cody. Plenty of fascinating stuff about gastric bypass surgeries and French-Canadian hockey players, but nothing about these two jokers. As far as I could see, they were off the grid and out of touch. Not even a Facebook presence.

Last night, Beth had given me a blow-by-blow account of her phone call with the guy named Cody. I was alarmed, although I admit it was more of a confirmatory shock than a complete surprise. I could practically hear Hat Guy's voice snarling at Beth over the phone, and I guess some of Beth's worries about Bella had spilled over to me. That's why I was here, waiting for the admittedly slim chance to poke around in the DeRoux brothers' compound. Check for signs of Bella, due diligence and all, maybe figure out what the "product" was.

Beth thought I was headed into Ellensburg to look at floor tile samples. She would not have been happy to learn that I had fibbed. Again. Although, technically, I considered it just a sub-lie, a venial addendum to the main lie, which she didn't know about so, technically, it wasn't even a lie yet. Anyway, Beth didn't seem unhappy to see me go away. With my insistence on keeping Bella's secret, the atmosphere in our little cabin wasn't exactly genial. She might cool off if I stayed out of range for a while. So, there I sat, my ends justifying my means, binoculars pointed, listening to the Subaru tick behind me as it gave up its heat to the early morning air.

Every few minutes, I'd unzip the daypack at my feet and reach inside to feel the unfamiliar contours of my uncle Bob's old service revolver—touching it sent a charge through my system every time. Bob was in the California Highway Patrol for 30 years. When he died, my Dad and I went through his stuff at his home near Lake Shasta. After we made a few runs to Goodwill and the dumps, my sister drove our father back home to Sacramento and I headed north to Seattle with a load of hand tools, books, lamps, and financial records. I was the executor of Bob's estate and, as my fingers on the cold steel kept confirming, his loaded gun.

Thinking about Bob and his gun set loose an even older memory. When I was around 12 years old, my father used to take me to a shooting range in an old quarry above Sacramento in the Sierra foothills. If we were alone, after he finished his target practice, he'd let me walk out to the firing line. He'd hunch up his tall frame to match my height, reach his arms around me, and carefully press the heavy gun into my right hand. Then he'd wrap both of my hands in his, and we would aim together. I'd squeeze the trigger, hear the slam, and feel the recoil through my father's hands.

One summer evening—I remember he'd just returned from a business trip somewhere in Central America—we stayed much later than usual, and I got no lesson. Two cans of Budweiser at his feet—unheard of for him—my father stood at the line and continued firing well into what should have been my time, sipping the beer with each reload, until darkness came on. I had to squint to read my paperback book, then I couldn't see the print at all. The air cooled, the blasts stopped, and the crickets started up. Dad stood at the line, a black figure silhouetted against the huge western sky beyond the range. He was looking away from the target toward an old wooden fence at the side of the quarry. Following his gaze, I saw the humped black outlines of a family of huge rats streaming along the fence top. Dad took aim, and with each sharp blast, a rat disappeared, leaving a spray of blood briefly suspended in the air like a handful of tossed flour.

Why did a government civil engineer need a revolver? Why did he need to take target practice? And what was he doing in Nicaragua? I figured it all out soon enough, but I'd nearly forgotten about that evening at the firing range until Uncle Bob's gun brought the memory back. I never told anyone the story, not even my older brothers. Certainly not Beth. It seemed like something private between Dad and me, his youngest boy.

I saw movement at the cottage below. The green jeep careened into view, crunching along the driveway and spraying gravel as it turned onto the forest road. Advancing my binoculars to the leading edge of the dust cloud, I thought I saw somebody in the passenger seat. But just as I steadied and focused, the jeep disappeared into the forest. If my fleeting impression of a passenger was accurate, the coast was clear for my snooping. If it was wishful thinking, I might be screwed.

I bounded down the slope and then lingered for a few minutes at the edge of the compound. Smoke still leaked from the cottage's chimney. A muscular Stellar's jay supervised the yard. The caged dogs let out a few barks and whimpers, but the barn looked dark, so I circled the perimeter of the property toward the back entrance, careful to stay in the trees. Creeping closer on soft pine needles, I heard low voices coming from inside the barn. I froze, my pulse pounding in my ears. But then the low voices morphed into those of the morning goofballs on sports talk radio. Jack and Jake. No wonder Penny was nervous about the Mariners. She'd probably endured quite a few games on this station.

I peered inside the barn. Just the dogs, so I decided to take a closer look. As soon as I stepped inside I knew I'd made a mistake. The dogs let loose with a mournful chorus, and I froze again. To my surprise, the yapping died down almost immediately. With my heart once again banging in my ears, my eyes adjusted to the dark and I could soon see that the 20 or so dogs—all Vizslas, many with cones around their heads—were uniformly lethargic. Most were on their sides and breathing heavily. Only two or three bothered to stand up to look at me. Their cages, surprisingly, all looked clean and well-tended. I took a few photos of the dogs and backed out of the barn.

Slipping again into the trees on the property's perimeter, I circled around behind the cottage. I found a moss-draped fir branch about the size of a Louisville Slugger and lobbed it high over the roof of the house. It landed with a hollow bang on the front porch dormer. The only reaction came from the noisy jay. Feeling confident, I walked to the front of the cottage, climbed onto the porch, and twisted the doorknob—unlocked. I pushed open the door and stepped inside.

Heavy curtains shrouded the windows. I switched on my headlamp to reveal a large, open room. A kitchen area and an oak pedestal table were in the back corner. In the living area where I stood the focal point consisted of two plaid recliners facing a modest-sized flat screen TV. The remains of a fire smoldered within the river-rock hearth. Stacks of boxes and piles of jackets, shirts, and shoes filled corners and edges of the room.

In front of the recliners, a glass-topped coffee table held a collection of neatly stacked magazines, a pile of mail, and a variety of remotes. I was leaning over the table snapping photos of the magazines—an eclectic mix of *Dog Fancier*, *Smithsonian*, *Guns & Ammo*—when a burst of small explosions rattled the kitchen window pane. A string of firecrackers? An automatic weapon? As I ducked down and struggled to get Bob's gun out of my pack, the pops and bangs assembled themselves into the sounds of a big four-stroke engine rumbling to life. Of course: a motorcycle.

I peeked out from between the curtains in time to see a powerful black bike roll out from alongside the compound's RV. The bike, some kind of beefy vintage thing, leaned heavily then burst from the driveway in a spray of gravel. The rider was a big guy in a white T-shirt. He was hunched low, practically lying on top of the gas tank. Muscular tattooed arms reached for the low handlebars and his legs, clad in lightweight pajamas or yoga pants, bent back to straddle the rear of the bike. A pistol was strapped to his side. I got one good look at his face as he cast a departing glance over his thick bicep. My mental freeze-frame registered Asian or American Indian features, a long black ponytail, and a really pissed look.

"How did I miss seeing a motorcycle?" I asked myself as the rider roared off. I was annoyed with my carelessness, but relieved that, in his hurry to depart, the rider hadn't seen me. Or had he?

The burst of adrenalin cleared my head, and I remembered I was working under a deadline.

I threw open cupboards and drawers in the kitchen—nothing unusual there—and then swept through both back bedrooms. The bedrooms were nearly identical, each holding a single bed neatly made up with a boldly striped gold-and-red spread. Piles of clothes carpeted the floors.

So far, all I had learned was that these guys could really use some coat hooks. It occurred to me that I didn't know what I was looking for.

Disgusted with myself, I retreated to the front door. I was reaching for the knob when I noticed a brown canvas daypack atop the jumble of boots, gloves, and baseball hats just inside the entry. Sewn on the back pocket was a purple patch with a swoopy logo forming the letters "FT," the same logo I'd seen on bumper stickers, usually alongside those extolling Bernie, vegan living, and coexistence. I hesitated, confused. I wouldn't have pegged the brothers running the puppy mill for liberals. I plunged back into the daylight and was hot-footing it toward the Subaru when I had an idea.

I turned and headed back toward the motorhome. The orange dirt bike I'd noticed on my first visit still hung off the rack on back. The RV's skinny door was open, and the aluminum steps were folded down. As soon as I gripped the metal grab bar and hoisted myself to the first step, the skunky smell of marijuana hit me. From some hidden speaker, a female's enthusiastic voice in an English-learning program spoke at polite ten-second intervals.

"This place is hands down my favorite restaurant."

I moved through the doped-up air past the pivoting leather passenger's chair and turned back into the main cabin.

"His eyesight is not good. He is as blind as a bat."

This would've been my third immersion into darkness within an hour if not for my headlamp and the images from an old *Bonanza* episode—Hoss Cartwright clutched his cowboy hat and talked to a pretty girl—flickering on the small TV fitted into the overhead cabinet.

"He is not in on the scheme."

On the fold-out table next to a leather love seat was another pile of magazines: *Japan Racing Association, Futurity Magazine, Equus.* I took photos of the magazines.

"William would play music until the cows come home."

Stuffed below the RV's bench sofa opposite me was an assortment of zipper-lock bags filled with what was very likely marijuana. Behind the bags were jars of honey, or maybe apple jelly. I took more photos, telling myself I'd investigate later.

"The job was a piece of cake."

Next, I aimed the beam of my headlamp into what seemed like dozens of cabinets. There was a chime from the hidden speaker. And then the soothing voice spoke again:

"Vocabulary. What is the suitable word for someone who is not honest? Underhanded? Or staunch?

The tiny glove box, so out of proportion to the Intruder itself, was completely empty. No registration. No insurance card. No pack of gum. Who owned this thing?

"Underhanded? Or staunch?"

I swiveled my head, looking for another likely place to stash ownership papers, but my internal clock was beeping. Time to go.

"Are you there? Underhanded? Or staunch?"

I jumped down the motorhome's delicate steps, snapped a couple photos of its exterior and license plate, and turned back toward the pond and the hill where I'd left the Subaru.

I was pushing through the brush when a willow branch lashed at my eyes and I fell, half-blinded, onto what felt like a mushy, moss-covered log. My knees sank into the unnaturally soft surface and my hands flew to my face, almost in time to protect it from the tangle of sharp protuberances. Something raked across my eye, and to this day I don't know if it was a tree branch or the antler of the dead elk.

For a moment, I knelt, stunned, on the swollen carcass. My brain urged caution before moving. Make sure the thing was, number one, actually real, and number two, actually dead. Once I was convinced, I grabbed some overhead branches to wrestle myself up off the beast. After testing my eye and assessing the damage to my scraped-up face, I pushed back the brush to take a closer look. It struck me as an undignified pose for an elk, like those horses you sometimes see lying on their flanks as you drive by their pastures, the sides of their bellies pushing up and their legs sticking out awkwardly. I looked for bullet entry points on the elk. None. Too intact to be mauled by a mountain lion. I became aware of the flies and the reek of rotting meat.

Looking back, it surprises me that after my head-on with the elk I had the presence of mind to take the empty specimen bottle from my pack and scoop up a sample of the compound's pond water.

* * * * *

I was still at Dave's bar, gently probing my eye and contemplating what that pond water might contain, when my phone vibrated. It was a text from Muriel. Strange that Muriel was texting me rather than contacting Dave, who, after all, was her husband and standing right there behind the bar.

Since the day Muriel had given Beth the handwritten notice about the missing girl, I knew that she'd been monitoring missing persons notices at the Forest Service office. So far, there were no official reports. And Muriel had hinted that the confusion of overlapping jurisdictions and Bella's age—consenting adult, we guessed—made it unlikely that anything would turn up right away.

So, I was taken aback by the text that Muriel sent to Beth and me.

Muriel   **5:22 PM**
Is this Emma Turnstone the girl you saw?

Attached to the text was a link to the photo page on the Washington State Patrol's Adult Missing and Unidentified Persons Unit website. When I scrolled down the faces of the missing, Bella's jumped out at me. Perhaps a selfie, it looked to be from year or two ago. She was halfway to one of those celebrity-mocking poses: eyebrows arched up, cheeks sucked in, lips pursed. She was wearing lipstick and eyeliner.

Below the photo was a name, Emma Turnstone. That sounded familiar. Tapping the name led me to a listing of physical attributes that also matched up to our Bella: age 22, height 6 feet, weight 130 pounds, eyes blue, hair blonde. The description said she was from Seattle and hadn't been seen in almost a month. Anyone with information was asked to contact the King County Sheriff's Office. A phone number was listed.

My phone vibrated with rapid-fire texts:

Beth   **5:25 PM**
Turnstone?! That's her!
Muriel

Did you call number on that flier?
Beth
Yep. Guy was mad at her. Hung up on me.
Muriel
WTF?
Beth
Meet you at Dave's pub now? You there, Nathan?
Nathan
Yep. See you.

Dave was again tinkering in back, so I searched "Emma Turnstone Seattle" and scanned hits from the *Seattle Times*, *The Stranger*, and even some national and international wire stories. The news reports, all from the beginning of the year, immediately answered the questions that had tickled my brain as soon as I saw her name. Is she related to Curtis Turnstone, one of the richest people in the country? And didn't she get into some sort of trouble recently?

Yep. Bella—or Emma, I reminded myself—was indeed the daughter of Curtis Turnstone. With slight variations, the stories all outlined the same sad tale. Emma was suspected of being a leading member of an animal rights group called the FreeThinkers, the same group whose purple logo I'd seen that morning on the daypack in the DeRoux's cabin. The bomb they set off in a university research facility managed only to start a late-night fire that belched a toxic black smoke, killing more than a dozen of the macaques and chimps they sought to liberate.

I moved behind the bar to pour pints for two young women who had just blown in off First Street, where the late afternoon wind was racing east, right on schedule. Across the street, next to the Chamber of Commerce office, an American flag so large I swear it could cover a tennis court flapped dangerously, with oceanic swells and snaps. Its edges were frayed by the wind tunnel test it received every afternoon.

As I was contemplating the flag's undulations, I spotted Beth with Lacey, my brother Andy's kid. Together they struggled against the gusts as they angled across the street toward Cenozoic. They popped through the door as if entering through the airlock of the space shuttle and paused, breathless, to reorient to the safety and stillness of the pub. Penny was immediately at their feet, stretching like a cat with her fat front paws out, hind quarters up, and tail wagging sleepily.

"So, you found your girl," said Muriel, whose sudden appearance at my side made me jump sideways into the bar's metal wastebasket. With a dull clang, it tipped its load of damp pretzel bits and spent lottery scratchers onto the concrete floor. Penny galloped over and gave the garbage an appraising sniff.

Dave closed the back door behind Muriel, and the four of us took over the round oak table in the corner. Using our two laptops, four phones, and an iPad we proceeded to gorge ourselves on information about Emma.

"Get this," said Lacey, before the rest of us could even unlock our phones. "Bella, I mean Emma, was down in Olympia, too. Protesting with PETA against something to do with cougars."

Lacey seemed to me a bit like Emma, one of those young women who is strikingly tall and self-possessed, with a complex arrangement of long hair gathered atop her head in some kind of bun approximation. That's the first impression, anyway. My niece is also incredibly smart and socially very adept. I attended her linguistics thesis lecture at the UW earlier this year and she managed the stage like it was a TED talk. I suspected stupendous nutrition and hours of yoga were helping to breed this new generation of superwomen, and I was all for it. Men weren't doing so well running the world.

"More." Lacey was still holding her phone up like a pocket prayer missal, apparently searching and scrolling with her thumbs, though I could detect no movement.

"This sucks," she said. "Those chimps they killed at the U-Dub. They were already scheduled to be sent away to a retirement sanctuary in just a week. And get this, Aunt Beth. The sanctuary is in La Likt. Did you know that?"

Beth did not respond. She was looking at her laptop, which I could see still displayed her screensaver, a shot of golden larches at Oval Lake. Her hand reached down beside her chair and she scratched Penny's raised chin.

"Listen to this," said Muriel, tilting her laptop open a bit wider and tapping as she talked. "They're talking like her father, the rich guy, somehow got Bella off, I mean Emma, and got her out of the country."

"The father was one of the first Microsoft millionaires," I said. "Then he started his own company. Big time venture capitalist. Billionaire now."

"Curtis Turnstone, 52." This was Lacey, supplying chapter and verse.

"The *Times* had a similar follow-up," I said. "Did you know that, Beth? It sounds like Emma burned some FT bridges during the trial."

"Jeez, she really ratted out her comrades, didn't she?" said Muriel. "Or maybe they just wanted a scapegoat. Blame the rich girl."

We all followed leads and shared factoids until the same nuggets started washing up again and again, retold by different sources. By this time, I was pretty worn out. Through the window I could see wisps of clouds over the pine-covered ridge above town. The clouds caught the last of the sun and soaked up its rich vermillion, the sky behind the clouds deepening into an electric blue. The massive flag hung down in utter exhaustion against its stout wooden pole.

"You know what we have to do, right?" said Beth staring intently at me and only me.

I drained my second beer, thought again of the daypack with the FT patch I'd seen at the DeRoux's cottage, and said, "We'll call soon."

As we all gathered up our devices, I checked my phone once more and saw an email from my 84-year-old father in Sacramento. He'd sent a note to his entire contacts list:

I have no idea how, I did not request it, but I am now apparently part of the Facebook. If you receive anything from me on the Facebook, please disregard. It may be a scam.

On the way to the door, I set my foamy glass in the bar-side wash rack.

"Red alert from Sacramento," I said to Dave, waggling the phone. "Old man's got himself in trouble again. Damn internets."

"That'll happen," said Dave.

Beth was waiting for me, hands literally on hips, outside the pub.

Chapter 7

Charlie Johnson-Medra

Excerpt from the journal of Charlie Johnson-Medra

Oct 3

Met up with Em Thursday! She was waiting near Peggy's Pond, with hardly any food AND big, purple, nasty puncture wounds on her arm. A dog at Fortune Creek attacked her! An old couple on the trail gave her bandages and antibiotic cream, but I think she's feverish. We moved north a bit to this spot below Cathedral Peak that Em heard about. Near a little creek that comes off Mt Daniel. Secluded and off the PCT. But she's wiped. We'll rest here another day or two. I've got plenty of food.

Oh, and by the way, stuffed inside some bear-proof sacks in her ratty old backpack is like 30 pounds of pot concentrate. Dab. The crumbly waxy stuff. I'm OK with having a motherlode of pot around, for sure. But carrying it to Canada is another thing. It's like carrying a case of Jif Chunky! And exactly who'd it come from, right? Those brothers on Fortune Creek? Place sounds grim. Em says they owe her for taking care of their dogs and for the damage to her arm. She says the whole FT thing is blowing up again and she wants to go to Canada to sell those honeybags and disappear. A minute ago, before she fell asleep, she was spouting crazy talk about genetic engineers in London. Not just your standard anti-GMO stuff but whole

spiels about editing the genome. Rants about her capitalist
father and whore of a mother. She said some detective talked
with Jack and then almost found her at her parents' place up in
the mountains. Or maybe it was some kind of journalist? I
couldn't really follow. Could be the fever. We'll sit tight until
she's stronger.

Even with all the drama... Em is back!

Chapter 8

MARY BETH DRAKE

October 3-4

When I saw the missing persons report, I knew I wasn't keeping any more half-baked promises, no matter what my husband said. I sat impatiently as everyone clicked and pecked their way through Emma's story. Then, after they all got up from the table, I motioned for Nathan to follow me outside.

"I'm calling Jennifer Menendez at SPD," I told him as we huddled on the side of the old stone building that housed Dave's brewery. "Then I'm calling the State Patrol Missing Persons Unit."

"OK, but let's wait one more day before we get the police involved," he countered. "Emma Turnstone's disappearance is a big deal, Beth, and we may have been the last people to see her. We need a little time to figure out what to do."

I admit I lost my temper. "When cops get a report of a missing girl, do you know what they think, Nathan? It's not, 'Oh, here's a pretty young woman from one of the country's wealthiest families who needs some 'me time.' They think kidnapping. They think homicide. And judging by the conversation I had this morning with whoever made that poster, in this case they might not be too far off." I took a step closer to my husband and had to clasp my hands together to stop from poking him repeatedly in the chest with my index finger. "So,

I'm going to call Detective Menendez in Seattle. I'm going to ask for her advice. Then I'm going to help find this woman before something happens to her." I turned and began speed walking toward the Subaru. "If it hasn't already," I added over my shoulder.

Nathan caught up to me and touched my shoulder. "Let me get Penny," he said. I'd forgotten that we had a dog now.

I'd known Detective Jennifer Menendez for almost fifteen years. She was one of the first people I met in Seattle when I showed up from California, brand new on the cops and courts beat. In those days, Menendez was the public information officer for the Seattle cops, and we had one of those love-hate relationships reporters often develop with the agencies they cover—love when the news is good, not such warm feelings when it's bad. Now Menendez was a case detective in the sexual and child abuse unit, a job that must tear her up, especially since she's got a two-year-old daughter herself.

"I've got a question about missing persons," I said when she returned my call a couple of hours later, just before midnight.

"Call the state patrol. They're the lead on unidentified and missing," she said tiredly. "Come on, Beth. You know I wouldn't get involved in troopers' business, even if I wanted to work a dead-end job like missing persons."

"It's about Emma Turnstone," I said, "Curtis Turnstone's daughter. Nathan and I saw her last week outside of La Likt, headed up to the Pacific Crest Trail." Now I had her attention.

"Last week? And you haven't told anybody?" She paused, then asked, "Are you working this story?"

"No, I'm not working this story," I said a bit defensively, though I must admit the thought of breaking a big piece of news after such a long layoff raised my heart rate. "And we didn't know there was anything to tell until we came across the missing persons report today. Which the troopers have kept unusually quiet for such a high-profile runner, if you ask me. So now I'm asking you: Who do I talk to?"

Menendez didn't answer, so I carried on. "Once it gets out, this'll be a hot story, Jennifer. I'm not going to be just another yahoo listening to the hold music on the patrol's 800 number, waiting around to report seeing a blonde who's going to inherit America's thirty-second largest fortune."

"No offense, Beth," Menendez said, "but how do I know you're not just one of the yahoos?"

I sighed. "Put me in touch with the right people in Missing Persons, and I'll tell you why."

She went silent, considering my request. "OK," she said finally, "but this better be good. How early can you get here?"

Six and a half hours later Nathan and I sat at a fake cherry wood conference table in the State Patrol's district 2 headquarters in Seattle, tiny bottles of water on coasters in front of us. It was still a half-hour before sunrise, but Menendez had managed to round up the state trooper in charge of Emma's disappearance, a pink and white guy who looked too young to shave. At the end of the table sat a sleepy FBI agent from the bureau's Seattle office. Due to Emma's involvement with the FreeThinkers, I figured, the Feds had more than the usual level of interest in finding a missing woman over the age of consent. The FBI guy, introduced to us as Agent Hardy, took the lead.

"All right, Mr. and Mrs.," he made a show of looking down at a notebook on the table in front of him, "Drake?" I felt my hackles rise. "Drake" is not a difficult name, and Menendez would have already made sure the Fed knew exactly who we were. Why ask unless he wanted us to know our place in the current hierarchy? I have to admit, that kind of rank-pulling drives me crazy.

"When and where did you see Emma Turnstone?" he asked, and when I opened my mouth to answer, he raised one hand to stop me. "That is, where do you *think* you saw Emma Turnstone?"

Now I was full-on irritated. "We met her last Tuesday as we were coming down the trail from Cathedral Rock," I said with a little more heat than necessary. I felt Nathan shift uneasily in his chair beside mine and told myself not to go adversarial. Not yet. "That's in the Alpine Lakes Wilderness," I added for the Fed's benefit. "She was going up. She said she'd planned to hike on the Pacific Crest Trail."

"And she told you she was Emma Turnstone?"

I glanced at Nathan. "No," I admitted. "She called herself Bella. But we spent a good twenty minutes with her, and I'm sure she's Emma Turnstone."

The cops exchanged looks. "Right," said Hardy. "What makes you so sure, Mrs. Drake?"

"She's a 6-foot blonde, early 20s, and troubled," I stammered, aware as I spoke of how flimsy my story sounded. "She was extremely upset and unprepared for a long backpacking trip. Her gear was ancient, and she didn't even know where she was headed. Also, she had her arm in a sling, like she'd hurt it. Maybe fell on it or something." I paused, shook my head and started again. "She was clearly running from something, and running so fast that she couldn't even take her dog. She left the dog with us." Nathan pressed his knee hard against mine under the table.

The cops waited in silence as I stood and dumped my daypack on the table, looking for the wanted poster Muriel had found at Buster's Hardware. "Look," I said, handing the crumpled piece of paper to Hardy. "We found this flyer, and I called the number two days ago. Someone who sounded like a young man answered. Told me his name is Cody. He said he needed to find this "Bella" because she'd stolen something he called his 'product.'"

Hardy looked at the blurry photo, then handed the paper to the Trooper. "This your girl?" he asked. "Could be," said Trooper Pinky, who to my horror, punched Cody's number into a landline that sat on the conference table. I imagined Cody seeing "State Troopers" showing up in his caller ID. How likely was it he'd answer? We waited. "Nothing," the Trooper said after a few uncomfortable minutes. "Not in service, I bet." Menendez sighed audibly.

"Well," said Hardy. "That's unfortunate." Was it my imagination or did he sound satisfied? Maybe even a little pleased?

"Maybe he got a new phone," I said. "You know, if he's doing something illegal, like with drugs, wouldn't he toss the used phone? Like on . . ." I stopped myself before I said it, but I imagined everyone in the room could complete my sentence for me: like on TV. Hardy looked at me with a flicker of amusement before his face fell back into its default expression. Professional. Noncommittal.

"Let's go over this just so I understand," he said. "You met a woman who identified herself as Bella on a trail in the," he looked at his notes, "Alpine Lakes Wilderness." I nodded. "That's what?" he continued, addressing Menendez, "something like 60 miles from the last known location of our subject?"

"Close to that," said Menendez. Hardy nodded and made a note. "The woman fit the description of Emma Turnstone," he continued. "She had old camping equipment and seemed to you unprepared for the rigors of the wilderness. Her arm—left? Right?"

"Left," I answered.

"Her left arm was injured. She had a puppy with her, which she gave to you." He stopped, and I felt Nathan tense beside me.

"This dog was her puppy?" he asked.

Nathan answered. "She said it wasn't her puppy. But Bella called her Penny. She—I mean Bella—had a leash and collar and a Frisbee. That is, for Penny. The leash was for Penny. The dog. She gave the dog to us because it was clear she—Penny, that is—couldn't make the hike."

"Penny," Hardy said, his pen busy. "And the girl, Bella, told you she was hiking the Pacific Crest Trail."

"At least she was thinking about it," I said. "It seemed like the trail was harder than she expected."

"North? South?" asked Menendez.

I was embarrassed now. "We don't really know which way she's headed. I'm afraid we just assumed she would go north, because the thru-hikers almost always go north."

"And the last time you saw her, she was walking toward this," Hardy looked down at his notes again. "Cathedral Rock?"

We nodded. "And she seemed upset," I added. "I mean, she'd just given us her puppy, so yeah, reason to be unhappy, right?" Hardy looked at me, professionally bored. "But still," I added, "She seemed very upset."

"Upset," echoed Hardy. "Got that." He capped his pen. "Mr. and Mrs. Drake, thank you for coming forward with this information. We rely on citizens like you to help us do our jobs." I flinched at that, since being an involved citizen clashed with my old school journalistic training, which tended more toward uninvolved observation and smirking. If Hardy saw my reaction, he didn't let on. "What I'm going to do now is write up my notes from our talk today, and with your permission I'll be contacting you again if I have any questions."

The cops shifted in their uncomfortable chairs. I imagined them thinking they might be able to drop by the house, say hi to the kids before their real workdays began. If I had any questions for them, now was the time. "So," I said too loudly, "if you don't mind my asking, will you be sending someone up to Cathedral Rock? I'm not sure if she decided to go north or south on the PCT, but there's a lot of roadless territory along the trail between Snoqualmie Pass and Stevens Pass. You might need quite a few searchers, and maybe her dog could help. We could take her dog up there." Nathan kicked me under the table, but I blundered on. "It's just I've been thinking about her parents," I continued, figuring it couldn't hurt to sound more sympathetic. "They must be frantic with worry."

Hardy put his chin in his hand and leaned over the table toward me. "Mrs. Drake, Detective Menendez tells me you're a reporter," he said. "A crime writer?"

"Was a reporter." I didn't like where he was headed. "Not anymore."

"Well," he said dismissively, as if my background explained everything. "Let me assure you that the Trooper and I follow up on all significant leads." He leaned away from me. "Now," he said, "thank you both for the information." The cops rose from their seats.

I caught up with Menendez as we hustled out of the building. "Look, Jennifer, I know that sounded bad," I said. "But the girl we met was Emma Turnstone, and I swear it, she was in trouble." Menendez looked skeptical, but I kept on. "So, maybe Agent Hardy has time to go up to the PCT, and maybe he doesn't. But what about the parents? Shouldn't they know we saw Emma, even if they decide we're full of it? Because it's their daughter we're talking about. Their baby girl."

The cop rolled her eyes and started again toward the door.

"Jennifer, I know what I'm talking about. I told you once. About my sister."

That stopped her. I silently apologized to Laura.

"All right, Beth," she said. "I'll talk to my guys about it."

* * * * *

"Lots of girls around here look like Emma Turnstone," Nathan said as we headed toward our townhome in Seattle. "Lacey looks like Emma Turnstone."

"So, you don't think we met Emma Turnstone?" Penny, happy to have the pack reunited, turned three times on my lap and settled in for the ride home.

"I didn't say that." Nathan went quiet.

I sat in the passenger seat, pouting. I was angry at being dismissed as just another nut job with a bad celebrity news habit or worse, a has-been reporter looking for a few morsels to base a comeback on.

When my phone buzzed, I jumped so violently that the seat belt restraints caught, and Penny braced herself. The caller ID said Jennifer Menendez.

"Beth, they want to meet you," Menendez said. "The Turnstones."

"You're kidding."

"I don't kid, you know that. You and Nathan can meet their security team at the West Precinct this afternoon at 2. They want to run a background check, of course, and if you come out

OK, they'll take you over to the house." She paused. "Or mansion. Whatever."

"Just Nathan and me?"

"Yeah. My guys aren't too happy about that, but it's the Turnstone's funeral." We shared an awkward silence. "I mean, who can blame them for wanting to hear about their little girl," she said quietly. "No matter the source."

* * * * *

The Turnstones lived, famously, on the shores of Lake Washington. The summer we arrived in Seattle, Nathan and I boarded a tour boat that cruised past their dock, the guide on a squawking audio system intoning facts about Curtis Turnstone as we squinted up at the acres of glass bisected by impossibly broad beams of polished wood—and that was only the boathouse, our guide told us. Curtis Turnstone was the billionaire founder of Mentor Core, the Puget Sound's venture capital firm of choice. The Turnstone's fortune, while only in the middle of the pack on the Forbes 100 Richest List, was still enough to attract plenty of attention.

Since retiring from active management of his fund ten years ago, Turnstone and his wife had turned their attention to philanthropy. The family had taken to veganism with a vengeance, and their grant-making focused on animal rights, a field neglected by other prominent donors. They quickly learned why. The public doesn't always take well to rich people telling them what they can't eat or keep on a leash. Despite their missteps, or perhaps because of them, it was safe to say that the Turnstones were even better known, if not better loved, than they'd been when Curtis Turnstone was a tech kingmaker.

The three Turnstone children, however, remained a mystery to those of us who never got closer to the family than the deck of a tour boat. We didn't even know the kids' names and ages, except, now, for Emma. Nathan and I tried not to gape as we were driven in an SUV the size of a shipping container through a series of security gates and up a long driveway. We were accompanied by the family's security team: two exceptionally fit young men and one exceptionally fit young woman, all dressed in khakis and impeccably pressed light blue Oxford-cloth shirts. It was a look straight out of my high school years: button-down collars and Bass Weejuns. At the door of the Turnstone's beams-and-river-rock estate we were met by what was either a concierge, secretary, or butler. He too wore khakis and a wrinkle-free shirt, this one in white. "Like a National Park lodge, only much grander," Nathan whispered to me as we followed the young man to the library, which overlooked a green expanse of lawn that swept down a gentle slope to the lake. Douglas fir and cedar trees massed along the periphery.

After the butler settled us in, Nathan got up to study the titles on the bookshelves lining the walls. He reached out to get a better look at one of the books, using two fingers to tip it up on its spine. "Don't!" I hissed, gesturing to the corners of the room. "They probably have security cameras." He shrugged, let the book fall back, and ambled over to sit next to me on an unfriendly sofa, bright white and chilly, with rigid buttons I could feel through my good summer-weight trousers. The house smelled of absolutely nothing, an absence of scent I associate with people who have money enough to locate the kitchen in another wing. We folded our hands in our laps like 8-year-olds waiting to be dismissed from catechism class. "Italian leather, you think?" Nathan whispered, unclasping his hands to lightly caress the sofa. "Weird choice for vegans."

The butler—or whatever he was, he'd introduced himself only as "Chad"—reentered the room carrying a sleek stainless-steel coffee carafe, four plain white mugs, and an exquisite glass tray in deep aquamarine that held a selection of brown, tubular plugs the size of shotgun shells. Stuffed dates, maybe? Whatever they were, they sure looked vegan.

"Curt and Caro will be down in a minute," Chad said. "Please help yourself to refreshments."

The Turnstones entered their library as Nathan and I were trying to figure out how to get the coffee out of the carafe. "For something that looks so simple," I was saying, "this thing is truly frustrating to operate."

"It's Icelandic," said a voice behind us. "You have to think like an Icelandic reindeer herder to make it work." Curtis Turnstone was smaller than I expected. As he took the carafe from my hands, I noticed he was only an inch or two taller than me and probably somewhere under my weight class—scrawny, in the way of serious runners. With a quick twist of the lid, he overcame the carafe's closure system and began pouring out the coffee in a smooth arc. "Soy milk? he asked. "Turbinado?" Nathan and I shook our heads "no" even though we both like cream in our brew.

"Thank you for coming on such short notice," said Carolyn Turnstone, who'd evidently slipped into the room behind her husband, along with a tall, unsmiling man carrying a black leather portfolio. Carolyn Turnstone seemed not to notice her escort as she settled across from us on another sofa, a match to the one we sat on. She perched on the forward edge so that her lean body barely touched the upholstery. The tall man chose an oversized mission-style straight-backed chair in the corner.

Both Turnstones had what my mother used to call "nervy" expressions: eyes red-rimmed, muscles taut, faces drawn. But what would you expect from a couple whose daughter was missing? "We're very interested in hearing about how you saw Emma, or thought you saw Emma," said Curtis Turnstone, settling in next to his wife. "But before we talk, I need to make one thing clear." He removed his wire-rimmed eyeglasses, held them out as if to inspect them for flaws, then replaced them on his nose. "Ms. Drake, I understand you're a journalist."

"Used to be," I said. "I'm retired." The word stuck in my throat, but I got it out.

"This," he said, indicating the tall man, "is John Bridges, our family counsel." The tall man nodded in our direction, and my heart lurched. It's never good to be introduced to somebody's attorney. "We're going to ask you to sign an agreement that states you won't use any of our conversation today in anything you might produce for publication or otherwise in the future."

I sat still for a moment, gathering my thoughts. Finally, I said, "As I mentioned, I'm not active in reporting."

"That's very good to hear," said Curtis Turnstone, "but we really do need to make that legally binding." With a sharp snap, the tall man unhooked the portfolio.

It was baffling, and a little flattering, too, that so many people still seemed to think of me as a journalist. I wasn't. Not anymore. But that didn't mean I was signing something that would stop me if I changed my mind. "Mr. Turnstone, it seems to me that you have the power to control this conversation." I said. "My husband and I are here to tell you what we saw and to answer your questions." I turned on my warmest smile. "Really, it's the two of us who are being interviewed, not the two of you."

"Ms. Drake, I'm sure you understand my position. I can't have reporters, even former reporters, talking with my wife and me about one of our children."

"I understand, Mr. Turnstone, and I want to tell you what we saw on the trail last week," I said, addressing the husband but looking at the wife. "But I'm sorry, I won't sign any agreement. Details of your daughter's case are bound to become public. I don't intend to be the source of them, but I can't put myself in the position of being legally at risk if they do come out."

I sat back on the sofa, took a deep breath and let it out as I silently counted to ten. It was an old reporting trick: sometimes if the silence becomes uncomfortable enough, a source will start talking just to relieve the tension. I finished counting, took another breath, and started over, this time counting down from ten to one. The silence wasn't a good sign, and I was certain that Nathan and I were about to be booted unceremoniously back through the security gates. But Carolyn Turnstone raised her eyes from her hands, which she held balled in her lap so tightly her knuckles stood out like enormous freshwater pearls, and asked, "When you saw Emma, was she all right?" The lawyer in the corner twitched, but he let me answer.

"If you mean was she all right physically, Mrs. Turnstone, for the most part, she was. She did have an injury to her left arm. It was in a sling and it looked like it had been bleeding." I watched Carolyn Turnstone's blue eyes, a match to her daughter's, as they filled with tears.

"We gave her a tube of antibacterial cream from our first aid kit, and some good bandages," Nathan added, "so with any luck it's healing up now."

"But she was bleeding," Carolyn Turnstone said. "Emma was bleeding." She turned toward her husband. "Curt, let them tell us what they know."

Curtis Turnstone glanced at his wife, then at his lawyer. The man inclined his head in a gesture that was hard to interpret. Yes? No? Could be either. It seemed to me a handy maneuver, and I filed it away for use in situations when ambiguity was a plus. Finally, Curtis Turnstone turned to Nathan and me and nodded. "Ms. Drake, Mr. Drake," he said, "we'd be grateful if you told us what you saw."

I knew enough not to start my story with the lawyer still in the room, so I pressed my leg hard against Nathan's to warn him into silence and watched as the man gathered his paperwork, stood, and moved smoothly on his soundless loafers toward the exit. The door had nearly closed on him when something shiny caught my eye. The silver tip of fancy-tooled cowboy boot had been inserted between the door and its frame. Into the room loped the boot's owner, a large man with a mustache as robust as a 1980s TV detective's. He had the rolling, uncertain gait of a big man who can't trust his knees and wore a dark brown leather blazer over a yellow snap-button shirt with a string tie, the kind my grandpa from Idaho had favored. As he took up the spot recently vacated by the attorney, I realized I was faintly disappointed that he had no hat to tip to us.

"Mr. and Mrs. Drake," said Curtis Turnstone. "This is Mr. Hawk. He's a private investigator who's helping us find Emma."

"Mr. Hawk," Nathan said slowly. "You mean, Sheriff Hawk? Sahaptin County's Sheriff Hawk?"

The big man pointed his substantial chin our way, smiled beneath his dark mustache, and held out both tanned hands, fingers spread. "Used to be," he said, his words uncomfortably like my own just moments ago. "I was sheriff in the Sahaptin, years ago." His voice, deep and slightly phlegmy, seemed summoned from somewhere below his naval. "Now I help folks out when they've got a problem in my county."

I'm afraid Nathan and I gaped. Jason Hawk was famous in our part of the world, and not entirely for the best reasons. He'd grown up not far from our little weekend hideaway in La Likt and made his way to the University of Washington on a football scholarship. After four glorious years wowing the adoring crowds at UW, he spent a couple more with the Seattle Seahawks as a tight end. Since then Hawk had owned car dealerships, lost his shirt promoting a failed sports bar franchise, and settled back home in a big house he'd had built just outside La Likt, sheriff for life if he had wanted to be. Still sheriff for life if you got on his bad side, some people whispered. His was quite the central Washington success story, if you paid no attention to the reports of his temper and his drinking.

Hawk came to a stop behind the sofa occupied by the Turnstones, and both turned an ear toward him while keeping their eyes on us, as if ready to act on an audible play. When none came, Carolyn Turnstone glanced up at Hawk and then stole a look at her husband before turning to face me. She drew in a quick breath and raised her chin. "Ms. Drake," she said, reaching over and touching my knee gently. "You were about to tell us how you met Emma."

Mostly I told our story, though Nathan did get in a mention of High Country Crapper and the toilet at Peggy's Pond. When I finished talking, Curtis Turnstone set his coffee cup on the teak table in front of us, placing it so carefully it made no sound when it touched the surface of the wood. "We have a few questions for you. I hope you understand. We need to establish that it was really Emma that you met."

"Of course," Nathan said. I nodded once and kept my mouth shut for a change.

"Your physical description sounds right, but it could fit any number of girls. Or you might have read it in the missing persons bulletin. Can you tell us what she was wearing?"

"Stretchy short-shorts," I replied, "like someone might wear for a yoga class. An old puffer jacket, powder blue."

"A wool hat," Nathan continued. "In one of those Scottish prints. What do you call it?"

"Fair Isle," I said.

"And a key on a chain," Nathan said.

The Turnstones shifted almost imperceptibly toward each other. "What kind of key?" Curtis asked.

"A big, old-fashioned key," Nathan said. "What are they called?"

"Skeleton key," I said.

He nodded. "It was on a thick silver chain that went over her head. She could wear it like a necklace, but when I saw it, she had it in her hands, wrapping the chain around her knuckles and then unwrapping it again." He looked at Curtis Turnstone. "Is it significant?"

"You said she had a dog that you've taken in," he replied. "What kind of dog?"

"A Hungarian Viszla," I said, feeling Nathan tense beside me at the mention of Penny.

"I just find it funny she'd give the dog up like that," Carolyn Turnstone said. "She must have trusted you, and trust doesn't come easy to my Emma." She made a sound halfway between a snort and a giggle. "Emma's not what you'd call trusting."

"Now, Caro," Curtis Turnstone whispered at her.

"Well, Curt, she's *not* trusting. Or forgiving, for that matter," his wife responded. "Emma's always loved animals, more than anything or anybody else. Maybe too much." She gave Nathan and me a defiant stare, as if challenging us to disagree. "But you probably know that."

Curtis Turnstone put a hand on his wife's well-toned upper arm and sighed. "You've read about the FreeThinkers?" Nathan and I nodded in unison. "Then you know Emma was a member. But there's never been evidence that she was involved with the explosion that killed those poor chimps at the UW. There's never been enough evidence, up to now anyway, for the prosecutor to, you know, bring charges."

Hawk made a low rumbling sound, like a mountain lion might make before pouncing on a house cat, and the couple again angled toward him. The billionaire exchanged a look with his hired muscle, then faced us and picked up his coffee cup. He didn't bring it to his lips. "Did she say anything about the FreeThinkers?"

"No," Nathan replied.

"Nothing about seeing her old friends, or why she'd need to go hiking right now? No reason why she felt she should hide? Nothing about new information coming out?"

Nathan glanced at Hawk, then turned back to Curtis Turnstone. "No, I'm sorry. She seemed to be in a hurry."

"Well," Turnstone said. "That's very helpful, right, Mr. Hawk?"

Hawk limped toward the space between the twin sofas.

"Very helpful," he growled.

He stopped just to the right of Nathan and me, his saucer-sized silver belt buckle at my eye level, then turned and placed a heavy left hand, no wedding band, on my right shoulder. Bolts of anxiety shot down my arm and curled my fingers into a fist.

"But she didn't say where she was going, Mrs. Drake?"

I tried to suppress a shudder. "She didn't," I answered. "She didn't say where she was going."

"Well, not exactly," Nathan said. "Like Beth said, Emma said she'd been thinking about heading up to the Pacific Crest Trail, and judging by the weight of her load, she probably could spend a week or two." He looked at Carolyn Turnstone, who was twisting a blonde lock of hair around her index finger so hard I was sure it hurt her scalp. "We gave her the first aid supplies and some extra nuts and breakfast bars, that kind of thing."

Hawk left his heavy hand on my shoulder, and I pressed my leg hard against Nathan's, willing him, for once, not to give up more information. I stared through the picture windows past the Turnstones to the water, where a tour boat had pulled up just beyond the dock. I could see the passengers lining the rail. Some raised their hands to their eyes. Maybe they had binoculars.

"Oh ho," said Hawk, rhythmically massaging my shoulder, each squeeze delivering another jolt directly to my nervous system. "So, she did say something about where she was headed, didn't she, Mrs. Drake? Thanks for bringing that up, Mr. Drake. Like Curtis said, those kinds of details are very helpful." He lifted his hand from my shoulder and used it to give Curtis Turnstone a two-fingered salute. Then he turned and began a slow walk toward the door. "Thanks for the tips," he said over his shoulder. "I'll check 'em out for you."

After Hawk left the room, Carolyn Turnstone faced her husband. "I don't like him," she said tersely. "Maybe he's a big deal in Sahaptin County. Maybe he knows where all the bodies are buried . . ." She stopped short.

"You'll have to excuse us, Mr. and Mrs. Drake," said Curtis Turnstone. "We have mixed feelings about Hawk."

"My feelings about him aren't mixed," his wife said. "I don't trust him. And he's expensive."

"We're told he's the one to see if you've got trouble in that part of the world."

"Well, he's awfully expensive if you ask me. For somebody who's really just a big jock."

"Actually" said Curtis Turnstone, leaning forward toward Nathan and me, voice lowered, "his story is fascinating. When Hawk was 12, both parents and a younger brother were killed by a drunk driver on Blewett Pass."

Carolyn Turnstone rolled her eyes toward the ceiling beams and sighed dramatically. "Oh, here we go."

"Raised on his uncle's farm in Ellensburg," her husband continued, palms up, almost beseeching us. "All scholarships. Football, then business, then elected office. All self-made."

"Self-made," Carolyn Turnstone snorted. "Right."

A frown passed quickly over the billionaire's face. Then he leaned back, arranged his features to a more neutral expression, and took his wife's hand.

"There's something about him, isn't there?" I finally said. "High creep factor." Everyone looked at me as if startled by my words, and I wondered how mixed the Turnstones' feelings really were when it came to Hawk. "It's just a feeling, right?" Carolyn Turnstone's big blue eyes were on me. "Like he's threatening you. Probably it's just his size or his reputation."

I paused to let someone agree with me. Someone like Nathan, for example. But no one picked up the conversation. "Anyway," I said just a tad too breezily, "maybe that's why I didn't want to tell you this in front of him. We gave Emma directions to one of our favorite campsites, and it seemed like she might set up there. Of course, that was a few days ago. She's probably farther along the trail now."

Carolyn Turnstone's words came out in a rush, "But she might be there. We can look. Or you can. Would you? Would you go up and check?" She gestured toward the tour boat on the other side of the windows. "I'd check myself, but I can't go anywhere. You, though. You could go check, couldn't you?"

"I'm not sure it would be a good idea for us to get involved," Nathan said, "since you have Mr. Hawk working for you. Too many cooks in the kitchen and all that."

"No," her tone was urgent. "Certainly not Hawk. Emma trusted you. You go. It would be a favor to us. A favor we could return when this is all over." She looked at me. "When it's time to tell our story, when it's time for Emma to tell her story, I mean, it makes sense we'd tell it to a journalist we know and trust. Like you, Ms. Drake."

"Call me Beth," I said as she opened a slender drawer in the coffee table and extracted a creamy rectangle of heavy card stock. She handed it to me. The card was embossed with the letters "CMT." A string of 10 numbers stood out in black ink beneath the monogram. "My phone number," she said. "Don't be afraid to call."

She turned to Nathan. "And your organization, what is it? The Crapper Coalition? It sounds like the kind of good work the Turnstone Foundation might be very interested in supporting." She turned toward her husband. "Isn't that right, Curtis?"

Chad entered the library just as we were struggling to get up without spilling our coffee. The butler walked toward us swiftly, relieved us of the coffee cups, and circled behind as if to herd us toward the door. Nathan made a grab for the snack tray and, to my horror, pocketed a few dates.

"I'm surprised they don't blindfold us," I whispered once we were buckled into the middle seats of the black SUV, with two security boys stationed in front of us and one security girl in back. We'd almost cleared the last set of gates when we heard the incongruous sound of a revving engine coming through the thick forest of Douglas fir that lined the private road below.

"What the hell?" said one of the security guys as a red SUV with California plates fishtailed into view. Behind us, the security girl began speaking urgently into a hand-held walkie talkie. "All units, code purple on the forest road. Repeating: possible perimeter threat on the forest road."

Our driver swung his monstrous vehicle sideways to block the way. The red SUV slowed briefly, then shot toward the narrow opening between our rear bumper and the vine-covered stone wall that lined the driveway. We heard the sharp shriek of metal on metal and felt a slight jolt as the vehicle squeezed past us. "Damn!" shouted one of the security boys as we all turned and saw the red SUV, side mirror hanging and engine still revving, halted on the lane we'd just descended.

Jason Hawk stood in the middle of the driveway pointing an impressively large handgun at the SUV's windshield. "Out. Now. Hands where I can see 'em," he yelled. By the time our security crew unbuckled and scrambled to the scene, Hawk had a lanky, long-haired man in tight black jeans and a rumpled tweed blazer pushed face-first into the stone wall. The man's arm was wrenched at a violent angle behind his back. From our perch, we got a glimpse of the side of his face. He'd managed somehow to hold on to the cigarette in his mouth, and it bobbed up and down as he talked nonstop. Hawk ratcheted the man's arm up a couple more inches, and the monologue ended with a scream of pain.

As I jockeyed for a better view out of the tinted windows, I felt Nathan tug my arm. "Beth," he said a little breathlessly, "I have a question."

"Yeah?" I said distractedly as I tried to memorize the red SUV's license plate number.

"What's turbinado?"

Chapter 9

Beauty in the Backwoods

Lawman tracks blonde heiress to remote Washington wasteland

Sweet Emma on the run?

By Nigel Turner
Informant Staff

La Likt, Washington: There's a belief out west that you can judge a man by his handshake. If that's true, Jason Hawk is a sadist.

Hawk, a former American football star and sheriff of rural Sahaptin County, Washington, is an awe-inspiring if not adored presence in this depressed, some might say depressing, mountain hamlet located a 90-minute motor drive east of Seattle. Ask around town and you'll discover he's accustomed to getting his way, or else. Now in the employ of famed investor Curtis Turnstone, he's twisting arms to find out who knows where the billionaire's wayward daughter Emma has gone.

"If anyone can track her down, it'll be Jason Hawk. Poor girl," said one raven-haired Hawk acquaintance who resides in La Likt, a town whose unusually descriptive name is derived from the Native American term for "salmon slime." (It is common, the *Informant* has learned, for place names in the region to refer to various aspects of fish or the cold swift waters in which they swim.)

Hawk's involvement in the search for Sweet Emma suggests that her family believes the former animal rights terrorist and girlfriend of gene tweaker Winston Drummond has fled to this rural central Washington county. If that's the case, the blonde beauty is indeed a long way from London, the city she suddenly left after Drummond's car spontaneously combusted last month, killing an unfortunate boy inside.

The villages strung along the river valleys here are undoubtedly picturesque, if dismayingly untidy in places, prompting a visitor to ask a local man what possible impending use he might have for a motorcycle, a snowmobile, and a wheelchair, all rusting near the front porch of his home.

"Never know what you might need," the man explained. "Motorbike was how I got around before that winter we had all the snow. Sled worked until the front track came off. Wheelchair was for when I got thrown off the sled."

One hopes that exact combination of circumstances will not occur again.

Hawk, meanwhile, seems to have escaped the necessity of holding on to spare parts in case the need for them arises. His recently completed three-level log home dominates the ridgeline above town, and local conversation.

"I don't know how he got the money for that place, especially after he had such bad luck with the sports bar franchise," said one resident who spoke on condition of anonymity due to the sensitive nature of her comments. "Plus, did you see he's got a brand-new truck? It's an import. They don't sell those around here."

Another local suggested the money might come from his work with Turnstone.

"I guess a successful man like Curtis Turnstone thinks he knows what he's doing," said the woman, who gave her name only as Serena. "But if he hired Hawk to look for his daughter, I'd tell him he's making a mistake. Hawk's just mean. I hope the girl can stay lost."

Keep up with the story! *Informant Online*.

--end

My phone pinged. Childe Editor again.

"Don't write, Nigel. Tweet."

And again, the ping.

"And give us a Tops to Watch on Emma. 150 words max."

Chapter 10

NATHAN DRAKE

October 6-9

During our interview with the Turnstones, I considered mentioning my little episode with the brothers at their Fortune Creek compound, but in the end I decided it wouldn't shed any light on Emma's whereabouts. She was gone and she wanted to be gone. That's why she asked us not to tell anybody we'd seen her. The farther away from Cody and Tommy she got, the better. And what if she did take their dog? How could you blame her? Penny was better off with us. Anyway, let things play out, is what I thought.

Even so, after meeting with Emma's parents, I agreed with Beth that we owed them a hike back up the trail to take a look around the spot we'd last seen their daughter. Now that my intrepid wife had stuck our noses in, we were on the hook. I mean, if the police weren't going to look, then we should. It had already been more than a week since we saw Emma and no one was in any hurry to follow her trail. No one official, anyway.

Our hike back to the spot we'd met Emma wasn't much fun. Muriel was watching Penny, which made us both anxious to begin with, especially me. Plus, it was slow going since we were hyper-alert for any evidence of Emma along the trail. I kept a printout of the missing persons report in my shirt pocket, and we stopped other hikers to ask if they'd seen a solo hiker matching her description. No one had.

But the real bummer about our three days on Emma's trail was how stubbornly out of sync Beth and I felt. She insisted I'd honored Emma's request for secrecy for too long. I thought she was too quick to betray a confidence. In my view, it was an honest difference of opinion, not right versus wrong. The missing persons report changed things, sure, and that's why I agreed to tag along to meet with Emma's parents. I mean, maybe Emma was OK with us telling her parents that we'd seen her. But I also worried that any new information about Emma's location that got out might put her in more danger with the puppy mill brothers, or even her former FT pals. For all I knew, it might even put us in danger. My thinking was, let's take it slow and see what Emma's running from.

My wife the journalist, on the other hand, believes the truth trumps everything else. Shine a light everywhere. No secrets. Nothing left unsaid. Publish every thought. Frankly, sometimes I can do without her seeker of truth act. Life isn't that simple. Tell the capital "T" Truth, I'd say, is just one imperative and it must always be weighed against another: Do no harm. There's always potential harm in the truth. Consider: what if your Truth, too liberally shared, results in a blown cover and a dead federal agent in Nicaragua? Just for example. Because my father could tell you about that. Not that he will. But more to the point—here, now—what if the Truth allows an old FT associate or Tommy DeRoux to find and harm Emma? Might one not make the case for staying quiet and allowing Emma to remain out of sight? Might one not consider the harm in dispensing excessive quantities of Truth and then calibrate the dose judiciously?

All these arguments spun through my head as we spent the second night of our search at Waptus Lake. Neither of us slept well. There was a lot of nylon-amplified tossing and turning inside our cramped tent.

We were wrapping around the flank of Cathedral Peak the next morning, headed toward the camp we told Emma about, when I tried once again to defend my reluctance to get too involved. "I'm just worried that we're going to have your old pals at the *Times* calling us when we get back."

"I'll deal with them," Beth said.

"And how much will you tell them?"

"I'll deal with them, I said."

"Great. And what will you say when they ask about Penny?"

"Why would they ask about her? They don't even know about her."

"You forget how clever reporters can be. Not to mention deceptive and disloyal. Duplicitous."

"Uh-huh. And you forget I used to be one of those reporters." Her pace accelerated, and the talking-distance gap between us became a solitary-thoughts gap. The trail over the low ridge, as smooth and neatly edged as a Japanese garden, curled through acres of red heather, the flower spikes now gone to seed. Mt. Daniel's snowclad northeast side loomed above. An idyllic setting. Too bad my wife and I hated each other.

By the time I reached the familiar cairn that marks the way to our secret camp, Beth was already boulder-hopping and squeezing her way through the creek-side brush. I heard the eager click-click of HiWI hiking poles approaching from behind, so I waited to make one more inquiry about our missing person. After letting the solo hiker move on, I discretely eased off trail and across the granite drainage.

Beth had dropped her pack in a gravelly flat surrounded by refrigerator-sized hunks of granite. Over the years, we'd spent maybe a half-dozen nights in this hidden hillside perch. It was only a quarter mile or so off the Pacific Crest Trail, and yet it always felt like our own private rock garden—the gravel bed always pressed smooth between our visits by the winter maid service of wind and rain and snow. But not this time.

"Holes from tent stakes," Beth said, pointing with her hiking pole to four small disturbed areas in the gravel. "Boot prints, too."

"Yeah, looks like some rocks have been moved here," I said. "Someone sat on this grass. Maybe even last night."

For ten more minutes, we looked closely at everything in the campsite except each other. On the hillside above us, the pikas cheeped warnings of our presence.

After all that poking around, we hoisted our packs and started busting our way back out to the main trail. I was shoving myself through the willows, head down and poles up like a downhill skier, when I nearly ran into Beth. She was facing me in the brush, holding up the skeleton key on its long silver chain.

"I found this just after the stream crossing," she said. "Maybe it broke off when they were filtering water."

"So, she was here," I said. "Which means she's likely moving north."

"Yeah, I guess we should've come here first instead of going south to Waptus."

Noted. Another mistake of mine.

"She must be long gone," Beth said. "She's young, she could be at Stevens Pass by now."

"Who knows where she is," I said. "She's injured, remember? She's got that ridiculous pack. Lots of stuff can go wrong. Anyway, we tried. We might as well keep heading north and then loop back via Hyas Lake."

"Yep."

Those were our last words until we turned on the La Likt River trail and descended to Hyas Lake. As we approached the valley bottom, we saw a couple of hikers near a smoldering fire. They'd just broken down their tent and were in that tedious phase of repacking their scattered gear into their backpacks.

"I'll go check with them," I said as Beth continued toward the main body of the lake.

"I'll be up around the corner," she said.

Moving closer to the smoky camp, I noticed two rifles propped against a log—and a sleeping dog. After a couple more steps, I realized with a start that the two guys standing side by side scratching their heads in unison were the brothers from the Fortune Creek puppy mill.

I immediately ducked low and pretended to tie my bootlace. They hadn't seen me yet, but I was exposed, so I remained on a knee and slowly pivoted to face away from them. When I was reasonably sure they were engrossed in their packing, I rose up quietly and headed down the trail.

Were they looking for Penny or the girl? Both? Were they headed up or coming back down? And were the deer rifles for high buck hunting season, or something else?

"We can be at the car in under two hours," I said, hurrying past Beth, who'd pretty obviously just returned from a pee in the woods.

"Yeah. I think? Whatever," she said, no doubt surprised to see me dart off before she had a chance to put away her TP.

Ninety minutes later we were in the parking lot, switching from boots into sneakers. As I pulled the Subaru onto the forest road, I saw the brothers' old green Jeep, the one with the roll bar, parked in a far corner of the lot.

I made good time down the forest road, considering the potholes, the washboard, and all my glances in the rearview mirror. When we reached smooth pavement, this time Beth didn't doze off. She just stared out at the river, the lake, and the woods.

* * * * *

The next day, I went on a dump run in the Subaru. The road from our La Likt cabin to the transfer station is just a few miles, but the drive seems to take forever. That's because the locals, so cavalier about fireworks bans and leash laws, have adopted a cult-like reverence for the 25 miles-per-hour speed limit posted here. How, I wonder, have the police cowed the entire local population into obeying this particular law, but not the others?

"What's up with these people, Penny?" I said to the alert dog who sat in the passenger seat, staring straight ahead as we crept uphill. I was now one of those guys who posed rhetorical questions to his dog while his wife engaged in aggressive vacuuming back at the suddenly too-small cabin. "Baffling and frustrating, isn't it, pup?"

The disappointment of missing Emma by just a day or two was hard to shake. We both just wanted to stew in our own juices for a while. Beth had agreed to call Carolyn Turnstone with the news. In fact, she was probably making the call right about the time I turned into the transfer station.

I was glad to be with Penny at the dump. I lifted the Subaru hatch and began the reliably melancholy task of hurling familiar objects one by one into the piles of garbage and recycling already on the concrete pad. A rusty fireplace screen that had come north from our first home together in Sacramento. My old training binders from the county. A boxful of antiquated landline equipment, modems, and phone cables. As each item emerged from the Subaru and arced through the air, the associated memory neurons flashed dutifully in my head, perhaps for the last time. You can't keep it all, I reminded myself. Penny poked her head between the two front seats and watched the spectacle.

As each object clattered to the end of its useful life, I distracted myself by reviewing the long list of bad things that could happen to a young woman on the trail. That arm for one. Maybe a bad infection, sepsis. There's always a broken ankle, a fall off the trail and down the hill, a head injury. Giardia wouldn't show up for a while, but it's surprising how many hikers are laid up by bad diarrhea or even routine GI stuff. I once read of a constipated hiker who suffered a massive stroke while trying to poop in the woods. What a way to go. Although, all told, I suppose you could do worse. For a more dignified end, I grant, that would be the one time you wouldn't want to be using a high country crapper.

I pulled out a small wooden tool box coated in green paint. For 10 years it sat on the lowest shelf in our garage, where it secured the musty drill bits and chisels of my Uncle Bob. Now empty, but still emitting that rusty tang of steel tools nearly a century old, the box sailed through the dust-filled air, hung briefly at the apex, and then dropped to the concrete and exploded into splinters, hinges and clasps. The tools would go to the flea market next month. Sorry, Bob.

Of course, there's always the sexy but rare stuff that might have caught up to Emma on the trail. Bears. Cougars. Lightning. Assault. Undiagnosed heart issue, like cardiomyopathy. Drowning. But you should really think common things first, I told myself. For her demographic, and I hate to say it, there's the bad ex-boyfriend, drug OD, or suicide. She *was* acting frazzled. Maybe she's just lost. Or most likely of all, I told myself for the umpteenth time, she just *wants* to be lost for a while.

Maybe we should've looked longer on the trail.

All the ruminating about old family stuff and missing young women made me think again about Beth's sister.

Where's Laura now? Who knows. The first time Beth told me the story, she mumbled something about the American River, the scene of several drownings each year. But she didn't sound convinced. She certainly wasn't comforted. It seemed more like a way to end the conversation about her sister than an explanation, and I never pressed her for more.

I sat on the back of the Subaru and looked beyond my personal contributions to the mounds of more anonymous detritus from upper Sahaptin County. Every speck in those heaps had meaning to someone at some time. Overwhelming to imagine all the memories lost here. Evaporated. All that substance without story. Penny was at my side sharing in my gaze, both of us trying to sense the meaning of the garbage-scape before us.

"It's the end of the road for this stuff, Penny," I told her, "it's the end of the road, girl."

We'd just headed back downhill toward home when my phone buzzed.

Lacey. I pulled off to the side of the road to take the call.

"What's up, Lacey?"

I watched the traffic creep by.

"Hey Uncle Nathan. I got a hit on the news alert... I... upset Emma.. and FT...strange... story."

I couldn't make sense of the words coming through my phone.

"She . . . *Informant* . . . London . . . Emma . . . online . . . bomb . . . tabloid . . ."

The sounds were disconnected, random utterances. Maybe not even words. Perhaps a kind of Aramaic. How does the brain ever connect a pile of sounds to make a story? My body felt odd in the car seat. For a moment, I thought I was having a stroke. The words stopped.

I raised my elbows out to the side, phone still at my ear, and leaned over to check my face in the rearview mirror. I peeled my lips back in a forced smile. Kinda creepy, but the cheeks matched up even.

"You still there?" Lacey asked.

I could read the dump receipt on my dashboard just fine. No stroke, I guess.

"Yeah sorry. Go ahead." Penny licked my protruding right elbow and gave me a puzzled look.

"I said she was mentioned in a story in the *Informant* online. It's a London tabloid. Sort of sleazy. So, what I found: It's a crime story, sort of a top-ten-unsolved-crimes-of-the-year thing. Along with these, I don't know, slasher murders and mom-cut-up-and-put-into-a-barrel things, there's one that says Emma Turnstone was involved in the car bombing of a biotech executive outside of London. They say it was another FT bombing."

"Geez," I said, snapped out of my dump-induced blues. Now Lacey's words made all too much sense. I was already recalibrating my faith in Emma. "Could explain why she left London."

"Yeah. If it's true. Actually, even if it's not true. The *Informant* isn't exactly the New York *Times*. They make a big deal about her dad and the money. They have a photo of her in a slinky dress outside a swanky London club. She's with some hunk in Armani."

Lacey read me the paragraph about Emma. It linked her to a car bombing in London that occurred six weeks previously. The writer briefly described her suspected involvement in the Seattle bombing, pegged her family's net worth at $14 billion and went on:

"The attractive heiress and acknowledged FT associate scarpered off to the U.S. shortly after the explosion that killed a 16-year-old boy and badly burned Winston Drummond, the dashing, 38-year-old CEO of Rational EvoAg, a biotech company that develops seeds and farm animals using genetic modification. There are rumors that the blonde animal rights champion may have dated Drummond simply to set him up for a fall. Although no charges have been brought, Sweet Emma is no doubt handsome, clever, and rich enough to feign romance in order to further her radical goals. And that's why she's one of our Tops to Watch this month."

Back home, over a BLT at our cabin's backyard picnic table, Beth was livid about the hyperbole and speculation employed by the *Informant* reporter, a guy named Nigel Turner. Using a mayo-free pinkie to jab at her phone, she located and quickly consumed, along with her sandwich, the three *Informant* stories mentioning Emma. I'd already read them by the side of the road.

"The guy convicts her and has no sources. Talk about a criminal writer."

I made a noise that I hoped sounded like agreement, and asked: "Why didn't we see all these *Informant* stories about Emma and the London bombing when we searched last week? You think the Turnstones know about them?"

But Beth still had her nose pointed at her phone.

"This Turner thinks he's so cute. The 'handsome, clever, and rich' line is straight from Austen's *Emma*, you know."

Of course, I didn't know. I was just glad the London reporter was deflecting some of Beth's anger and impatience away from me.

"Sounds to me like he wants to create the next Sexy Lexy," I said, finishing off the corn chips. "Or whoever that girl in Italy was years ago. From Seattle? Attractive girl in school overseas? A reputation for partying, according to the press."

"Sweet Emma," spat Beth. "Not quite the same ring as Sexy Lexy. But she's rich, so people will eat it up."

"Did you see the previous story? The longer one? Turner says the *Informant* is sending him to Seattle."

"Well, if you're going to cook up your own news," said Beth, "why not use the juiciest local ingredients, right?"

"Those Brit paparazzi know how to pursue their prey." As soon as I said it, I was sorry, because now we were both thinking of the sad end to Princess Diana's story. "Thanks for making lunch," I added, on my best behavior. "I'll clean up."

After washing our dishes at the backyard hose (the kitchen plumbing was weeks away from completion), I relocated to the darkened living room and settled into the cabin's only upholstered chair with my laptop. Beth started toward downtown La Likt on foot to pick up some sausage for tonight's pasta. Penny settled in at my feet. Beth and I had an unspoken agreement that there was no need to advertise Penny's whereabouts around town to whoever might be lazy enough to lose her in the first place. My wife's guilt about not seeking Penny's previous owner lessened with each passing day.

I nodded off for about five minutes, old-guy behavior that always disturbs me just a little. To make up for it, once I woke up, I found a few earlier stories about the London car explosion from sources other than the *Informant*, all of them much more circumspect about suspects. None mentioned FT or Emma, or any other animal-rights or anti-genetic modification angle, for that matter.

The explosion made the news, of course, because of the death of the teen in the car and also because of the public's fascination with Drummond as one of London's most eligible bachelors. I found more than a few photo-driven stories featuring the dark-haired Drummond shepherding some damsel into a Jaguar or Mercedes. The guy definitely had the looks and the money to attract someone like Emma.

From all indications, he had the smarts, too. His company was an interesting one. The idea was to use genetic engineering, including CRISPR and RNA-based techniques, to alter soybean and corn seeds and maximize crop yields. His people did some animal stuff too, and they were expanding and capturing a big share of the global agriculture market. Anti-GMO groups regularly boycotted their products, but never, according to what I found, was the company targeted for violence.

Beth listened to my synopsis while we took an evening stroll along a side channel of the Yakima River to see if there was anything new among the bird community there. It was something we'd liked to do together before Penny dropped into our lives, and now the pup skittered around our feet impatiently, unused to the leash we'd hooked to her collar. A squadron of tree swallows flew by like toy fighter jets to feed over the still water and then landed, one by one, on a stump in the river channel. It was late in the season for tree swallows. We raised our binoculars in unison, just another going-gray couple who will soon be checking the birdwatching box on the AARP hobby survey. The low sun caught the metallic blue-black feathers on the bird's blunt heads. Their bellies were white, soft, ruffled by the breeze. We watched their shiny heads swivel left then right then left again against a grainy backdrop of insects. We watched them watching us.

When Beth finally spoke, her voice was so soft that I became aware of the nearby roar of I-90.

"Well, Drummond sounds pretty full of himself. I hope Emma had nothing to do with him."

This was a briefer and altogether less sharp-edged reply than I had come to expect from my wife. She was still annoyed with me, no doubt. Perhaps tired after our work on the cabin that day and, just maybe, anxious about her drive over the pass to Seattle tomorrow, where she planned to check in on our townhouse and her vegetable garden and maybe make resupply stops at Fred Meyer and Trader Joe's.

Or, maybe not. What did I really know about this woman next to me? Maybe she just wanted to watch the birds.

Chapter 11

Charlie Johnson-Medra

Excerpt from the journal of Charlie Johnson-Medra

Oct. 6
  Yesterday Em saw the two guys from the Fortune Creek
place walking south on PCT with hunting rifles and a dog. Em
was really scared and had us break camp, pack up, in case we
had to run. But they came back today going north, passed us by,
and kept going. We'll wait another day to be sure. We can get
more food at Stevens Pass, I think.

Oct. 7
  So today Em saw the old couple who gave her the bandages
for her arm. We had already broken camp, and so we just
dragged our packs and hid way high off the trail. They snooped
around our camp then continued north on the PCT. We gave
them a head start and then went north ourselves. When we saw
them turn off down the La Likt River valley, we scooted to the
pass and scrambled up Trico Mountain. We'll hang out here for
one more day. Em had a little cry, who knows why. But she's
feeling better. We had some power bars, a walk up the ridge,
and a nice afternoon session in the tent. All of Em's drama
definitely worth it for that.

Oct. 9

Yesterday we set out for Doelle Lake, where we are now. Very steep climb (we stashed bear sacks at the bottom of the hill), but a beautiful spot. Mist burned off over the lake like steam from coffee this morning. But now Em's worried about leaving all those reeking terpenes in the bear sacks down below.

We got a cell signal on Surprise Mountain. So, Jake will do food drop at Stevens Pass day after tomorrow. North to the future!

Chapter 12

MARY BETH DRAKE

October 9-14

I held the silver skeleton key in my hand and rubbed my thumb over its rough teeth. I was going through my usual pre-interview breathing exercises—in and out slowly while concentrating on a favorite spot fixed in my mind's eye, this time the vine maples that rim Cooper Lake. Right now, I told myself, their leaves should be touched with the vibrant reds and oranges of fall. I let my breath out in a whoosh. The trees had a long way to go before snow fell. I put the key on the cot beside me, picked up my phone, and tapped in the number printed on the cream-colored card.

"Mrs. Turnstone," I said when she answered. "It's Beth."

"Beth Drake," she finished with the authority of a person used to commanding department head meetings. The vulnerability she'd shown during our in-person meeting had evaporated. "Did you see Emma?"

"No, I'm sorry," I said. "We got back late last night. We didn't see her. But we did find some signs of her." I looked at the key and concentrated on telling the story the way I'd practiced as we drove home from the trailhead. Nathan and Penny, each thrilled to be reunited with the other, were out celebrating at the dump, and the cabin was quiet except for the anxious hiss of the west wind in the aspens. "We found the skeleton key," I continued, "the one we talked about during our last meeting. It was near the camping spot we told Emma about." I hesitated. "We found signs that maybe there was more than one person in that camp."

"Do you have the key?" Carolyn Turnstone asked.

I was taken aback. I'd expected the mother to be more interested in the possibility that her daughter had met up with someone than in the old key. "Yes," I answered. "I'm looking at it right now."

"Hold on to it."

"All right," I said uncertainly.

She exhaled, and when she spoke again, her tone was warmer, as if she and I were friends who'd mended a falling out. "What I mean is, don't give it to Mr. Hawk or the police, OK, Beth? I'll need it back." She paused. "Actually, keep it for now. Do you have a safe place for it?"

A memory of Sunday afternoons spent watching cowboy movies on my grandpa's RCA console flickered in my mind. Heroines were forever squirreling something precious under the flooring in their rooms above the saloon. I scanned the cabin's dusty floor. "Sure," I said. "I can find somewhere to put it."

"Good. Thank you."

"Sure."

"And I'm sorry if I was short with you just now. It's hard to tell who I can trust, you know? I've trusted the wrong people in the past."

"I suppose it's hard to know people's motivation. I mean, given how prominent your family is, you have to wonder what people expect from you, or how they plan to use whatever they get from you." An internal alarm rang in my head. I was talking too much. "That's probably too obvious, but that's how I'd look at it."

"That's it exactly. When I'm talking to people, even people I consider my friends, I'm constantly asking myself, 'What's in it for them?' It's cynical, I know, but the times I've let my guard down." She paused. "Well, let's just say it's been a mistake to let my guard down. But I feel I can trust you to help me find Emma." She hesitated once more, "because of your own family's history."

A jolt of adrenalin blasted through my body and I almost dropped the phone. Once I had a secure hold on it again, I overcompensated by pressing the hot little rectangle tightly against my clammy cheek. The phone chirped like an injured bird. "Sorry," I said, forcing myself to back off my grip slightly. I should have known that the Turnstone's background check on Nathan and me would unearth Laura's case, but I'm never ready when someone brings it up.

It was still my turn to speak. "Yes, my family," I began. "My sister . . ." My voice trailed away. Social conditioning will take you only so far in these situations.

"I know," she said.

I struggled to catch my breath, and to turn the conversation away from Laura and me. "Mrs. Turnstone," I said at last, "Carolyn. What Nathan and I were wondering is where did Emma go after she camped in our spot? We scouted along the PCT and, like I said, we didn't see her. So, I'm wondering, do you have any idea where she'd go? Or who she might be with?"

"I don't know what she's doing out there at all. We're not a camping family."

"What about her friends, do they camp?"

She answered with a low, rueful laugh. "If you call flying out to the San Juan Islands and staying in a summer house with a wood-fired hot tub camping, then yes. She and her friend Wren used to go out to their family island. Lovely, but off the grid. They'd come home after a week, usually sunburned and dying for some kombucha. Otherwise, the closest Emma has ever been to the wilderness is our place at Skylandia."

"I don't suppose you can call that camping," I said, imagining the luxury resort just up the state highway from our La Likt cabin. The multimillion-dollar homes there sat on half-acre lots that abutted the fairways of plush golf courses. It was a world away from the ramshackle bungalows on the other side of the gates. "I didn't know you had a place at Skylandia."

"Rocky Ridge," she said absently, naming the development's most exclusive quarter. "We're not there often."

"Well, what I'm trying to figure out, Carolyn, is why Emma would take a sudden interest in the Pacific Crest Trail." I listened to the susurrus of the phone line. "Is she an impulsive person?"

"Impulsive, no. Maybe a little headstrong." Carolyn Turnstone emitted a snort-giggle. "You know young people, Beth. They've got all the answers. They see the truth so clearly. It drives me crazy. Absolutely no gray areas. At least, not with Emma. When she was little—just a preschooler—she decided animals were better than people. She informed us they had rights equal to humans, if not superior to them. We all had to go vegan just to keep peace in the house." Snort. Giggle. "Not that Curt minded. He's kind of a health Nazi, and Emma's always been his favorite anyway. But me, what I wouldn't have given some nights for a hamburger like we used to get back home at U-Tote-Em." She sighed. "I'd kill for a Dick's Deluxe right now."

"I can imagine," I said, snort-giggling a little myself. "But all little kids love puppies and kittens, right? What do you think made Emma so adamant about animal rights? Was there something that happened, or . . ."

"Look, I'm sorry, Beth, but I've got to go. I've got an," she stumbled on the word, "an appointment. Emma wasn't particularly impulsive, at least she wasn't before all this FreeThinkers mess. She was a good girl in school. Never any problems that Curt or I knew about."

"What about her friend," I asked, "Wren, is it? Can I talk to her?"

* * * * *

The day after my conversation with Carolyn Turnstone, I woke up early, put on my cleanest pair of Levis, a plain white T-shirt, and my slightly soiled Converse All-Stars and commandeered the Subaru for a trip to Seattle to talk with Wren

Wilson. Carolyn Turnstone had brokered the meeting in art studio, where she put together tiny three-dime collages, like miniature dioramas, mainly of crime sce. quick internet search told me they sold for $10,000 and up. waved goodbye to Penny and Nathan and headed up our drive, I felt a surge of happiness. It felt good to be driving opposed to being driven. It felt good to have a purpose.

Wren's studio was in a converted warehouse sandwich. between the tasting room of a boutique winery and a small batch distillery specializing in aquavit and absinthe. Just down the block was an artisan chocolate maker and a craft brewery, and beside that an exclusive showroom specializing in a highly processed form of marijuana that you could ingest via a vapor pipe. That way, you could get your high without suffering the negative health effects of either smoking or eating. Or so the signs on the door informed me. I stood outside the expensively draped façade of the pot shop and wondered at our booming city's evident need for relief from our success.

I suppose I was expecting a parody of a spoiled rich girl, but to my surprise, Wren Wilson resembled nothing more than her namesake. She was a bouncy, friendly young woman, as round and brown as Emma was tall and blonde. She flitted to an electric kettle that sat on an ancient wooden table painted robin's egg blue, then hopped over to my seat in a chintz armchair that leaked fluff. She handed me a chipped mug full of green tea mellowed with honey and soy milk.

She and Emma had been friends at school—Eastside Prep, known for the number of tech billionaires on its alumni roles. They bonded, she said, not because they were particularly compatible, but because they shared a longing so perverse that it was almost unspeakable in their circles: after graduation, they didn't want to go to college.

"We sort of wanted to get on with it, you know?" said Wren in between sips of her tea. "We were desperate to find our own tribes—people who got what we were about, if that makes sense. Neither one of us was what you'd call popular in high school. I had my art ideas, and Emma had her animal rights

Wren nodded in mock solemnity. "And finally," she said, "the kitten gets tangled up in a ball of yarn and accidentally hangs herself off the back of an original Stickley side chair. Who provided the toy that became the noose?"

"Oh no."

"Oh yes. Mrs. Carolyn Turnstone. It didn't do much for her relationship with her daughter, I can tell you." Wren sighed and placed her mug on the blue table. "I've always wondered if the cat was suicide."

"Wow," I said. "That *is* a string of bad luck." We let the pun hang between us for a moment before I asked, "What did you think when Emma's name came up in the UW bombing investigation?"

Wren frowned. "I wasn't that surprised, considering the guys she was hanging out with at the time."

The guys, Wren said, were FreeThinkers, and not just wannabes, but the hard-core, lead-the-revolution types. Their inflexible regard for the righteousness of the cause had appealed to Emma. "She's always been attracted to people with the answers," said Wren. "I mean, she can be headstrong herself, and maybe a little wild. So, I wasn't too surprised when I heard her name mixed in with the other suspects, those guys from Eugene. And I wasn't surprised when everyone but Emma got charged with a crime, either."

"How so?"

"Obviously, coming from a wealthy family has its advantages," Wren said, warming to her subject. She smiled wryly and cocked her head. "The FreeThinkers knew that. I think it was one of the reasons they took Emma in. They figured her money and status might come in handy down the road. What they didn't figure on is Emma's got a manipulative streak herself. What I think is when things got hot, she out-maneuvered them, with a little help from her dad. Now her friends are facing charges and she's what?" Wren blinked at me. "She's no longer with the movement. She's in London going to school." Wren put air quotes around the last word. She looked up from her tea and met my eyes. "Or at least, we all thought she was."

"How do the FreeThinkers feel about her now?"

"Oh, you know. People are mean," said Wren. "From what I hear, a bunch of them have sworn revenge on Emma. That's the reason I'm talking to you now. They say they're going to hunt her down on behalf of their jailed comrades and I don't think they've got anything particularly nice planned once they find her." She got up to plug the kettle in for more tea. "But a few of them think she's still on their side and this whole thing is vintage Emma."

"Vintage Emma?" I asked.

"You know," Wren said over her shoulder. "Show the world one face and your true friends another."

* * * * *

It should have been a good year for the tomatoes. The sun had been reliable throughout August and September, and we hadn't had anything close to a freeze yet. An hour after my interview with Wren, I stood, hands on hips, scowling at the plants struggling in the raised beds alongside our townhouse. I once was casual about my tomatoes, as befits any gardener raised in Sacramento. But Seattle was different. Here, gardeners care for their plants as if they're preemies in the neonatal ICU: protecting them under clear plastic sheeting, warming their roots with hot water bottles, gently rocking them to distribute pollen.

It was clear my poor Early Girls had been left on their own too often. I bent down, removed a gardening glove, and stuck an index finger into the ground near the base of one anemic plant, testing soil moisture. My elbow grazed a tiny green fruit, which fell silently to the earth beside my hand. I cursed under my breath.

So, I admit that I wasn't in the best of moods when I heard the motorcycle. It must have been one of those for which excessive noise is just as important as performance, because I could mark its progress down the hill long before it turned on our street and, emitting a series of mid-sized explosions, shuddered to a stop in front of our place. As I peeked between the slats in our offset fence, a man in black riding leathers and an open-faced helmet set the kickstand and dismounted in flurry of jerky motions. When he removed his goggles, I could see he was young, Asian, and angry. I watched at what I thought was a discrete distance as he stomped his boots on the sidewalk and yelled something I couldn't understand. I was shaking my head slowly back and forth in annoyance until I realized with a start that he was yelling at me.

"You, lady!" he screamed, raising his heavily tattooed right arm to point directly at me. Stupid offset fence slats, I thought. They let a little sun in, but they're no good when you're trying to hide. "Where's your husband?" the young man demanded.

He may not have meant it this way, but in my current mood, the question struck me as insufferably paternalistic. Why did I need a husband to unsuccessfully grow tomatoes in my side yard? It rankled. So, I straightened, opened the garden gate, and yelled back, "Who wants to know?"

This seemed to confuse him, and I got the sense that English wasn't his first language.

"*I* want to know," he said, sounding bewildered, as if this should have been clear by the context of the question. "Where's your husband? Why was he sneaking around my motorhome and barn?" He paused and thought for a moment. "Slinking," he added. "Creeping around my motorhome. On tiptoes." His lips turned up into a satisfied smile as he tasted the word. "Tiptoeing."

I have to admit, I admired his creative use of vocabulary. So many people have given up on anything other than a basic noun-verb speech pattern enlivened only by the tedious overuse of profanity and the most predictable profanity at that. Not everything is *that* awesome, I want to scream at them. In fact, most things aren't even just plain awesome. I shook my head and focused on the intruder.

"My husband wouldn't tiptoe around your motorhome," I shouted at him. I may have thrown my gardening gloves in his direction at this point, because later I found them stuck behind the azaleas in the rock garden. "He hates motorhomes!"

"He was sneaking! Drake was slinking around, like a no-good, tiptoeing spy," the young man insisted. "You tell him he better not. He better not," he stopped and glared at me. "Skulk," he concluded, kicking at some invisible bit of detritus on the sidewalk. "Private property!" he yelled, his voice going louder on the last syllable. "He better not trespass anymore." We glared at each other in seething silence. "Private property!" he repeated. "Trespass."

Have I mentioned I sometimes have a problem with people telling me what to do? I cannot abide that imperious tone they take. Plus, I thought, private property, my ass. The guy was probably camped out somewhere on Forest Service land. The thought of him emptying his sewage, maybe even near a water source, made me absolutely livid. Now I see that, based on the facts at hand, this was quite a leap in reasoning. At the time, though, it all seemed plausible.

"Yeah?" I yelled back, my tone challenging, "He better stop trespassing, huh? Or what?"

I don't know if it was the words or the regrettable smirk on my face, but the young man seemed to take my meaning this time. He charged up the granite steps that led from the street to our garden, pushed me out of the way, and made directly for the raised beds. There, he seized one of the tomato plants by the stalk and jerked it violently from the ground. I gasped in horror.

Turning back, he met my eyes as he coldly broke the spindly plant in two and threw it to the ground. Unsure whether to charge him or head for the street, I stumbled a bit, then steadied myself on the gate. The young man unzipped his jacket to reveal the handle of a gun strapped to his rotund torso, and my head went all swirly, the way it sometimes does when I've been bent over weeding for too long. "Or what?" he mocked in a high, faintly sing-song voice. His voice lowered, "Or this." He tapped the gun handle. "You tell him. Stay away from the motorhome." He stalked back to his motorcycle, and after a long series of pops and bangs, the thing was sufficiently ready to roar off again.

I called the police, of course, and for the second time in as many weeks I had a rather unsatisfactory interview with a law enforcement officer, this one sent to take my report.

"So, you're saying the man pulled up one of your tomato plants," the officer said, and I could just imagine him back at the precinct house later that evening, relating the latest on what passes for crime in the minds of middle-aged women living in the rarified neighborhoods north of downtown.

"He did. But really why I called is I think he had a gun and was making a threat against my husband."

"Right. But you don't *know* he had a gun."

"I saw the handle. It looked like a gun. I know what a gun looks like."

"Right. But you didn't see a handgun in its entirety."

We went on this way for some 15 minutes. Finally, the officer and I thanked each other for our service to the community, he left, and I called Nathan, who remained in La Likt with Penny.

"Huh," he said mildly after I told him the whole story. "Probably the guy just got us confused with someone else." He paused, and I could hear Penny's nails scrabbling on the old pine floor. "Sorry about your tomato plant, though."

"Thanks, but you know, Nathan, he had a gun." Was it me, or was every man I came in contact with today unable to understand my explanation of basic concepts, such as the connection between guns and violence? I tried the direct approach.

"And not only did he seem to know you—and know you by name, Nathan—he threatened you. With the gun."

"Huh," my husband repeated. "Well. He probably meant to threaten someone else."

It was enough to make a person give up on the whole gender.

Chapter 13

NATHAN DRAKE

October 15

I hate to admit it, but I was enjoying being on my own at the cabin. Progress made on cabin plans. New biography of Darwin, with a focus on his infamous stomach problems, started. Long walks with Penny up to the ridge. A bike ride down to Ellensburg and back. Not a thought about Emma. Or Beth. Until she called.

Yes, her story about the motorcycle guy was worrisome. But also understandable. First, he got my contact info off my driver's license, now forever stored on Cody's phone. Second, he decided to check me out for himself. Third, he yelled at my wife; she has that effect on some people. Anyway, I didn't think it was likely he'd follow through on any half-assed threat. Exactly where would that get him? No, he was just trying to scare me away from whatever illegal crap was going down in his motorhome, and that was fine with me.

But like I said, otherwise it had been a good couple of days, including some fine long evenings spent at the Cenozoic brewpub, where I now sat nursing a pint.

Dave the owner is one of that dying breed who naturally track the percentage of conversation coming out of their own mouth and ensure that the other party gets a reciprocal share. Dave's set point was about 50-to-60 percent and I was by nature a 20-to-40 percenter (more after a couple of beers or if the topic is water quality) so you can see how we might get along.

And tonight the topic had turned—what's this?—to the paucity of backcountry toilets in the Golden State.

"But there are so many more people in California than Washington," Dave said. "What is it? Forty million versus seven million now? Wouldn't you figure that the rangers down there would plan for all those hikers?"

"Precisely!" I practically yelled as the pint of beer headed toward my lips abruptly reversed course and landed with a thud back on the bar. I raised both my hands hosanna style. "And that's the whole point of High Country Crapper. Accept reality. Pull off the blinders. Acknowledge that you've got a ton of people on the trails. And what do those people do?"

"They poop?" Dave asked evenly.

"So, the thing you have to understand," I said, "is that native Californians are inherently different than native Washingtonians."

This theory had been taking shape in my mind for some time.

"Californians are idealistic and dreamy. They follow their inner tie-dyed spirit. Washingtonians like a good sensible plan, a set of rules so everyone is on the same page."

Dave stood behind the bar and nodded, probably mentally calculating my blood alcohol level but nonetheless politely waiting for the payoff.

"So anyway," I continued. "My theory is that this legacy of go-natural, follow your woo-woo in California has led to a situation where they simply deny the need for placing communal toilets at the most popular backcountry camps. I get it. I like wandering off to find my own little private spot. Who doesn't like the wind whistling through the wickets? Nothing better to put you in touch with your inner homo sapien. Up here in Washington though, as you and Muriel know, you can pretty much count on a serviceable little wooden box hidden in the woods above all the big camps." I was exhausted by my little speech and took a tug on my beer.

COURTER P. DONNELLY

Dave paused in his behind-the-bar work. "I think I get it," he said, wiping his hands on a small towel. He hailed from Maine and had no horse in the race. "I mean, your thing about California and Washington. Just look at Jobs versus Gates, the poster boys. Jobs was all about the free-form Mac, be here now, mouse instead of keyboard, and maybe that's because he grew up riding his stingray around the California suburbs on winding roads and into random cul-de-sacs named for local flowers and people. It was all local, loopy, organic."

He chucked the towel into a box and gave me a slight smile. "Gates, on the other hand, was imprinted in a place where all the roads are on a grid—456th St Southeast, 235th St Northwest—you can't go anywhere around the Puget Sound without the streets reminding you where you are in relation to everyone else. Gates required that external mental map to know himself. He existed only in relation to other people and places. Jobs created his own reality. He was an island.

"So, in California," Dave continued, spreading his arms as I had done only moments earlier, "the crapper is seen as unnatural, an intrusion into the random wilderness experience. Do your own thing, baby! And do it when the impulse strikes."

It's a beautiful thing to be truly understood.

"Gentlemen, I give you the John Muir Trail," I said, raising my glass in a mock toast, "where the camps are a mess of amateur cat holes and toilet paper ribbons. It's a tragedy of the commons. Why not accept reality! Add a couple well-designed and artfully placed crappers at the most popular spots. That's all my Foundation wants to do!"

As Dave returned to his tanks, I tended my beer and mentally tightened up the elevator speech I had just field tested. It'll need to be crisper to win a Sierra Club grant, I thought. And I'll need to do it without a pint and a half in my belly.

A bit later I was scanning headlines of the rumpled *Northern Sahaptin County Localizer* someone had left behind—the above-the-fold stories were "Kiwanis Picnic Raises $350 for Fire Relief" and "Second Property Tax Payment Due Next Week"—when the phone I'd stuck in my hat on top of the bar gave a long vibration and lit up. An actual incoming call. From Beth.

"Hey Beth," I said. "Where are you?"

"La Likt," she said. "Novik's, getting sausages. Like we talked about? Listen, I was looking at the community bulletin board here."

"Don't tell me. There's a pancake breakfast at the La Likt Senior Center?"

"Ha-ha. Yeah," she said, "horse trailer for sale, too. But listen: somebody lost a dog. The flyer says a red, short-haired dog."

I waited.

"So where are you and Penny?"

"Well," I said, "Dave was just closing early and we were heading to Patrick to pick up a book I ordered."

"Penny?"

"With me. Looking at her right now."

"I'll see you at the bookstore in a half hour."

It was nearly 5 o'clock when Dave, Penny, and I pulled into the little town of Patrick, which is only a couple of miles up the state highway from La Likt but somehow manages to jump ahead several social classes. Dave parked the Tacoma in front of the post office and a minute later the three of us were pushing through the door of the town's combination bookstore, coffee bar, and hipster hangout. Except, of course, there are no true hipsters in Sahaptin County, even in Patrick. That's a considerable part of its charm. Instead, there was a friendly mix of flip-flopped 20-somethings up from the university in Ellensburg, 30-something moms with strollers, and ball-capped retirees with all the time in the world.

I was just getting into my new book, "Raising the Introvert Canine," when I saw Beth charge through the front door, scan the crowd, and heave a sigh. We were out on the back porch, and so I stood and waved my Mariner's hat in her direction. I watched her make the rounds of the crowd inside, peering into the face of man after man, like Diogenes with his lamp. Finally, she spotted me and clambered through the swinging door, which responded by whacking her in the backside.

"When did you get home?" I asked, giving her a quick kiss on the cheek.

She slapped the lost dog notice down on our picnic table hard enough to slosh Dave's large drip with steamed milk right out of its Italian stoneware. I picked up the paper and looked at it closely.

"It's the same handwriting as Bella's poster. I hope you see that," she said. "It's that Cody again, and now he's after Penny." To my surprise, tears started to her eyes.

I looked closer at the photo in the poster. "It's not Penny," I said.

"What do you mean, 'It's not Penny?'" she demanded. "Of course, it's Penny." She reached down to scratch the puppy's favorite spot between her floppy ears. Penny looked up at Beth and furrowed her brow. "Look at the picture, Nathan. It looks exactly like Penny."

"No, not exactly. There's no white blaze on the chest." I held my breath, then blew out a long, slow sigh. "It's one of the other dogs."

For a moment, Beth seemed so relieved that I thought my words hadn't completely registered. Which might be to my advantage. Then Dave said, "One of the *other* dogs?"

Everybody went silent.

"Nathan," Beth said. "There are other dogs?" Muriel arrived holding a bag from the pastry case and took the seat next to Beth. "What dogs?" she asked eagerly as she extracted a chocolate chip cookie. "What'd I miss?"

"Yeah, there are other dogs," I said reluctantly. I reached across the table and patted Beth's hand, "I was going to tell you, but I thought you'd just get upset. You remember the day we got Penny, I went to look for her owner in the campground?" Beth nodded. "Well, I ran into a couple of guys living off the grid on some land up the side creek a little way." I turned toward Dave. "There's a stagnant pond up there," I said. "It's got a trace of cobalt and some blue-green algae and . . ."

"Nathan," Beth interrupted. "The dogs?"

"Well, they had a couple of dogs that looked like Penny. Poor things were in bad shape, though—mangy and skinny like Penny used to be." I reached down for the puppy, who rolled over to ask for a belly scratch. "They have some kind of motorhome up there, and I could hear dogs going crazy in the distance."

"Could be a puppy mill," Muriel said. "People can get up to all kinds of no good on those checkerboard pieces of private land out there."

"And they had a pit bull or Rottweiler or some kind of mix," I said. "That's how my arm got hurt, Beth. The dog came after me. I got a tetanus shot, but I've also been getting the rabies series."

"A dog bit you? Why am I hearing about this only now?"

"Well, you get upset. I don't like to upset you with extraneous information." I glanced over at Muriel and Dave, who had both lowered their eyes as if to give us some privacy while still catching the juicy details.

"Yes, well, I'm certainly upset now. I can't believe you didn't tell me this, Nathan. When exactly did I lose my security clearance? What else?"

"So, these two guys, they had a gun, and they kind of beat me up a little, too. Kind of cuffed me with the gun handle, and punched, or more like slapped me. And I thought it would be best just to take their advice and forget I'd run across them, since there's no way I'd ever give Penny back to them."

I reached down and rubbed Penny's belly vigorously while her leg bounced in time. I didn't plan what came out of my mouth next. "But knowing about this London bombing stuff," I said, "and now knowing what Emma's friend Wren told you about those FT guys out to get her—maybe that's why Emma was running when we bumped into her." I regarded Penny's pink belly and concluded: "Guilty or not, maybe she needs help. Maybe we should try to find her."

"Oh, what a great idea. Maybe we should try to find her," Beth said acidly. "Hey! And maybe it'd be easier if we started working together. That is, unless you have any other secrets you should tell me first?"

* * * * *

So, there it is: My new worries about Emma's safety plus my growing doubts about her innocence finally trumped my promise of secrecy. Yes, the proximity of a livid wife may've tipped the scales toward this new position, but I like to think reason, some weighing of new evidence, was involved as well. Probably a combination. Maybe 20:80, wife:reason. Hard to say.

Anyway, it was a relief to have all my cards on the table with Beth. (Well, most of my cards: Who would benefit from knowing I had made a second trip to Camp DeRoux? No one. And that was a sub-lie anyway.) Beth had grunted very few words in my direction ever since my coffee shop confession. The atmosphere wasn't exactly friendly around our little cabin, but I was pretty sure my wife would cool off if I stayed out of range for a while.

The lost dog poster, I decided, was a two-for-one opportunity. We hatched a plan for Beth to call the number listed on the notice, convince whoever answered that she might have the lost dog, and arrange a meeting to see if it was a match. This would lure the brothers away from the cottage long enough for me to swoop down and snoop.

As I explained it to Beth, Dave, and Muriel at our kitchen table the following morning, if all went according to plan, Beth would get a face full of the inimitable DeRoux social sensibilities while I looked for clues about Emma, or their "product," or . . . frankly, I knew exactly what I wanted: that little rucksack with the FT patch that I had seen on my second, secret sortie to the brothers' compound. Anything else was a bonus. With new facts in hand maybe we could figure out who was the good guy and who was the bad guy.

If all went according to plan.

Chapter 14

Charlie Johnson-Medra

Excerpt from the journal of Charlie Johnson-Medra

Oct. 17
Feels good to be moving. Days getting shorter. Em is
looking better. We'll take the side trip to Stehekin to get my
food drop. And then, Canada Ho! I'm thinking of taking a year
off with Em, maybe on Vancouver Island. And when things
cool down, I can see myself going back to school and living
with Em in one of those big, old houses near Green Lake.

Chapter 15

MARY BETH DRAKE

October 18

It felt good to have a plan, even if I wasn't convinced that it was well thought out. But, as Nathan kept telling me, if both DeRoux brothers left the compound to meet me, he'd have a good chance to look around for evidence of Emma, which might tell us whether she was either *a* danger or *in* danger. And if one brother stayed behind, Nathan reasoned he'd simply turn the car around and head home, or even just hunker down in trailhead parking until the coast was clear.

"I don't think they got a look at the car last time," he said, "and even if they did, what are the chances they would suspect our silver Subaru?" He laughed quietly. "A silver Subaru is the most common car in the Northwest, Beth. They issue one to you when you register to vote."

Nathan seemed almost giddy, or as close to giddy as he gets. Looking back on it, I suppose he could have been filling in the space I usually take up, because I was not in the mood to talk—at least not to my husband. "I didn't lie, Beth," he insisted when I confronted him. "I just left out a few details." There are details, I coldly told him, and then there are falsehoods. "Next time, leave out the part about how you slipped on a rock and got a boo-boo. Put in the stuff about being attacked by a dog and then beat up by some thug with a gun." I was so angry at Nathan that it scared me.

It didn't help that he looked so pleased with his self-assigned mission as he readied his binoculars and daypack, which as usual was bulging with supplies like headlamps (one primary and one secondary in case the primary failed) and Ace bandages (essential for twisted ankles and can also be used, if primary and secondary bandages are braided together, to belay oneself down an unanticipated cliff). He started toward me as if to kiss me goodbye, took a look at my face, and changed course. "Remember, just keep them talking as long as you can and call me when they're heading home."

I relaxed as soon as my husband left. I'd set up the meeting about the lost dog the previous evening using the last operating pay phone in the upper Sahaptin, a dingy, windblown box located next to the town's gas station. The number for the lost dog was different from the one I'd called after seeing the poster for Bella, but I wasn't taking any chances with caller ID or anything else. And sure enough, the man who answered sounded a lot like Cody.

"Yah, you have missing dog, I think?" I said, wincing at my attempt at a German accent, which owed a lot to American TV shows of the 1960s. "I picked up this dog, yah?" After a few more "yahs" and a round of "dankes," the man agreed to meet me in town to see if my dog was the one he was missing. "You know the Smoke-N-Spit?" he asked, choosing one of the more descriptively named businesses in town as a rendezvous point.

"Of course," my German alter ego replied, even though I'm pretty sure she didn't smoke.

"We'll be there in a green jeep at 10," Cody or someone who sounded eerily like him said. "Bring the dog."

"You bet," I said, and we ended the call.

I obviously couldn't take Penny to the meeting, so I needed to borrow a pup fast. I headed out the front door of the cabin and started downhill toward the home of our neighbors, Bill and Kathy Chaney. It was Kathy's pet I had my eye on: Roxy the Chihuahua. The improbably bold Roxy had been through a couple of play dates with our still skittish Penny, and, God forgive me, I thought I could probably get the little dog away from Kathy, whose big heart made suspicion an impossibility.

"Well, sure, I guess," Kathy said slowly when I asked if Roxy could come along on our chores that day. "If you think it'll help with Penny's socialization."

I did think it would help Penny, though not in the way Kathy imagined. The way I saw it, Roxy would be assisting Penny in saving her brothers and sisters, if that's what they were, who were starving in the cages Nathan glimpsed on his first visit to the compound, if that's what he really saw. Perhaps this conclusion is a stretch, given the facts I had, but still, I needed a dog and Roxy was very conveniently located.

As 10 o'clock drew nearer, I bundled both dogs into the 1975 VW Beetle that Nathan gave me the day I left the newspaper. It was ChemTone green where it wasn't rusty, and a near match for the car I kept all through high school and college. I'd been driving that bug the summer we met. Nathan and I both had a soft spot for the old V-Dubs, in spite or perhaps because of their quirks. We kept the car on the La Likt property, and someday, once we built the magnificent garage, we were going to restore it. Maybe even convert it to an electric vehicle. For now, the bug's tiny engine started with a familiar loud rattle, and the dogs and I chugged off toward the Smoke-N-Spit. On the way, I explained the plan to Roxy, whom Kathy had dressed against the fall mountain air in a cunning pink coat printed with bright green cacti and sombreros. I'd come up with a disguise myself: a red and white polka dot bucket hat that fit low over my forehead and a pair of oversize sunglasses. Neither one of us, it occurred to me, was doing much for international understanding.

"OK, Rox," I said, mainly to bolster my own confidence, "Listen up. This is how it's gonna go down."

Roxy stood at attention in her carrier, braced herself on her four rat-like feet, and barked without pause. Penny, who'd evidently heard the plan before, settled into a ball on the back seat.

"We're going to drop Penny here with Dave and Muriel, who'll be surveilling from their truck across the street, just in case we have any trouble."

Roxy barked.

"Then you and I are going to try to convince the two guys who pistol-whipped my unnaturally secretive husband that you're Penny, or a dog very much like her." Roxy momentarily shut her mouth, perhaps in awe of the plan's brilliance. "So, if you could act like Penny," I said to the little dog, "and also maybe appear larger?"

Roxy resumed barking happily.

We came to the state highway and waited while a string of hay trucks rolled through town, leaving behind swirling clouds of straw held aloft in the west wind. Once the road cleared, we pulled out through the straw storm toward the meeting place.

The handoff of Penny to Dave and Muriel went without a hitch, and Roxy and I took up our spot in the Smoke-N-Spit's lot. At 9:50 a.m., the customers mainly seemed to be after Smokes.

"Don't take it up," I advised Roxy, now out of her carrier and standing at attention on my lap, her oversize ears pointed toward the steering wheel. "It's a hard habit to break."

By 10:20 a.m. we were beginning to attract some attention from the Smoke-N-Spit proprietors, one of whom came up to the store's glass door and made a point of taking a good, long look before turning her back on us and waving her hand dismissively. There aren't too many vintage Beetles in town, and if you thought about it, there aren't many good reasons a woman of a certain age would be parked for a half-hour in front of the Smoke-N-Spit while having a one-sided conversation with what looked like Kathy Chaney's Chihuahua. I was wondering which would be considered the odder behavior: going into the store after such a long wait in the lot or staying put and pretending I was on a long, one-sided phone call. Before I had to choose, a green, open-top jeep pulled into the lot and skidded to a stop. "Here we go, Roxy," I said.

The Beetle's driver's side door emitted its usual ear-piercing creak as I forced it open. "Hallo, hallo," I cheerfully bellowed in my faultless German accent. "You are the losers, yah?"

Both brothers had made the trip into town, thank goodness, and now they walked slowly toward me, the skinny one—Cody, according to Nathan—slightly in the lead, and the beefier one—Tommy—lagging behind. Cody almost lost his baseball cap in the wind but caught the brim just in time. He removed it and ran his grubby fingers through his tangled nest of sandy hair. I could tell he was sizing me up, and as he stuck the hat back on more securely, he smirked. I was used to this kind of response from guys who thought they held all the cards, and it never failed to piss me off. Never mind, I told myself, I've been underestimated by better men.

"Where's the dog?" demanded Cody, who evidently was the brains of the operation. As if in answer, Roxy took up her barking again. She pranced prettily on the passenger seat's cracked upholstery. ("It's original," Nathan had proudly stated the day he handed over the keys. "It's all original.") With her tiny front paws, she made a valiant effort to scrabble through the window. "Stall them," I thought, glancing back at Roxy. "Just stall."

"It's a beautiful day, isn't it?" I countered, wondering if simply appending "yah" to the end of each sentence would be enough to fool Cody. "You come here to Smoke-N-Spit often, yah?"

"That the dog?" the other brother asked. He shifted his big body sideways to get a look around me into the VW. I jumped between him and Roxy to block his view and stuck out my right hand. "Gudrun Weiss," I announced, pronouncing the last name as "Vice." I smiled broadly. "And I am speaking with who?" Momentarily confused, the skinny brother—Cody, I reminded myself—stepped in to take my offered hand. He gave it a quick shake before swiftly dropping it like he'd just latched on to a piece of decaying meat. I placed my hands on my hips, elbows out at sharp angles as Tommy attempted to get around me for a better look at Roxy.

"Where is the dog?" Cody said in a loud voice, pronouncing each word as if it were a sentence unto itself. His cadence reminded me of my call seeking information about Bella, when the man on the other end of the line mistook me for aged.

"Well, yah, before we get to that," I said to the brothers, "We talk about reward."

Cody laughed. "What reward? We got no reward."

"Well, yah, there is reward," I insisted. "I am sure there is reward listed on your dog lost notice."

"No reward listed on that notice. That's one thing I'm sure of."

"Yah, yah," I said, stomping my sneakered foot for good measure. "There is a reward. Maybe I have some confusion about where it is listed, maybe it's not on the poster, but I am sure I saw it somewhere. There is reward."

"No reward listed anywhere," Cody said with growing impatience, "because there isn't no reward."

Tommy managed to sneak around my arms akimbo defense and got a look at Roxy, who was still bouncing and barking inside the Beetle. He didn't like what he saw. "Ah hell, Cody," he said as he watched the little dog's head bob in and out of view with each leap. "It's nothing but a puny rat dog." He kicked up a spray of gravel that hit the Beetle's tinny door like a burst of gun fire in an old gangster movie. Anger flooded his voice. "It's not our dog," he said. "It's nothing like our Scout."

"Well, yah, it is like your Scout," blathered Gudrun Weiss. "I am sure you don't recognize the dog because you have not seen her in several weeks."

"Scout's a boy. That isn't Scout. No way. Is it, Cody?"

"How do you know she is not Scout?" I asked, "How can you be so sure?"

Tommy turned toward me and balled his hands into fists. "Lady, they got anything besides wiener dogs where you come from? This is nothing like the dog we lost." He looked into my eyes with something close to rage. "This is a Mexican dog, is what. Whaddya call 'em?"

"Chow chow," Cody supplied. "China chow. Something like that."

"How can this dog be Mexican if she is from China?" I asked. "Maybe we go to beer garden over here," I gestured to the wind-toppled chairs in front of Jake's Tavern next door. "And maybe we discuss some more, yah? I will buy. We take it out of the reward money."

Roxy's long toenails made a scratching sound against the bug's window. Tommy turned and looked at her, then took a step back and in one smooth motion peeled off his faded blue T-shirt. He wrapped the dirty rag around his right hand so quickly you'd have thought he'd practiced the move a million times in front of a mirror. He seemed to compress like a spring, then brought his arm back and smashed his muffled fist hard against the glass. With a sound like sleet falling on a frozen lake the window shattered into tiny, diamond-bright pieces. I screamed in spite of myself, pushed past Tommy, and spotted poor Roxy, skeletal tail between her legs, cowering underneath the brake pedal. There was a roaring in my ears as Tommy grabbed my shirt by the collar and spun me around. My hat flew off toward the Smoke-N-Spit, where a few people had gathered at the door.

"It's not our dog, lady," Tommy said quietly, giving me a close-up view of his ravaged teeth and scruffy beard. His head tilted to the right, as if he was genuinely puzzled, and he pulled me closer to his mad black eyes. "It's never been our dog, and I think you know that."

"Tommy," Cody yelled. "Jesus Christ. Let her go, OK?"

Tommy eased his grip, placed his palms on my chest, and pushed hard. I fell rear first on to the gravel, biting my tongue so hard when I hit the ground that I tasted blood. Looking between Tommy's stout legs, I got a good view of Dave's truck, shooting out of its hiding place and pulling a U-turn in the middle of First Street.

"OK, OK," said Cody, rushing over and placing his hand on his brother's beefy arm. "I guess that's done, Tommy." He looked down at me. "You're all right, huh? No real damage?" I was figuring out my response when he added, "Waste of time anyway. Nothing but crazy old women in this town." The brothers turned in unison, climbed into their jeep and, grinding the gears, Cody backed up and then lurched onto First Street. Seconds later, Dave pulled up beside me. Muriel was next to him holding Penny, who wrinkled her forehead at me and yipped as if she regretted allowing me out of her sight. "You OK?" Dave yelled.

"Fine," I said shakily as I rose to my feet. "You follow them. I'll call Nathan." Dave opened the truck door and shoveled Penny out toward me. I grabbed her around her soft puppy belly, raised my left knee, and balanced her on it while I tried to regain my equilibrium. Show apparently over, the little knot of people inside the Smoke-N-Spit began to disperse. One thing about living in a town where people do what they have to in order to get by: Folks aren't inclined to butt into one another's business.

Dave gunned the Tacoma onto First Street as I reached into my back pocket for my phone, noting grimly that the screen was now partially obscured by a network of spidery cracks. I tapped in Nathan's number and listened as the call went straight to voicemail.

Chapter 16

DAVE SCHMIDELL

October 18

It'd started blowing earlier than usual. Even for La Likt, this was windy. My truck creaked on its springs as the wind sped unobstructed down First Street. You'd think this town's wide streets had been carefully platted to funnel the wind that races, every damn afternoon, over the pass and down this valley to the county seat at Ellensburg, 25 miles away.

"What do you think they're gabbing about?" I asked Muriel. "Roxy is pretty clearly not their dog."

My wife looked up over her copy of the *Northern Sahaptin County Localizer*. Penny was lying on the bench seat between us, sniffing and occasionally licking the leather knob on the Tacoma's stick shift as if it was an ice cream cone and she wasn't quite sure she liked pistachio. Leaning forward, Muriel scanned the skies as if to check the weather, then snuck a glance across First Street to the Smoke-N-Spit parking lot.

There Beth stood alongside her little green VW Beetle, engaged in a vigorous back and forth with two men we figured were the DeRoux brothers. All three had assumed a wider than usual stance to deal with the sideways gale. Beth seemed unusually animated, rocking stiffly from side to side and making odd choppy gestures with her arms to punctuate whatever she was saying.

"Well," Muriel said, leaning back, "if anyone can pump you for information without you being aware, it's Beth. Ever see her at one of the bookstore's art openings up in Patrick? She's always cornering some local watercolorist and getting them to admit their pretty little landscape is really a manifestation of some inner turmoil."

"Once a journalist," I said.

We watched the brother in the black baseball hat expounding about God only knew what. He pointed at Roxy and then back at his brother.

"People want to talk about themselves, don't you think?" asked Muriel, who really seemed to enjoy playing this undercover role on her day off. "Beth just helps them do it."

"She's the catalyst," I said. "The enzyme."

Whatever they were discussing over there, Beth was doing her best to give Nathan time to look around the DeRoux's place up in Fortune Creek. I kept checking my phone for texts announcing he'd finished his tour of the property. We were supposed to warn him if the brothers headed back his way.

I looked up from my phone just in time to see the burly brother rear back and smash his fist through the VW's passenger-side window. Muriel let out a yell and I must have grabbed for the ignition, because next time I looked, Beth was on her ass next to the Beetle and the DeRouxs were headed back to their jeep.

I cranked the engine, threw it into gear—thanks to Penny the shifter was a slick leathery ball of dog slobber—and whipped across the street. The DeRouxs had just pulled out of the lot, heading west on First toward Fortune Creek.

"Jeez, what creeps," yelled Beth as we pulled in. She insisted that she and Roxy were OK and told us to follow the brothers. We let Penny hop out to Beth's embrace and took off after them. We didn't get far.

"Wait a minute," Muriel said. "Look. They stopped. At the taxidermy place."

We pulled to the curb and waited. Plenty of parking in La Likt.

"This is like an old Hollywood car chase," my passenger said excitedly.

The taxidermy shop was an enterprise that, in my opinion, deserved to stay in business no matter the financials, just because everybody enjoyed the name: Trompe l'oeil Taxidermy.

"I've never seen anybody go in there," I said.

I barely had time to imagine a Trompe customer making plans for their recently departed before the brothers burst back through the door. After a brief delay—the smaller one's cap was violently stripped off his head by a wind gust and he had to chase it across the lot next door—the jeep was moving west again. I followed from five or six cars back and handed my phone to Muriel.

"Ick," she said, "it's got dog slobber all over it."

"Just be ready to text Nathan," I told her.

But the brothers weren't going back to Fortune Creek. Instead, at the stoplight near my pub, the jeep blinked its intention to turn left toward South La Likt. Idling two cars behind, we could feel the concussive snaps of the big American flag in front of the Chamber of Commerce. The light changed, and our little convoy eased through the turn and proceeded slowly under I-90, over the railroad tracks, and then across the concrete bridge spanning the white-capped Yakima River.

The jeep took the first right after the bridge onto Jefferson Street.

"Let's go Adams," I said, turning right on the next street up. Now we were paralleling the DeRoux brothers, headed west. Looking to our right across empty lots, we spotted the jeep as it pulled up in front of an impressive metal garage. The shiny structure, maybe 500 or 600 square feet of space, had an opening with a roller door big enough to accommodate a bus, an RV, or maybe even a semi-truck. In fact, a Freightliner hauling a standard-size shipping container—a dull red Hagan-Lloyd—was parked on the street in front of a white, single-wide trailer that seemed to share the lot with the spiffy garage.

We parked where we had a clear view of the garage across a dirt field dotted with piles of split firewood. The jeep's horn blasted twice. From this angle, I could see a dog carrier in the back. A moment later, the big garage door rolled up, the jeep pulled in, and the door closed.

"You think the garage belongs to the white single-wide?" asked Muriel.

I eyed the trailer and also a tiny pink house near the garage. "Don't you mean which house belongs to the garage?"

Around here, living quarters are subordinate to garages. Just like where I grew up along the Aroostook River in Maine. East coast or west, away from the big cities it's all about trucks and ATVs and dirt bikes and snow sleds. I've heard Nathan riff on big-ass garages and oversized trucks plenty of times at the pub. He can be a sour guy, but he's basically a suburban kid and he's been living in the Seattle bubble for a long time. Out here, people have a different way of thinking. Different priorities. No, they will not be knocking out that dining room wall to make way for the open concept kitchen with French doors to the organic garden. Yes, they will be buying that almost-new 4x4 Dodge RAM 2500. Sometimes the priorities don't make economic sense, but whose priorities ever do? Unfortunately for Muriel and me, the local worldview usually doesn't include a craving for artisan beer.

By now a couple of neighborhood dogs were loping matter-of-factly toward our truck. These mutts, a lab-shepherd mix and his smaller black-and-white companion, seemed close to retirement age; they let out only a few perfunctory barks. No doubt they were waiting for us to exit the car, at which time their jobs would require a more full-throated protest.

We texted Nathan and Beth with an update on our whereabouts and waited, trying to act casual with the newspaper and our phones as props. We avoided eye contact with the dogs. The wind carried a steady stream of plastic Safeway bags, McDonald's cups, and pine needles directly past us. Looking west five blocks to the end of Adams Street, I counted at least a dozen late-model full-size trucks parked in driveways, most of them with massive engines under their hoods and all of them with completely empty beds. I couldn't help thinking of Nathan's familiar diatribe about the American male's requirement of a truck even if he didn't have a rational use for one. More than once, forgetting that I owned a truck, he would gaze out the window at traffic and mutter his bumper sticker idea: Empty Trucks, Empty Minds.

Maybe he's right. Like my small town in Maine, La Likt has a nice riverside setting and good bones—handsome brick buildings on a wide main avenue—but it lacks an economic pulse. What kinds of jobs are available for the young people, even with good high school diplomas, if they don't leave for Seattle? It's a hard go. Even the booming luxury resort development just up the road doesn't seem to goose our local economy. Those second-home owners hardly ever stray from their 4,000-square-foot estates and their manicured golf courses. Hell, they're only up here two or three weeks a year. And from what I can tell, most of their architects and contractors come from the Puget Sound side of the state, too, or maybe the bigger central Washington towns like Wenatchee or Yakima. The young men and women of La Likt, meanwhile, are installing landscaping and making 15 or 20 bucks an hour. Or if they're lucky, they got on with an electrician or carpenter and can actually start saving if they get some overtime hours. They're the guys I see ducking in the side door of Sparky's bar at two in the afternoon for a quick bourbon with a Coke chaser, the coke left untouched as they scurry back out to the job site.

After about twenty minutes, activity behind the big garage caught our attention. To get a better view (and to ditch the neighborhood dogs around our truck, who now numbered five) we looped back around to Jefferson Street and parked two blocks down from the garage.

Inside, they were up to something. We could hear a generator and sharp pounding, but our view was still partially blocked by a collection of snowmobiles and outbuildings. I decided to get out and walk the river trail upstream to get a look from behind. I took my fishing rod along as cover.

"Be careful," said Muriel over her half-opened window. "No need to get too close."

"I need to take a piss anyway," I said. Fly rod on display, I headed through the high grass between the empty lots to pick up the river trail. I'd fished this stretch of the Yakima many times. The heavily wooded trail popped out into a muddy clearing alongside the swollen river—they must've still been releasing water from the lake in advance of the winter rains—and I could see the back of the metal garage through the cottonwoods.

The roller door on the backside was wide open and the interior was brightly lit. Inside, the two brothers and one older guy were working intently on what looked like a washing machine. I crept closer, pulled the pocket binoculars from my fishing belt, and raised them to my eyes. What I thought was a washer was in fact a big bale of hay wrapped in white plastic.

Premium green timothy hay, prized for its sugar content, is Sahaptin County's most lucrative export. The wind helps reduce bleaching of the timothy's much-admired deep jade color. Some farmers I met at one of Muriel's Forest Service seminars on habitat preservation told me they can get $300 a ton for the high-grade stuff. I'd bet there were a dozen trucks around town driven by guys who made their living hauling the wrapped bales to the port in Seattle, where it was loaded on ships headed for Japan.

Which might explain the container truck out front of the garage.

This particular bundle of hay was getting special treatment. Inside the garage, the three men seemed to be stuffing pint-sized packages into the bale. I saw about a dozen packages go in. After some final adjustments, the bigger brother, the one who had busted Beth's car window, worked alone to repack the outer layer of hay. He used a pencil-sized object to bind it, and, with help from the older guy, grappled with a large roll of white shrink-wrap and a blow dryer the size of a shop vac to re-compress the bale.

My arms got tired, and as I lowered my binoculars, I noticed movement upstream. A fisherman was standing calf-deep in the river, casting his line in an easy back-and-forth, side-angle motion to avoid overhead branches. A camera with a long lens hung from his neck. Extremely odd, not only because cameras and water don't go together, but in my experience neither do the pastimes of fishing and photography, except for the trophy shot. And you got that with your phone.

The fisherman looked over at me and nodded and I raised my rod in salute. He looked familiar, and with a start, I realized it was Hawk. The former sheriff was one of my few regular customers and I knew from Nathan that he was leading the Turnstone's search for their daughter. At the moment, though, he was not somebody I cared to engage. I moved downriver.

When I was out of Hawk's view, I turned again to the garage. The older guy was out on the street pulling pins from the corrugated doors of the shipping container that sat on the bed of the Freightliner. A small forklift carrying two wrapped bales advanced out of the garage and made a stuttering turn toward the semi.

I felt a vibration in my pocket and reached for my phone. Two text messages from Nathan had come in:

Nathan   **11:44 AM**
I'm headed back home. All OK. Found Emma's daypack.

Nathan   **11:55 AM**
Back in La Likt now. Just saw your text. Motorcycle guy just made turn toward South La Likt. Where U now?

While I stared at the newest text, I heard the sub-base rumble of a big bike. At first, I thought the locomotive-like sound was somehow coming from my phone, but then I spotted a heavy, dark-haired guy, no helmet, advancing toward the garage on what looked like a customized Indian Chief racing bike.

If there's one thing an American male wants more than a pickup truck, it's an Indian. And this low-slung café racer looked tricked out, with a leaf spring over the front fork, a retro leather strap around the black tank, and a long banana saddle.

I'd never seen anything so cool. The front roller door opened, and the biker glided inside. He yelled something at the brothers and pointed with a jabbing motion at the garage door. The forklift swung around and trundled back inside. By the time the door rolled shut, I was headed back to the truck.

Muriel was drumming the dashboard nervously.

"Hurry up," she said through her open window. "That guy on the motorcycle stopped and looked at me. Did you see Nathan's text?"

"Don't worry." I said. "We're out of here."

As I was stashing my fishing gear in back, the garage's front door rolled open and the motorcycle swooped out and rocketed straight toward us. Hands on the low handlebars, chin out, its rider seemed intent on ramming our truck. In the bike's wake, a large, light-colored dog sprinted low across the pavement. The biker skidded to a stop near the front of my truck. He was wearing leather pants, a white T-shirt—the flimsy kind you get in a six-pack at Walmart—and a gun. It was strapped to his chest. He began yelling at me, but I couldn't hear him clearly over the growling pipes of his bike.

I moved around the front of the truck. By the time the snarling dog arrived, I had the pepper spray out of my fishing belt, unpinned, and pointed at the dog's head. "Call your dog!" I shouted. "Call him right now or I spray him!" I shot off a taste of spray. The dog slowed, lowered his head, and showed me his teeth. "Call him off, I said! Right now!"

The green jeep pulled up behind the motorcycle, and while it was still rolling, the stocky brother leapt out, yelling for his dog. "Monty! No! Leave it!" He approached the animal and snapped a leash to its studded collar. His brother joined him, and they walked toward me, the little one holding a Colt .38 and the big one some fat-snouted thing, probably a .357 Magnum.

"What are you doing here?" the stocky one shouted over the rumble of the idling bike and the growling dog.

I held up my fly rod, which I still clenched in my left hand, and glared at the man. "Next time I kill the dog with my fish knife. And I sue the hell out of you."

The brothers looked at each other. One smirked, the other snorted.

The Toyota's passenger door creaked open behind me.

"But if you need another reason to back the hell off," I yelled, "there's my wife."

Muriel half-crouched alongside the Toyota, hands steadied on the hood as she gripped and aimed her service pistol. I knew she wouldn't sit still while the DeRouxs were waving guns around out here.

The brothers leaned back in unison. Guns now hanging down in their right hands, their empty left hands drifted up into identical easy-there-little-lady poses. Simultaneously, they turned to look at the motorcycle guy, who stared at me with distaste.

"This is not the crapper man Drake," the motorcyclist said disgustedly. The information apparently was intended for the DeRouxs, but he never took his eyes off me. "Tell Drake to stay away from my property. Tell him," he paused and revved his bike. "Desist!" he concluded proudly. "Cease and desist, or else there will be consequences." He hunched over the gas tank and blasted off between the brothers and me, headed back toward town.

I was glad to see him go, but that still left the DeRouxs standing in front of me, identical scowls on their faces. "Somebody could get hurt snooping around our property," said the Colt .38, his eyes following the popping progress of the Indian as it crossed the Yakima. "But, you know. I guess no harm done, right? Dog just doing its job, man." I didn't answer, and as the sound of the bike finally faded, the brothers and the leashed dog scuttled back to their jeep and spun it around toward the metal garage.

Muriel drove us back to town.

"That was crazy, you know," she said. "Won't be good if it gets out I drew my gun, especially since I wasn't even working."

"Well," I said, "those guys aren't in any hurry to show off what they're up to in that garage, so I doubt they'll say anything."

As we crossed the river and headed into town, I was thinking of old high school classmates left behind in Maine, wondering if they were alive or in jail. "I don't think those two brothers are FT animal huggers, Muriel. But whoever they are, I can see why Emma Turnstone might want to stay lost."

Chapter 17

MARY BETH DRAKE

October 18. Midday.

Of course, I was most worried about Roxy as I struggled to get my rear up off the Smoke-N-Spit lot, where Tommy had unceremoniously dumped me moments before. But the Chihuahua had already recovered from the shock of feeling the Beetle's passenger-side window shatter over her and now stood on the driver's seat, barking as if to alert the town to our mishap. Penny, whose collar I clutched with my left hand, joined in. I stuffed her in the back seat of the bug, crossing my fingers that she wouldn't step on anything sharp. Then I picked up Roxy. She was still wearing her bright pink coat, which seemed to protect her from the rain of glass. As far as I could see, she hadn't been hurt at all. I sighed with relief, placed the little dog inside of her carrier, and headed into the Smoke-N-Spit to borrow a broom and dustpan.

The clerk was a pretty, plus-size woman in her late 30s whose light brown hair was pulled back in a ponytail so tight it hurt to look at her. Her green eyes were set in an oval face that was pale and make-up free. She gave me an appraising look as she handed over the broom. I could see her take in my dorky knee-length shorts and my fleece pullover, my stupidly expensive wool crew socks and my lime green sneakers. I imagined her contrasting it all with her own rhinestone-encrusted flip flops, leopard-print yoga capris, and black T-shirt emblazoned with a rearing stallion and the words "wild and untamed" in flowing script. She held my gaze for a minute to remind me she wasn't the one who'd ended up on her butt in the parking lot, but she didn't ask any questions. She probably figured she didn't have to. She knew the score, or at least she thought she did.

"Well," I said as she handed me the broom over the counter between us, "that was embarrassing."

"Happens to a lot of women." She said it as if she were simply stating a fact, like the price of a pack of Camels. I grasped the broom handle just above her hand-hold and kept it still over the counter. "Really?" I said. "A lot of women?"

She looked me full in the face, as if trying to decide whether I was worth the effort. Then she let go of the broom and ducked behind the counter for the dustpan. On the wall behind her I saw a glossy calendar, the kind real estate agents send out at Christmastime. October's photo featured a stand of screaming yellow aspen. A roan horse posed in the foreground. Below the horse's rear, smack in the middle of the calendar, an oval photograph of the real estate agent was superimposed on the image. With a start, I saw it was Jason Hawk.

"Geez," I said, nodding toward the calendar as the clerk reemerged with the dustpan, "that guy has his hand in everything."

She turned to the calendar and, I swear, I thought she might spit. Instead, she only snorted. "More like he's got his hand *on* everything."

"Is that right?" I said with a low chuckle, trying to keep her engaged. "Well, it doesn't really surprise me. I've met him a few times, and," I leaned over the counter just slightly and lowered my voice. "I probably shouldn't say it, but there's something about him, isn't there?" When she didn't answer, I prompted, "Something creepy?"

Her bitter laugh surprised me. "Creepy," she repeated. "Yeah, I guess you could call it that." She offered me the dustpan, but I held tight to the broom handle with both hands and began counting silently to myself. When I reached seven, she said, "See, it's not just men like your Tommy who do wrong." She shook her head. "Tommy DeRoux. He never had anyone or anything to help him do right, except maybe his loser of a brother. And the Army, it helps some of them, but it didn't help Tommy."

She glanced up at me. "Not that it excuses what he did just now," she continued, "but it's the ones who act like they're better than the rest of us that grew up in this town who really piss me off. Men who run around this county like they're the only goddam reason anybody's got a pot to piss in and we all should be grateful they don't knock us down and take it away."

I stared over the clerk's shoulder at the calendar. "Jason Hawk, you mean," I said.

She laughed again. "Oh yeah. Jason Hawk, he's a real pillar of the community. A true *ass*et." She put a strong accent on the first syllable of the word. "You can ask Serena down at Safeway about that, or Jen over at the Marijuana Superstore. Ask them how it feels to be the girlfriend of the famous hero Jason Hawk."

"You're saying Jason Hawk?" I asked again. "The sheriff? He's," I searched for the right words, "violent with women?"

She straightened behind the counter and again offered me the dustpan. When I didn't move, she gave up a tight nod. "Jason Hawk." She spat the name out. Then she hooked her bright pink thumbnail over her lower lip, extended her pinkie, tilted her head back, and made the universal glug, glug, glug motion.

"He drinks, too?"

She gave me a long, disgusted look. "I thought you said you'd met him." She thrust the dustpan at me and turned away.

* * * * *

I'd just dropped Roxy back with her ecstatic owner when my phone rang. I grabbed it, hoping to see Nathan's name, but the number on the screen wasn't one I recognized. I conducted a fast and familiar internal debate: pick it up or let it go to voicemail?

"Beth?" a woman asked when I picked up, and my heart sank. No doubt this was another opportunity to get my carpets cleaned. "Yes," I responded warily.

"This is Carolyn Turnstone," the woman said. When I didn't reply right away, she added, "Emma Turnstone's mother?"

"Oh, yes, Carolyn, of course. I'm surprised to hear from you so soon, is all."

"Yes," she said. "Listen, Beth. The thing is my husband doesn't know I'm calling you or about our talk the other day." She paused a moment. "I felt we had a connection when we spoke, and I wondered if you felt the same?"

"Yes. I mean, sure."

"The thing is," she began again, "I've been thinking about what we said about trust. And, I've decided. What I mean is, no one is looking for Emma in the right places. And no one has seen her or talked to her in the last three weeks, except you and your husband." I heard the tinkle of ice cubes against glass. "The police tell me that she'll turn up, as if she's just late getting back from a game of tennis or something. And Curtis keeps reminding me that she's our wild child, and the best we can do is wait to hear from her. But Beth, you know what it's like." I held my tongue and waited for her to continue. "I know my Emma better than they do." I heard a sniffle. "I know more than they do, period."

"You do?"

She hesitated. I made it to a count of five before she spoke.

"I'm sorry I didn't tell you this last time we spoke, but I've been in touch with Emma," she said. "The last time was a couple weeks before you saw her on the trail. After we got her home from London, after Drummond and the exploding car. Or the bombed car. Whatever it was." Carolyn Turnstone took a ragged breath, and I could hear ice kiss glass again. "But you don't know about London, do you? Curt is so careful not to let details about the children get out, and I know he's right, most of the time. But if we don't tell someone this time, who'll help us?"

"That's true," I said. Of course, Nathan and I knew one salacious version of the story thanks to the London *Informant*, but I wanted to hear Carolyn Turnstone's take. "What happened in London?"

"After the trouble at the UW, Emma enrolled at University College London. You know, to get a fresh start. She was going to study global agriculture so she could help people affected by climate change. Isn't that great?" Carolyn Turnstone sighed. "But then, there was trouble with an explosion in a car owned by Winston Drummond. The police suspect the FreeThinkers have something to do with it because Drummond's company is into genetic modification of animals. And because they suspect FT, Emma is under suspicion too." She took another slow sip of whatever she was drinking and I could feel the dust in my own throat. "It didn't help that Emma ran around with Drummond for a while, or that his company is in competition with a genetic modification start-up that Curtis has invested quite a bit of money in."

"But I thought you were vegans," I blurted.

"Never mix business with your personal beliefs."

"So, after the explosion, that's when Emma came home from London?"

"Yes, we brought her home while we still could. The Metropolitan Police were starting to sniff around, and they were putting pressure on the FBI to reopen the UW case. And believe me, the British tabloid press makes the gossip websites here look like a grade school newsletter."

She took another sip and I waited for her to continue. "It seemed like a good idea to get her back under our roof. Only," the ice tinkled again. "Only everybody knows where her home is, that's what we thought. The police and even the more intelligent reporters could find her whenever they wanted her. You can see why Emma and I decided it would be a good idea if she disappeared for a little while. Just until the car explosion became a little less . . . explosive." She did the snort-giggle thing, which I chalked up to stress. "Excuse me," she said.

"So, Emma really wasn't missing at all?"

"Not at first. She was staying in our place in Skylandia. We thought no one would look for Emma there. As I told you, we're hardly ever there, so why would anyone think Emma might move in? Besides, Rocky Ridge has a highly regarded security team. It seemed like a good spot for her, just until the Drummond explosion dies down."

"I see what you mean."

"But I'm afraid there's something else. Maybe you should know. I made a mistake."

"A mistake?"

"I sometimes go to Skylandia on my own to relax for a night or two. Meet old friends. Did you know I grew up in Ellensburg?" I shook my head, as if she could see me over the phone. "I know," she said. "Small town girl, that's me. So, I shop a little at the Skylandia Boutique. I play some tennis and get a massage. Glass of wine or two at the club."

"Yes, of course."

"Well, I wanted to see Emma, so I went to the cabin. The thing is, Emma came back from a hike early one afternoon. She was supposed to be in Leavenworth until dark. And the truth is," she took a breath in and let it out again, "Emma saw me relaxing in the spa."

I willed myself to stay quiet. Ten, nine, eight, seven . . .

"I was," Carolyn reluctantly continued, "in the middle of things with a male friend."

Six . . . five . . . four . . .

"With Jason Hawk, actually." She rushed on. "Of course, Emma was upset. I understand that. It was my fault. She left the house then, and she stopped returning my phone calls. And, as you know, we haven't been able to locate her. Of course, I never told Curtis why she disappeared."

Holy cannoli, I thought. Three . . . two . . .

"The thing is, Beth, I'm really calling to ask for a favor."

"A favor?"

"Will you go up to our place in Rocky Ridge and see if Emma's back there now? Or if she left a note? Or anything? I'd go myself, but, you know, I think I'd just scare her away again."

"Why not send Hawk?"

She gave up a bitter little laugh. "Oh, I'm through with Mr. Hawk."

* * * * *

My right hip was sore. I must have bruised it when Tommy knocked me down. I massaged it with one hand while I slowly pedaled my ancient mountain bike up the dirt path toward Skylandia. After Carolyn Turnstone and I said goodbye, I put Penny in the dog run Nathan had cobbled together next to the future site of the magnificent garage. Then I stared at the poor shattered Beetle for a while, rubbing my right forearm and wrist. My muscles felt drained and my psyche shaky after the attack at the Smoke-N-Spit, but I reluctantly decided not to take the car to Skylandia. It would be easier to stash a bike in the trees. Most of all, I didn't want the old car with the broken window to attract attention. I didn't want to find myself explaining to Jason Hawk what I was doing inside Curtis and Carolyn Turnstone's mountain retreat.

I panted my way up to the resort's main entrance and managed a rather imperial wave at the guard as I skirted the retractable gate and turned onto the spotless bike path. I must look like I belong, I thought. Either that, or the security team is off its game today. After a couple of minutes of pedaling on the well-swept bike path, I was presented with a choice: Turn right on Snowdrop Loop or left on Pinedrop Loop? I looked both ways. As usual, there was nobody in sight except for yard crews focused on blowing pine needles from one client's driveway to another's.

I took out my cracked phone and glanced at Carolyn Turnstone's directions. Pinedrop Loop it was. Slowly, I cruised by homes on half-acres, homes that backed up to the golf courses, and homes that featured a peekaboo view of Rocky

Ridge from the second story master suite. The drone of lawnmowers filled the fall afternoon. I cycled by the children's playground. It was empty. I passed the practice putting green. Deserted. Tennis courts lacked players and there was no splashing in the pool. Good, I thought. Fewer eyes.

I passed the Turnstone's driveway and, checking to see if any of the neighbors were visible, I circled the long loop again just to be sure. When I reached the drive a second time, I dipped behind a screen of vine maples that hid the home from the street and stashed the bike in some snowberry that grew alongside the driveway. It seemed the Turnstones had stopped their yard service after Emma arrived. The lawns in front and back were brittle from lack of water, and the pine needles, twigs, and branches that drop in the inevitable wind storms had been neither raked from the lawn nor swept from the walkways. I looked up at the house. For a multi-billionaire's place, the Turnstone home was remarkably ordinary. With the exception of the unkempt garden, it looked like the neighboring properties: tall, dark, and handsome.

Carolyn Turnstone told me I'd find the spare key hidden under an imitation boulder to the right of the detached garage. I kicked tentatively at the rocks until I booted away the one made of lightweight plastic and picked up the key. Once I opened the door, I'd have 30 seconds to override the alarm. It made me shake with nerves, but after pushing open the door I found the keypad in the entry, punched in the code, and was rewarded with a solid green light.

"Hello?" I squeaked, suddenly timid in the empty expanse. "Emma?"

Inside, the Turnstone's place was like the rest of Skylandia, as tidy and roomy as the surrounding towns were cluttered and cramped. The Turnstones had chosen a lot that backed up on the community forest, and the enormous panes of glass that made up the back wall of the first floor provided a private view of cedars, Douglas fir, and western hemlock. Two steps down and to the right, a kitchen that surely was bigger than our entire cabin stretched toward a formal dining room on one end and a great room on the other. I searched the acres of barren granite beneath the cherry wood cabinets for a note or any signs of habitation. Nothing. The doors of the stainless sub-zero freezer were likewise unadorned and smudge-free.

Behind me, in the foyer, an open staircase led to what I thought must be the sleeping quarters. I tiptoed up the risers past what seemed to be the guest wing and continued to the third floor. There, I dipped into the four bed-and-bath suites—one for each kid and shared accommodation for mommy and daddy, I bet. Emma was the middle child and the only girl, and I guessed her room was the one decorated with oil portraits of what may have been the ill-fated Turnstone family pets: a golden retriever streaking past a grove of aspen in stunning fall display, a black and white long-haired kitten creeping through a patch of green grass, and a surprisingly expressive tortoise staring determinedly forward, one stumpy foot lifted from the ground. All three seemed to be making a break for it.

I took a quick look in each of the brothers' rooms, then Curt and Caro's, and headed back downstairs, intending to check the basement level. As I reached the last steps and turned into the entry hall, I lifted my eyes to the forest view.

Outside the vast middle window, a man stood with his back to me. He was dressed warmly for a mild, mid-October afternoon in a red buffalo plaid wool shirt and black down vest with western piping at the yoke. His skinny jeans ended in pair of black Doc Marten boots, Brit punk style. Beneath a hunting cap in bright orange camo print, unruly brown hair hung in luxuriant, shoulder-length curls. I leapt into the great room and dropped down behind an overstuffed armchair, but I needn't have worried: he didn't see me. He was too busy peeing on a small fir tree.

After he shook off, tucked in, and zipped, he placed his hands on his slender hips and looked off into the tawny buzz and chirp of the forest, rotating his head slowly, first left, then right. He shuddered and turned abruptly toward the house, pulling on a pair of fleece mittens as he approached the expanse of windows. "Good Christ," he said in a voice loud enough for me to hear through the triple-paned glass. "What a thoroughly desolate wilderness!"

I recoiled behind my armchair, grateful that the Turnstones, or more likely their interior designer, had furnished the place in the kind of oversized pieces meant to accommodate modern American proportions. It meant I had plenty of space back there to move around and get a look at the intruder, who was muttering to himself in what sounded like an English accent as he worked his way down the windows, hands cupped to the glass to facilitate viewing. Every few feet he'd stop and tap the panes, then muttering afresh, continue down the line. He showed no sign of seeing me. I suppose the reflection on the glass was working in my favor, because now I could see that the curls escaping from under his cap were frosted with gray and the lines on his face ran deep—sexy, in a Mick Jagger kind of way. When he got to the end of the windows, he turned around, strolled toward an Adirondack chair placed amidst the drying pine needles on the lawn, dropped into it listlessly, and lit a cigarette.

And there the two of us sat as he smoked his cigarette and I hatched and discarded escape plans. Call 911, then disappear under the cover of sirens? Monkey crawl through the entry hall and out the door? Text Nathan to drive out to the Turnstones and cause a diversion? I tried that one, sending a trial "u there?" but Nathan was apparently still out of range.

Outside, the intruder dropped his expended cigarette to the ground and lit a new one. We both settled into position. He was seated at a right angle to my field of vision, my view partially blocked by an end table holding a hand-blown glass cowboy hat, full-size, that I recognized as the work of a local artist. After a couple of extravagant inhalations and shuddering exhalations, he clamped the cigarette between his teeth and began excavating the pockets of his skinny jeans. He probed anxiously, eventually extracted a phone from the right rear pocket, and stabbed dejectedly at the screen.

Whatever he saw there, it wasn't good news. "Blood-dee hell!" he howled. The cigarette fell from his mouth to join its fellow butt on the pine needles below his chair. He patted furiously at the ash on his chest, then began digging in the vest's pocket. During the search, a couple of pens, a notebook, and a black item the size and shape of a slim pack of gum joined the cigarette butts on the lawn. I was puzzling over the identity of the black object when I noticed a thin line of gray-white smoke trailing upward from the tip of the man's right boot.

The intruder clamped a hand on his hat as the prevailing west wind made a grab for it, and I saw a tickle of yellow-orange flame flare beneath the smoke. "Oh no," I breathed aloud. Our state has a reputation for rain, but fire is no joke during a central Washington summer. We've lost hundreds of homes and thousands of acres to wildfires in the last few years. The man fished a silver pack of cigarettes from his vest pocket and lit up a fresh smoke. A gust of wind lifted the curls away from his shoulders and the flames began a run up the rear legs of the Adirondack chair and toward the house.

"Fire!" I yelled, rising from my hiding spot. I raced through the front door, down the driveway, and around toward the back of the house, registering in my peripheral vision a massive red vehicle. It was a model whose name particularly annoyed me because it showed the makers had no idea of the meaning or history of the word. The "Dreadnought" was parked at an angle perilously close to my hidden bike. "Fire!" I yelled again at the intruder, who managed to hold onto his current cigarette as he popped out of the Adirondack chair. "Who in God's name are you?" he screeched when he saw me. "There's a fire!" I responded.

"Where did you come from?" asked the startled man. Then, in a warmer voice, "Mrs. Turnstone?"

"Fire!" I answered. I pointed to the ground behind him, where the flames were already consuming a strip of pine needles along the base of the shingled house. "Fire!" I repeated as I began stamping on the flames.

"Dear God!" the man exclaimed. "Fire!" He joined me in stamping wildly at the ground as the flames took full possession of the Adirondack chair. He took off his vest and began beating it against the new eruption, at the same time stretching with his right leg in an effort to kick his notebook and—now I saw it—his voice recorder away from the blaze.

We carried on in this fashion for a few seconds—me stamping, he beating—more or less fighting the flames to a draw. After a time, the intruder's silver cigarette pack came loose from the vest's pocket and fell directly in front of my dancing feet. On it were the words "Lambert & Butler" and, in serious black against a white background, the warning, "Smoking kills."

It became clear to both of us, I think, that while the fire wasn't exactly gaining strength, neither were we. I could hear the man drawing huge, wet breaths into his spongy lungs as he slapped the singed down vest against the chair with decreasing vigor. I became aware of my aching hip as my stamping steps steadily became less nimble. The edges of several cedar shingles along the base of the house were smoking. I desperately scanned the back of the house for a faucet. And, of course, there it was, with a shiny black garden hose attached. I made a dash for it as the intruder gasped, "This is no time to be leaving, especially since we've just met."

I twisted the faucet's handle to the right until an impressive stream of water shot from the hose. I trained it on the Adirondack chair, the shingles, and the intruder, who, as the freezing water hit him, yelped and abruptly abandoned his firefighting efforts. It must have taken less than a minute to douse the flames, but of course, it seemed longer.

Afterward, we stood at the periphery of a roughly rectangular burn in the dried grass, gazing with shared satisfaction at the blackened Adirondack chair, which had been saved, sort of, by our heroic efforts. The man's sopping, smoke-damaged down vest hung from the chair's right arm like a drowned thing. The intruder sighed contentedly and patted his shirt pockets as if searching for something, then seemed to think better of it. He turned toward me.

"Mrs. Turnstone?"

I considered my answer. "Who are you?"

He paused as if choosing between identities, then said, "Have you seen your daughter recently?"

It was a good trick, and one I had used before myself. Get them flustered by asking a more incendiary question before they can respond to the first, but I was wise to it. "Why do you ask?" I responded.

"Is she in any trouble?"

"What kind of trouble?"

"Have the police told you about their leads?"

"Why would the police contact me?"

"Is there a man involved? A boyfriend? Or a girlfriend?"

I ran a sooty hand through my hair and sighed. "Look, Mr. Turner," I said. "Maybe you should just give me a ride into town and we'll talk about it."

Chapter 18

NATHAN DRAKE

October 18. Evening.

The brewpub closed early that night. Dave and I ate sandwiches while sitting in the pub's red plastic Adirondack chairs just outside the back door. We didn't talk much, just listened to the flow of traffic on the interstate and watched the mountain called Peoh Point turn pink against a blue sky and then black against a pink sky. We had already swapped highlights of our busy day, but we were saving the details for the arrival of Beth and Muriel.

I think we both craved a dose of normality, which must be why we decided to run a batch of Bachelor Creek IPA from the primary fermenter into the conditioning tank through a rough filter I'd mocked up. Remove a bit more yeast and protein, unmask the hops, that was the idea.

Two hours later, mission accomplished, we'd just finished hosing out the stainless steel fermenter when Beth and Muriel tromped through the back door.

"I can't believe you're working tonight," said Muriel, passing rapidly over the wet concrete floor toward the front room.

"Beer never sleeps," said Dave.

I toweled off my hands and gave Beth a hug. Her hair held a distinct scent of campfire. "You OK?" We'd talked just briefly on the phone after she got back from Skylandia, so I'd heard about her run-in with the DeRouxs, and somewhat less about a competing reporter at the Turnstone's place.

"Yeah fine," she said. "Just mad at those guys, Cody and Tommy, and I'm sorry about the VW's window." She looked tired, but also a bit antsy. "But Penny is fine. Roxy too."

The blinds in the tasting room were drawn against curious passersby. We sat at the round oak table, facing each other over glasses of Dave's stout. There was a lot to take in. An RV that reeked of weed. An angry biker. Hollow hay bales. Two-fisted brothers. Curtis Turnstone's curious investment portfolio, his wife's bad luck with house pets, and a British tabloid journalist named Nigel. We sipped our dark brews and sorted the pieces.

Beth took the first shot. "OK, let's keep things simple. Emma stole Penny to get her out of that rat hole you saw, Nathan. Penny and the other puppies are the 'product' Cody was talking about. The doofus brothers are clearly running a breeding mill. Meanwhile, their motorcycle friend is selling a little pot, and apparently testing a strain that makes him paranoid. End of that story." She frowned.

"And Emma?" I asked. "Why's she suddenly hiking the Pacific Crest Trail?"

"Let's say she had nothing to do with either of the bombings," Beth continued. "Even if law enforcement isn't actively seeking her whereabouts, she's still got the DeRouxs mad at her, not to mention her former pals at FT. The British media are poking around about the Drummond case, and her mom is up at Skylandia messing around . . ." Beth left off abruptly, took a deep breath, and then added, "Her mom is a disappointment in many departments. No wonder Emma started crying when we met her."

"Yeah," I said. "But if you have the kind of resources Emma does, why not just make up with Daddy, buy everybody off, and go to, I don't know, Costa Rica?"

Beth lifted her hands in exasperation. "I'd head for the hills too if my parents were celebrity billionaires and every time I turned around Nigel Turner was there with his camera and his vivid imagination. But, hey, who knows."

"What's eating the motorcycle guy?" asked Muriel.

"And do you think Hawk was watching the DeRouxs in South La Likt?" asked Dave. "Does he know Emma has a connection to the puppy mill?"

"And while we're at it," I added, "why are the DeRouxs so fired up about one missing dog? They've got trouble enough keeping all the others alive."

In the silence following this cascade of questions, I reflexively looked in the corner for Penny, but then I remembered she was up at our cabin in the dog run. Muriel and Dave gazed, glassy-eyed, at each other across the table. Their upper lips sported identical stout-foam mustaches.

"Yeah, lots of puzzle parts," said Dave. "Like, your pictures of the magazines in the RV? They looked to me like horse racing mags. Japanese versions. That might explain the hay. I've heard that the Japanese buy a lot of timothy from the lower Sahaptin for their beef cattle and fancy horses."

"So, the motorcycle dude's a paranoid junkie hay exporter?" asked Muriel.

Dave duplicated Beth's hands-up gesture. "If he's stuffing the bales full of pot or guns, maybe so."

Muriel scraped her chair back from the table. "Right. When do we tell the police about all this?"

Silence again. This time not even Beth moved.

"Let's concentrate on Emma," Beth said.

"Well then," I said, "let me show you the daypack I found in the DeRoux's cottage." Everybody leaned back in their chairs as I hoisted the daypack onto the table. I pointed to the FT patch sewn on the front and said "Pretty clearly hers, especially when you see what's inside." I then proceeded to describe each item as I pulled it from the pack.

A six-page lecture outline from a graduate-level class on agricultural economics.

A paperback copy of "Sustainable Global Development," signed by author "To Emma – keep fighting"

A Google map printout of the DeRoux property on Fortune Creek, with directions from downtown La Likt.
A menu from the Cabin Café in La Likt.
A receipt from La Likt Safeway for groceries, toothbrush, toothpaste, and a Seattle *Times*. Six weeks old.
Four Luna bars, three pens, one pencil.
A phone charger.
I placed all the items back in the pack and, my stout having vanished, went to pour myself dessert: a robust porter.
Muriel reached into the pack and extracted the Google map by its very edge, as if fingerprints may be required at some point. "Where's a beautiful young heiress on the run to hide?" She let the page float to the table. "I know. Why not stay in a sad puppy ranch with scary hosts?"
"But other than the owners," said Beth, "not a bad choice, on the face of it, for an animal-lover with no access to her cash machine?"
"And aiming for the PCT?" added Muriel.
"I'm not sure she planned that," I said. "All her gear looked pretty makeshift. Probably stolen from DeRoux."
"Yeah, gotcha," said Muriel, reaching again into the pack. "I mean, you can hide up there, that's for sure. But you're also exposed to the elements. You need resupply."
"And then winter comes," I said. "Eventually."
Beth exhaled heavily and said "Yes, Nathan, winter comes. Eventually." She stared down at her hands, examining her blackened nails. "Although," she finally added, a bit grudgingly, I thought, "that's probably one reason Carolyn Turnstone is extra frantic to find her daughter right now. Before the snow falls, I mean." She looked up at me. "Did you know Caro is a local girl? Grew up in Ellensburg. Like Hawk."
Muriel piped up again. "Anybody know who Ron St. Clair is?" She was holding the Cabin Café menu with her fingertips. "Somebody wrote his name on the back of this. 'Ron St. Clair.' Then it says, 'Bakery, Columbia City.'"
"Somebody," we agreed, was probably Emma, since the handwriting matched the notes on the syllabus and in the

margins of the book. After zipping all the evidence back into Emma's pack, we decided that once one of us got back on the west side of the state, it was worth checking out the bakeries in Columbia City, a rapidly gentrifying neighborhood in the south of Seattle. Ron St. Clair would get Googled, too.

"Back to Emma," said Beth. "Let's assume she returned from London because she was scared of the accusations in that *Informant* article."

"But she'd just gone there for a fresh start. Why come back if. . ."

"Precisely! That's *precisely* what I wanted to know! Why run, Sweet Emma, if you are innocent?"

The voice, high-pitched, with a working-class British accent like a young Michael Caine, came from behind the bar.

"Can a fellow get a decent pint of bitter here? That's what I heard."

He had a mole-like face with a goatee struggling to make a claim on his chin. His wet hair was pulled back in a barely sustainable ponytail, and his worn T-shirt, commemorating a concert tour by some band I'd never heard of, hugged a decidedly concave chest. His bony, white arm hovered near the tap handles.

"Nigel," said Beth. "You found some dry clothes?"

"I did indeed, Mary Beth, at that quaint store you recommended. A thrift shop you called it, and it did make me feel very thrifty." He plucked at the T-shirt. "Nickelback isn't a special favorite of mine," he said in a thoughtful tone.

Dave and I had propped open the door to the back room to help it dry out. That must be how the little weasel got in. I wondered how long he'd been lurking and listening by the tanks of finishing beer.

"Everybody," announced Beth, "this is Nigel Turner, reporter from the London *Informant* here to cover Emma's disappearance. Maybe after Dave gets Nigel the beer I promised him, he'll tell us why he's so sure Emma was involved in the London bombing."

The reporter shook our hands in turn and after extracting phone, cigarettes, lighter, and notepad from the pockets of his jeans (it was a wonder how he stowed all of it in there), he wedged a chair next to Beth's and joined us at the table. I lifted Emma's daypack off the table top, discretely I thought, as if simply making room, and placed it under my chair.

Turner had no trouble filling the silence left by our mistrust.

First, he took one long pull on his beer, during which his beady eyes assessed all those around the table. After tucking his chin to suppress an appreciative burp, he aimed a fleeting and complex nod-smile-wink combination at Dave and then launched into a longer and more vulgar version of what already had been published in the *Informant*. Although the facts were basically the same, he hinted strongly of incriminating evidence to come.

"But you know how editors can be, Beth," he fake-whispered in her ear. "Weak knees. No balls. Ehm?"

There were a few new pieces of information in his gassy discourse, if you listened for them carefully. Turner told us he believed Emma and a FreeThinker leader named Jack Scanlon were still in touch. He stated unequivocally that Curtis Turnstone's investment in a competitor of Winston Drummond's biotech company was no coincidence. And Emma's disappearance, he said, chiding us as if we were gullible children, could not possibly have happened without collaborators.

"And your sources are," Beth prodded in tired voice. She clearly had no hope of a satisfying reply.

"Ah. Must protect them." He reached a bony hand toward Beth and patted her arm. "You know this, Mary Beth."

The four of us exchanged glances and sipped from our beers. Nigel was clearly chumming the waters, fishing for more of what we'd pieced together. He didn't seem to know how deeply involved Beth and I were in Emma's story, other than we'd met her on the trail. But if he'd been in our part of the country for almost two weeks, wouldn't he have discovered more? And how long had he been listening to us at the back door?

"The high and the low of it, dear Mary Beth," he summarized, having now drained his pint, "is that your Sweet Emma is in much deeper trouble than you realize."

"Oh, I don't know about that." A new voice resonated from behind the bar. Jason Hawk stood where Nigel had been a moment ago.

"I gotta latch that door," mumbled Dave, rising wearily to his feet.

Hawk took the liberty of pouring himself a beer, and it wasn't his first of the evening to judge from his ruddy face and the seeming misplacement of his normal voice.

"These things have a way of working out," he said in a rich baritone, one muscular eyebrow rising toward his impressive hairline. "Give it some time and it'll blow over."

He stood with one paw on the bar and the other gripping his pint glass and added, now in a Nick Nolte growl, "The Turnstone's pretty little girl didn't do anything wrong."

Nigel stood and raised an empty palm toward the sheriff turned private investigator. "Well," he said. "How fortunate to see you again, Mr. Hawk."

I glanced at Beth, and she nodded at me. Of course, it was Nigel we saw spread-eagled against the wall at the Turnstone's Seattle mansion. Nigel continued in a genial tone, "Finally, someone proffering the answers we seek."

Hawk was in the middle of a long swig of beer. He took his time, eyeing the Brit over the upturned heel of his emptying glass.

"Nigel," said Beth as the former sheriff continued to pour beer down his thick neck, "I know you've met Jason Hawk. I suppose you also know that he's been engaged by the Turnstones to find Emma and bring her home?"

"And we all wish him every success, I'm sure," squeaked Nigel. "But I wonder if Mr. Hawk could tell us if he has been in communication with the girl. Perhaps he could explain why, if she is innocent, she suddenly vanished from London after the bombing of her former flame, Mr. Drummond, whose bioengineering business must be, what shall I say, distasteful to her? She's on record saying as much."

Hawk smiled and, wiping his mustache on the back of his right hand, waited for Nigel to go on. The journalist obliged him.

"And I must note that Sweet Emma's undoubted qualms about her former love's business activity were followed by a bombing. Curiously similar to the scenario that played out at the University of Washington not so long ago."

Hawk set his empty glass on the bar and stared at it. "That's a lot of bull," he hissed, now a menacing Clint Eastwood. He placed his vast palms on the bar and exhaled impressively out of the side of his mouth—though, I don't know, it might've been just an exceedingly well-controlled burp. He raised his bloodshot eyes to us.

"Look, I assure you all that Emma Turnstone is innocent, and she's safe," he said. The voice finally seemed to resemble his own. "Everything is under control. You're only making the situation worse with your snooping around. Leave it to the professionals."

Nigel, seated again, was jotting in his pocket notebook.

"So, you found her?" asked Beth. "She told you she's innocent in the Drummond bombing?"

Hawk stopped in the process of reaching for his wallet. He looked at Nigel before repeating, "Her guilt or innocence isn't even a question at this point, Mrs. Drake. Hell, she hasn't even been charged, has she, Mr. Turner?"

He slapped a fifty on the bar. "I'm buying tonight," he said before turning to look at Dave. "Hey, any luck on the river today?"

I was thrown by the change of subject, but Dave just shook his head. "Nah," he said. "It was a little bright for that late in the afternoon. Windy too." He smiled at the big man. "How about you? You get some good pictures?"

Hawk stiffened behind the bar, then tipped his chin up a fraction. "Yeah, I sure did. My little grand-niece loves those ducks. Mergansers, they're called. I like to send her a few pictures." He raised his hand in a salute to the rest of us as Dave went to unlock the back door. "You all have a good night," he said. "Have a good trip back to England, Mr. Turner. Sorry about that arm." He turned toward Beth and me and gave us his grimace of a smile. "Drive safe back home to Seattle, you two."

"We're not going to Seattle," I blurted. "We've got a home here."

"Oh, I know that," Hawk said, "but you'll want to be getting out of the mountains before the cold weather comes." He fixed us with a stare. "Better do it soon."

We heard the back door bang shut after Hawk's exit. Dave went to re-latch it. Beth's eyes were glassy. As Nigel tilted the last of his second bitter toward his mouth, she tried to wrap up the day's events.

"Well," she said, "that guy may be full of B.S. and Carolyn Turnstone may not have all her facts straight, but I believe them when they say Emma didn't have anything to do with the Drummond bombing."

"But Mummy hid her at Skylandia," said Nigel, a terrier unwilling to give up his chew toy. "Right?"

"Yes," sighed Beth. "We know she stayed at Skylandia for about a week or so until somebody—or something—scared her off. And that's all we know." She thumped her empty glass to the table as if gaveling the meeting to a close.

Beth and I walked the Brit out to his SUV, its massive haunches claiming two-thirds of the sidewalk. We mumbled our goodbyes and dispersed.

* * * * *

Dave and Muriel were running Beth up to the cabin in the truck. I was planning to follow on her bike, but first, I took my remaining half-glass of porter out back, waved to Dave in his departing truck, and eased into one of the red chairs. The October air chilled my exposed arms and neck.

"My favorite time of year," said Hawk, stepping out of the building's shadow. "That chill in the air. Makes you feel alive."

After all the day's surprises, it seemed almost natural when Hawk lowered his bulk into the empty red chair next to mine and took a long pull on one of Dave's big bottles. Either the stout or the red. Too dark to tell.

"I think I must be a top customer at this place," he said.

"Well," I said, "you gotta reward the best with your business."

We sat at the outer edge of a puddle of light thrown by a bulb on the neighbor's back stairway, drinking our beers, listening to the thrum of the freeway.

"Look," he said after a full minute, "I'm just doing my job here. I know I ruffle some feathers. People tell all kinds of stories. But I get the job done. Always have."

I waited to hear what he really wanted to say. Something about backing off the search for Emma. Or forgetting the DeRouxs. Or going back to Seattle.

He swallowed more beer and said, "We need more people like you up here, Nate. Trying to do the right thing."

That caught me off guard. I said, "Hard to say what's right sometimes. Or who."

"Tell me about it," he grunted, stretching his long legs out in front of him. "My whole life. Family. Sports. Law. A little bad always mixed with the good."

"Not many straight-up heroes or villains left," I said.

"Just people," he said. "Trying to get by."

"I figure it's a matter of percentages," I said.

I could feel him watching me as I took a sip of the porter. "I mean," I continued, "we have to decide, society does, when somebody crosses the line. What's a crime? When does indiscretion become injustice? And what about mitigating factors? Or intentions?"

"What?" he said. "You got a justice meter there in your pocket, Nate? Some kind of Ghandi-to-Hitler sliding scale? I could've used that when I was sheriff."

I let his chuckle run its course. "Yeah," I said. "It's just, sometimes, right and wrong isn't so obvious. Degrees of guilt and all that."

"Nah, I gotcha," he said.

"The gray area thing," I said.

I'm not sure he heard me. He had thrown his head back, the bottle tilting almost straight up. Finished, he blotted his lips with his sleeve and lay the empty bottle on the gravel between us. "All right then," he announced, "I should take a piss and get going." He began rubbing his knees in preparation for standing, but he didn't move to get out of the chair.

"You know, when I first joined the sheriff's department," he said, hands now quiet on knees, "we had a run of trouble with gang members up from Yakima. Meth labs. Bodies turning up in the river canyon. Not just rivals. Teenage girls. Mutilated."

He let the diesel rattle of a semi-truck pass before continuing. "One night I followed a junky car out of the canyon. Driving real slow. Up into the Badger Pocket. I mean this guy wasn't an apple picker out there. Not in January. So, I pull 'em over. Teenager, nervous as hell, practically crying. I find out why when I pop the trunk and see the body."

I wondered why Hawk was telling me all this.

"I don't know why I'm telling you all this," he said. "You woulda made a good priest maybe. Confession."

"Church of the Hops and Barley," I said.

"Anyway, even with a bullet through his head, I recognize the guy in the trunk. Leader of the most vicious gang in Yakima. The driver, now he's really bawling, tells me his uncle was pissed at the L.A. drug gangs causing trouble in town. So, when he came home and found this guy harassing his nephew, he just shot him. Sent the kid to dump him up in the canyon."

I had no idea where this was going.

"So, here's what I did," Hawk continued in low voice. "Tell me what you think. I have the kid follow me to an orchard up Thrall Road. I know the owner. Played ball with him in high school. Borrow his backhoe. Bury the bastard good and deep. The kid goes back home. Easy enough to spread some stories about Mr. Big going back to L.A. I talk with the uncle later. Turns out he's the first grower in the Yakima valley to go big time from apples to vineyards. Couple years later, he's rich. Made some nice contributions to my campaign fund."

Hawk let me chew on all this long enough to feel implicated. "So, what do you think? Did I do the right thing, Nate?"

I hesitated. "Well, obviously it's not by the book. I guess you were thinking about the greater good? The best outcome for the community?"

"That's it exactly."

"Although," I added, thinking vaguely of how I might need to recount this conversation to a jury at some later date, "there was the chance that wasn't Mr. Big in the trunk. Or your info on the gang connection was wrong. Or the kid's uncle was also dealing."

"Yeah, sure," he said, "but in that moment, I was 80 or 90 percent sure I had it right. Sometimes it's hard to do the calculation. Right? Wrong? Intentions? Prejudices? Best outcome for the community?"

"Who knows?" I heard myself say.

"It gets complicated, but I'll tell you one thing, Nate. We didn't find any bodies in the canyon after that night. So, sometimes it's not as simple as good versus evil. Maybe sometimes the ends do justify the means. Go ahead and tell me about gray areas."

It was unsettling to hear words that often played in my own mind come out of Hawk's mouth.

In the silence that followed, I thought about the Blewett Pass head-on that had killed Hawk's mom and dad and brother. After Curtis Turnstone mentioned it, I dug around a little and found out from my neighbor in La Likt that the rumor was both drivers were drunk. Happens more than you'd think my Uncle Bob the cop had told me once. "That's what we call a weekend double-header, Natie" he had whispered to me over his can of Budweiser at the dinner table in Sacramento.

Carolyn Turnstone certainly knew about Hawk's father's drinking too. That must have been why she rolled her eyes when Curtis recited the Seahawks-sanctioned Hawk origin story. Anyway, I'm not sure how you apportion guilt in that terrible situation. Blood alcohol level? Speed? Who's over the double yellow? History of DUIs? Maybe assign weight to each factor. Do the calculation.

"Look at us," Hawk grumbled amiably, slapping his broke-down knees, "dealing with the big issues. Good. Bad. Justice." Now he leaned forward, hands pressed down on the chair's molded plastic arms in preparation to launch himself up and out. I wondered if the chair could withstand that thrust.

"The girl," he sighed, holding the take-off pose. "Emma. She's got some explaining to do. Don't you think? At least to her parents?"

"To be honest," I said to him, "we wonder the same thing."

"Maybe a little monkey blood on her hands?" he asked in a jokey voice.

"Who knows what else."

"That's probably why you sent your buddy to snoop at the DeRoux's garage in South La Likt, right?"

I waited just a second before replying. "Dave was just fishing."

"Right," he answered. "Like me."

"Right."

He set his feet, and with a weightlifter's efficient grunt he was out of the chair.

"When all this is over," he said, taking a moment to let his joints orient to the upright position, "get in touch. You fish?

"Not really."

"Hmm." Now he was moving. "I'll see you 'round." And then he was gone, a door slamming shut and the tires of his fancy SUV scrunching out of the back lot.

I pulled out my phone to text my brother Andy. Just had a beer with Jason Hawk. That would get a quick response.

But when I saw my Dad's name in my contacts above Andy's, I remembered his visit was coming up. And I remembered I had a question for him. After his career with the federal government, my father worked for an insurance company as a skip tracer. His job was to track down mobile home owners who were behind on their payments so the company could repossess their trailers or RVs.

I pressed "Jack Drake," then "Call."

"Hello, who is it?"

"Hi Dad, it's Nathan. How are you?"

"OK. Hey, did you see *60 Minutes* last night?"

"No. What was on?"

"Great story. Very inspirational. Police getting into football coaching. Inner cities. Getting gang toughs on their side. Less violence. Just a great story."

"It sounds like it."

"Well. How are you?"

"I'm OK. Beth's fine. We're up in La Likt."

"We were 95 degrees here in Sacramento today. Perfect."

"About 65 here."

"I'll see you and Beth later this week. Thursday morning?"

"Yes, of course. We're glad you're coming. You haven't been to La Likt yet. It's not exactly Tahoe, but the cabin's a real gem. You'll see."

"I can look over your sketch for the garage."

"That'll be great. Hey, Dad, I wanted to ask a favor. Do you think you'd be able to figure out who owns an RV if I gave you the license number?"

I listened to the faint squeal of my father's hearing aids as I waited for his reply. My phone vibrated with an incoming text.

"Dad," I said, "it's OK if you can't do it."

"What do you need it for?"

"It's kind of complicated, but there's an RV causing problems up here in La Likt. Just want to contact the owner directly."

"You try knocking?"

"It's kind of abandoned. That's the problem."

"You try your police up there?"

"They told us there's nothing they can do." I didn't like lying to the old man, but I was pretty sure that's the answer I'd get if I did call the local cops. I soothed my guilt with that thought and plunged on. "I tried some online services that track ownership, but they looked like scams or they just tell me that the plate number isn't available for purchase."

"Fourth amendment."

"What?"

"The fourth amendment. No search or seizure. Now it's all spelled out in Title 18 of the U.S. Code. The DMV can't give away your private information."

"Oh."

"So, give me the license number. I can do it."

"Really? How?"

"Once a skip tracer, always a skip tracer. I still know some people at SpanAmerica. That's why you asked me, right?"

"Well. Yes."

I believe my dad enjoyed those ten years with the insurance company. The bus commute to J Street downtown, the 9 to 5. A normal life, without a gun attached. I thought he might enjoy this little assignment as well. Something to do. So I gave Dad the information and was ready to let him go—I could sense his growing eagerness to break away for the beginning of the ten o'clock news—when he asked a surprising question.

"So, does this RV have anything to do with the girl who's missing?"

I was sure I hadn't said anything to him about Emma.

"Lacey called and told me about it," he said. "The bombing at the University. And London."

"Oh. Well, I was going to tell you."

"You still have the dog?"

"We do. Penny. That's her name."

"I'll get you the owner of the RV."

"Thanks, Dad. I'll see you next week at the airport."

I looked up at the sky and its array of damp little stars. I had a premonition of my 84-year-old father walking down the ramp at Sea-Tac, his beige golf jacket standing out in the sea of darkly clothed 30-somethings. A steady walk, but slower now. Pulling his carry-on. He has not seen me yet. Face inscrutable.

I heard a freight train rumble, probably at the river crossing up near Elk Lake Road, and only then did I remember that my phone had vibrated as I was talking with my father.

As I expected, it was from Beth:

Beth   **9:58 PM**
Where are you? Penny's gone.

Chapter 19

MARY BETH DRAKE

October 20

Run, Emma, Run!

EXCLUSIVE: Wealthy Girl turns
Stealthy Girl as tech heiress
Emma Turnstone hides from
Drummond car bombing woes in wild
western wilderness

By Nigel Turner
Informant Staff

La Likt, Washington: Emma Turnstone, the 22-
year-old daughter of venture capital
billionaire Curtis Turnstone, is on the run
from her past in the wilderness of Washington
State, sources tell our *Informant* reporter.

Blonde babe Emma, who sparked international
suspicion after her hasty departure from
London this summer following a car bombing
that seriously injured her boyfriend, gene
tweaker Winston Drummond, was spotted dashing
up a rough hillside in the remote mountains

here, far from the comforts daddy's money usually provides.

"Oh, come on!" I snorted, flipping my phone over so that I couldn't see the offending words on the cracked screen. "'Sources tell our *Informant* reporter?' More like '*Informant* reporter overhears while skulking around lapping up beer.'" I looked around the cabin for confirmation, but Nathan was in Seattle picking up his dad at the airport, and Penny, I reminded myself, Penny was gone.

It was my fault. I never should have left her alone in that rickety dog run, especially after the scary run-ins we'd all had with the DeRoux brothers. Maybe I didn't latch it right. Maybe something spooked her and she jumped over the flimsy fencing. Maybe somebody walked right in and took her. Or maybe a mountain lion. I didn't let myself think about that one. Whatever. She was gone and I was under strict instructions to stick close to the cabin in case she made her way back to us, *Incredible Journey* style. Muriel and Dave volunteered to do the active searching for our pup and I wanted to be out there with them. But Nathan said someone had to stay home, just in case.

Actually, what he said was, "Based on the last couple of days, who do you think will do a better job of finding Penny and staying out of trouble at the same time?" He gave me a stern look. It didn't help that he was packing up his toothbrush as he said it, a move that never fails to annoy me. Why not invest in two toothbrushes, one for Seattle and one for La Likt? Why shuttle the same damn toothbrush back and forth? I got so mad that I kicked aside the rock we use as a stop and slammed the bedroom door, causing a framed picture to bounce off the wall—the two of us grinning stupidly in front of the yawning crater of Mt. St. Helens, like we had personally overseen the explosion or something. For his part, Nathan left the picture where it landed, and neither of us said goodbye when he took off in the Subaru to get his dad.

To pass the time between frequent, forlorn sessions of calling Penny's name down by the empty dog run, I was drinking coffee and checking in on Nigel's latest dispatch from his reporting outpost at the Sno-Cap Motel. As usual, I was appalled.

The golden girl of the animal rights movement, Sweet Emma has reasons to run. Sources in the movement tell the *Informant* that she was having it off with both Drummond and a leader of the FreeThinkers anti-viv group, Jack Scanlon.

Though suspected of involvement, neither Emma nor Scanlon ever faced charges in connection with any of FT's crimes. That includes February's botched attack on a University of Washington laboratory animal facility, which killed 14 of the very chimps the bumbling bombers said they wanted to free. While two of her radical pals await appeal of their convictions in that act of terrorism, others in the movement believe Emma's privileged upbringing and her papa's ready hand with cash shielded her from scrutiny. Now they worry she'll tell all if she's brought up on new bombing charges in the UK.

I brought my cup to my lips, but the coffee had gone cold. So, Nigel had figured out that Emma had reason to run not only from the London explosion, but also from her former friends at FT. I set the cup down. I had to admit, he'd done some pretty good digging to get Emma's "radical pals" to talk. I stood up and stalked around the room once, then twice. I was irritated, and I didn't like to admit the reason why. Nigel Turner had himself a good story. And I was jealous of him.

I was headed toward the two-burner camp stove to reheat my coffee when I heard a sharp scraping, like fingernails raked across an old-fashioned blackboard. My first thought was that Penny had come back and was scratching like a wild thing at our front door. When I threw the door open, though, I saw the red Dreadnought parked at the end of our gravel drive, near the future site of the magnificent garage. The SUV's door was open, and the idiot chimes were insistently gonging. Nigel Turner stood alongside the vehicle, examining three jagged scratches that ran the length of the driver's side, near matches to the gouges on the passenger's side left by the Turnstone's security barge. The remains of Penny's dog run lay on the ground next to him.

He looked up at me. "Bullocks," he pronounced. "Give a friend a cup of tea, Beth?"

"Friend?" I said. "Or source?"

"Both, I hope," he answered with a smile that showed me his teeth, just crooked enough to be sexy. I sighed and waved him in. Two can play at this game, Nigel, I thought.

"Where's the absent-minded husband today? Off building sustainable sanitation for woodland creatures?"

"Do you want me to make you some tea or not?" His body brushed against mine as he inched through the cabin's narrow doorway. He paused half-way and gave me frank stare. I caught the faint scent of something spicy. Body spray?

"I see you've read my latest piece," he said once I had him settled at the cabin's rough wooden table, a mug of Earl Grey steaming in front of him. "Sweet Emma," he said. "That's not exactly accurate, is it? I should have named her 'the Turnstone Turn-on.' He frowned. "I wonder if it's too late to use that."

"Yeah," I said, retrieving my phone from its spot on the table in front of him. "Who would expect a woman to have two boyfriends? I thought that kind of behavior was reserved for the men you write about."

"Now, Mary Beth. Is that fair? I'm ecstatic whenever one of my subjects has a little something extra on the side, man or woman." He thought for a moment. "Preferably man *and*

160

woman. And at the same time." When I didn't respond, he put his hand on mine. "Oh come, now. Not even a smile?"

I looked up from my reheated coffee and met his eyes. It *was* kind of funny, the sort of newsroom banter that I missed. I struggled to keep the grin off my face. "What do you want, Nigel?"

"I was hoping you might give me the benefit of your superior knowledge of the region," he said cheerfully. "I know you saw Emma on a trail, you see, but I don't know which trail. And I was hoping you might be able to tell me, as an outdoors expert, where you think Emma is right now."

"As an outdoors expert, I don't know where she is. And if I did, I don't see how it would profit me to tell you."

"Oh, profit. Why must we always bring profit into it, Beth? I know you're, how should I put it?" He gazed at me appraisingly. "Curious," he concluded. "Yes, you're curious. Or you wouldn't have been sneaking around inside the Turnstone's massive cabin." He sighed. "Surely 'cabin' isn't quite the word for it." He glanced around the room. "*This* is a cabin. But the Turnstone's place. What would you call it? Not a country house. Not a villa."

"Lodge."

"Lodge," he repeated delightedly. I thought he might clap his hands. "Of course. You Americans have such a beguiling way of naming things. A lodge, as if we were all sleeping rough, without Wi-Fi or climate control." He grinned at me. "See what a good team we could make?"

I took a sip of my coffee just to have something to do. It had turned bitter on the stove, and I made a face.

"You can't tell me, dearest Mary Beth, that you aren't at all curious about what happened to young Emma. You can't tell me you don't want some answers about the Turnstone Turn-on." He smiled, and I noticed the two dimples that made twin commas beside his pouty lips. "You do want it, you know."

Was it my imagination or was the man coming on to me? It had been so long since anyone had bothered with anything close to flirtation where I was concerned that I couldn't be sure. I put my mug down and studied the rough wood of the table.

"Of course, you want to know. So why don't you help me? The two of us, working side-by-side? Joint byline?" he offered. "Anything you want." When I didn't respond, he scooted his chair closer to mine and took both of my hands in his. "Look, Mary Beth, my love, I know some details that could make this a good story. A very good story. But I need to find Emma, and the only way I know to do that is to follow the leads. And the only good leads I have are the rather promiscuous Jack Scanlon and the very fetching you." He smiled at me again, dimple one and dimple two deepening. "I've found you, thank God, and our meeting has been the best part of my visit to your rustic part of the world. But I haven't found Jack Scanlon."

"You asked his attorney?"

He gave my hands a squeeze. "Now, that's the kind of incisive thinking I need. But yes, of course I asked his attorney. She had no comment on Jack's whereabouts or activities, beyond saying that he's being a model citizen. Seems he's learning to become a vegan baker, whatever that may be, and staying as far away from his frightening friends at FT as he can."

A baker? I thought back to the notes we'd found scrawled on the Cabin Café menu in Emma's backpack. We'd all wondered why Emma would take an interest in a bakery back home in Seattle. Could Jack Scanlon be hiding out with the man whose name she'd printed on the menu, Ron St. Clair? Or maybe he's hiding *as* Ron St. Clair? OK, I know that's a leap in logic. But still, wasn't it possible?

"Beth," Nigel said. "Please, love, stay focused here. Look at me. Can't you see I need you?"

"Nigel," I said, and now it was my turn to smile at him, "what do you think about taking a drive into Seattle?"

He leaned across the table, took my face in his hands, and kissed me.

162

Chapter 20

NATHAN DRAKE

October 21

"Holy Mother!"

The Tesla accelerated soundlessly through the sweeping curve of the downtown tunnel, the white walls and arched ceiling with its twin ribbons of lights sucking us—the only car inside that gleaming chute—deeper and faster into a leftward bending infinity. When the tunnel finally leveled and straightened, I inhaled sharply, goosed the speed, and then swooped across lanes and rocketed up the long rightward bend toward the rectangle of sunlight. As we shot into that blinding sunlight, I lifted my foot off the accelerator and gravity reclaimed the heavy slab of batteries under our seats. We landed at a sedate 50 miles per hour on the section of southbound State Route 99 squeezed between the baseball park and the harbor.

That rare stretch of empty Seattle roadway in the tunnel had allowed me to test the 0-to-80-in-four-seconds claim made by my "customer experience specialist" back at the Tesla dealership. I'm not exactly a driving enthusiast, but I'm as red-blooded as the next guy, and so, knowing full well the odds were against me, I looked ahead for another open stretch of road.

The test drive idea had been a complete surprise.

"How about we take a walk in the South Lake Union neighborhood?" my father had asked me just an hour before, as the stolid little Subaru carried us northbound from the airport on the bottom level of this very same SR 99 tunnel. We were headed toward the townhome, where we planned to spend the night before making our way to La Likt the next day. When I'd asked my father if he felt up to an afternoon stroll, I was expecting him to name a favorite route: the ship canal, Discovery Park, maybe the crown of Queen Anne.

"Really? South Lake Union?"

"I've heard it's all new development."

"That's for sure." I replied. "When we moved here, South Lake Union had a Hostess Twinkie factory, a flower wholesaler, trophy shops, ship upholsterers, that kind of thing. It's all Amazon and biotech now. Sort of hustle and bustle down there."

"Sounds interesting," said my dad. "But whatever you would like."

So, after dropping his roller suitcase in the guestroom, we stood in the kitchen and shared a sleeve of Fig Newtons before heading back toward downtown.

We found an empty parking spot on 9th Avenue and set out for Westlake, where we gawked at construction cranes and dodged the Amazon-badged hoards. As I negotiated the sidewalks and crosswalks with my fleece-vested father, I saw he was surely the oldest person in a mile radius. I was, quite possibly, the second oldest.

We were relieved to find an uncrowded coffee shop where we could hear each other. Our agenda included the family trust and, I hoped, the La Likt RV.

While Dad used the bathroom, I peeked into his old leather briefcase and saw, between his copies of the *Economist* and *Foreign Affairs*, several manila folders with neatly typed labels: LIVING TRUST, SEATTLE, and POWER OF ATTORNEY. Two additional files bore his angular penmanship: LA LIKT RV and DRUMMOND.

What the hell did he know about Winston Drummond?

Before he worked the skip tracer gig, my father spent his career with the federal government as a civil engineer specializing in failure analysis. His job was to figure out what went wrong on classified projects. At least that's how he explained it to us kids. As we got older, of course, my brothers and sisters and I grew more curious about what really happened on those long trips to Malaysia and Pakistan and Central America. Some of the Drake kids suspected CIA—I was certain of it—but Dad refused to be pinned down, pleading that even after retirement he couldn't risk sharing classified information. He was, foremost, a man who could keep a secret.

Why was I so certain of the CIA connection? Because he took me there, to Langley. CIA headquarters in Virginia. This was the late 70s, a family vacation to Washington D.C. But on that day, it was just me and him in the rental car, a purple Chevy Impala. We drove up Route 123 and then turned up a long, forested drive, went through a security gate, and parked. He told me to stay put and read my book while he saw his 'client,' then disappeared inside a concrete building. A while later, I heard a sharp rapping on the passenger window, now bleary with rain. He was standing there, gesturing for me to get out of the car. He led me across the parking lot and deep into a grove of trees that surrounded a life-size statue of a man dressed in breeches and a cutaway coat. His feet were bound and his wrists were tied behind his back, but his head was held high as he gazed proudly into the distance.

"This is Nathan Hale," my father said. "Revolutionary War hero. The first spy in our nation's history. He was discovered, captured, and hanged by the British."

We stood together and watched the rain drip off the coppery green face.

"I smoked a cigar right here the morning you were born, Nathan." He put a hand on my shoulder. "This is who you are named after. Nathan Hale."

I don't remember what I had to say, if anything, to this bit of information. I do remember what he said next, though, as we headed back to the car. "Can you keep quiet about this trip today, Nathan? Keep it just between us?"

I could and I did.

"So, I found your RV owner," Dad said, easing himself back into our booth.

I waited as he pulled the file.

"It's actually owned by a Japanese company, the Oba Corporation. It's a privately held investment group owned by Yoshio Oba."

He took a sip of his coffee and opened the file. He seemed in his element here, licking his fingertips and spinning a short stack of pages across the vintage Formica table toward me. Since adulthood, most of my business with my father had been conducted over holiday dinners, frozen computer screens, episodes of *Jeopardy*, or bodies of dead relatives. This was a side of him I had not seen.

"The thing about Mr. Oba," he said, now in full debrief mode, "is that although he has never been convicted of any crimes, the consensus is that he is an elder in the *yakuza*."

I looked up from the page.

"The *yakuza* are Japan's mafia. Tough bunch. Criminal network. Extortion. Gambling. Fake imports. Oba was the family head of one syndicate. They call him the *oyabun*. But," Dad added, "it looks like he's retired now. He lives in Tokyo and spends most of his time breeding race horses. Big deal for Japan's wealthy, horses. You can get half a million for a top runner. And that doesn't even count stud fees or baby horses. What are they called?

"Foals?"

"Yeah. Speaking of, Oba himself has two sons, Junichi and Toshi."

He took another sip of coffee and let me peruse the neatly stapled printouts.

The RV, I saw, was registered to Oba Corp. but at an address in Freedom, an old mining town in the hills above La Likt. Most of the remaining pages, laser printed from unidentified sources, described Oba and his *yakuza* connections.

"Wow," I said. "Where'd you get all this, Dad?"

"SpanAmerica. The agency. Contacts. I still know some people." A slight smile crossed his face. "Oh, and here," he said, pushing a glossy brochure, all in Japanese, across the table to me. "This is a horse breeder's catalogue. Shows the Oba Corp. stallion farm in Hokkaido. Profile of the whole operation. Soup to nuts."

I opened the brochure to a page marked with a Post-It note and saw a photo spread of healthy-looking horses grazing on the flanks of undulating green hills. A few close-ups showed sleek racehorses in action. And here was a dark-suited Mr. Oba himself, arm on barn door, eye to eye with a handsome horse's head.

"That's him," my father said. "Who says crime doesn't pay?"

On the next page, hay fields glowed emerald in dramatic late afternoon light. My father reached over and pointed to a cluster of English words below one photo. As soon as I read 'Upper Yakima River Valley,' I recognized the rows of white wind turbines in the background and, in one particularly fine shot, snow-covered Mt. Stuart looming over barns filled with coiled bales of green hay.

"The Land Park branch of the Sacramento library just happened to have this brochure?" I asked, turning the page.

"Guy I know. Probably on the internet too. But you know me and computers. And anyway, FedExed hard copy is more secure than Google."

I turned the page and I lowered my head to look more closely at a photo of a jumbo-sized, Armani-clad fellow with a ponytail standing by a row of hay bales. He was shaking hands with a farmer. A smaller close-up showed the same guy—identified this time as Junichi Oba—pinching a cluster of green hay between his fingers.

"That your RV occupant?"

"That's him. Minus the big Indian motorcycle and the dirty look."

* * * * *

It was on the walk back to the Subaru that my father suggested we stop in at the Tesla dealership. Kicking some tires was one thing, but when he asked the eager salesman if we could take a test drive, I thought of my sister Janey's suggestion that we all start watching Dad for signs of impulsiveness.

Sooner than seemed advisable we were alone in the car, blasting through the tunnel and back out into the open by the sports stadiums. There, I was amazed to find another wide-open stretch of highway and before I could think we must've topped 100 miles per hour. That's when my father said, "Take the West Seattle Bridge."

That he even knew there was a West Seattle, much less that getting there involved a bridge, was news to me.

Without fully registering my own surprise, I reacted to the paternal command. We veered onto the ramp at 60 miles per hour, the sheer density of all that nickel and lithium hugging us to the pavement, and then the hot electric motors behind each wheel vectored us onto and over the high span.

"And now, Southwest Admiral Way," Dad calmly said.

Something was up.

Soon enough he directed me to a free Tesla charging station, one of hundreds the company has set up for owners across the country.

Once parked next to the charger, we were alone on a bluff looking over the giant white and red shipping cranes of Harbor Island. The high-rises of downtown Seattle seemed to float just beyond the cranes. Dad's old leather briefcase was on his lap, and he held an open file in his hand.

"August 29 this year. Winston Drummond, CEO of Rational EvoAg, files insurance claim with Avita Insurance. Related to damage from fire resulting from explosion, two days previous, during recharging of experimental Croatian electric vehicle at his personal charging station—similar to this one, but apparently unauthorized." Dad waved his hand in the direction of the charger posts in front of us. "Located at his home in

London. Seeks compensation for total replacement of brand-new cTomic Model E99 plus medical costs for burns to hands plus salary replacement for lost time at work. September 1, claim approved, all damages verified."

"Wow," I said.

My father looked over at me. "It gets more curious."

He flipped to a new page. "September 3. Drummond files paperwork with Avita to retract all previous claims. Returns check. Cites pending lawsuits with cTomic on behalf of himself and the family of the boy killed in the explosion. Two days later, several news reports come out calling the Drummond explosion a bombing and linking it to FT and Emma Turnstone."

He looked out of the passenger window and casually studied the recharging station. "FYI," he added, "no lawsuit v. cTomic ever filed, and not a word from the family of that poor boy. Not yet anyway."

"That's odd," I said.

"Some things are dealt with quietly."

Through the windshield, we watched containers being stacked like colorful Legos onto ships below.

"You can connect the final dots, I think," he said, handing me the file. "I've been curious about these charger units." He opened the door, carefully twisted his torso, and extracted himself from the low-slung car.

As he inspected the charging stations in front of the Tesla—they looked like a row of those powerful vacuum cleaners you see at a car wash—I leafed through the contents of the file and found photos of Winston Drummond that Dad had thoughtfully included. I could see why Beth referred to Drummond as 'Tom Ford handsome.' One can never be sure, but I got the sense from his athletic build, impeccable attire, and exquisitely manicured six-day stubble, that he had been neither romantically pursuing nor chased by Emma Turnstone.

On the final page of the file, I saw a custom stock chart showing shares of Rational EvoAg's major competitor, MetaMorphDNA, at $89 per share on August 19, $93 on

August 26, and $92 on September 1. By September 8, the price had fallen to $41. Not good news for the company's Chairman of the Board and majority shareholder, Curtis Turnstone.

"So," I said, once my father had struggled back into the passenger seat, "Drummond confirms the rumor in the tabloids that FT and Emma Turnstone might be responsible for the car bombing. Simply whispering to certain members of the financial media about her presence in London is enough to get fertile imaginations flowing. And to make investors nervous. Drummond not only avoids liability for the explosion, he also decimates his chief rival's reputation and market cap."

My father took the file back and placed it in his briefcase. "If you say so."

* * * * *

Two hours later I was again looking down at the harbor's array of insect-like cranes, this time from the other side of Elliot Bay and 44 stories up in the Wells Fargo Center downtown.

Curtis Turnstone had returned my call within two minutes. Now I sat in a thousand-dollar swivel chair in his Seattle office, my knees touching the glass that displayed a floor-to-ceiling panorama of sailboats and ferries dodging tugs and container ships on the dark blue waters of the bay. Farther to the west, clouds piled against the Olympic mountains.

"Thank you for coming, Nathan," said Turnstone as he entered his office, closed the door, and shook my hand. "I appreciate your discretion. Best that we talk in person." He wore the standard VC get-up: dark leather Chukka boots, expensive jeans, and a grey V-neck sweater over a black T-shirt. He looked freshly and professionally shaved and smelled vaguely of eucalyptus. I sat down again while he crossed his arms tightly across his narrow chest and leaned back against his desk. "You have news."

I spent ten minutes outlining Drummond's shady dealings and then handed Curtis a printout with a few specifics— insurance company, original claim number, and policy information. I knew he'd want it to support the story. I didn't tell him about my father's role in digging up these facts.

He looked up from the paper. I expected questions, disbelief, surprise.

"Knowing Drummond," he said, "this makes sense."

"You know Drummond?" I asked.

He cracked open a small bottle of spring water—just a few ounces—and took a swig. "He came here to pitch us several years ago. Very brash. When we funded the second round of MetaMorphDNA instead, he called me and told me I'd regret it."

"But how did he know Emma was in London?"

Turnstone paused, then raised the back of his hand to blot his lips.

"Actually," he said, "Emma told me she contacted him. A project for one of her classes. An interview about the ethics of the new gene editing techniques."

"And he knew she was your daughter?"

"I presume so," he said. "Look, as you know, my daughter has strong opinions about animal rights and genetic modification. Last time I talked with her she tore into me about our MetaMorph investment. Don't bother telling her about trying to feed 9 billion people in 2030. She doesn't want to hear it. I'm guessing she also pissed off Drummond, who certainly knew about her FT days. Emma showing up in London was a gift dropped in his lap."

He started to take another hit off the tiny water bottle, then stopped. "Come to think of it," he squeezed the bottle so it gave a hollow click, "he's probably the one who placed the boatload of shorts—short-sell options, you know—so he made money when the price fell on MetaMorph after that story broke in London. The bastard."

The plate glass made a slight pop as the building shifted in the wind. We both turned our heads to check on the giddy view over the bay with its toy-like boats.

"Nathan, I can't thank you enough for this information," he said, "and also for your discretion. I feel like I can trust you."

I thought of Beth, at this very moment dying to dig up a story on his daughter, maybe even thinking about teaming up with that tabloid reporter. I hoped she was at the cabin, waiting for Penny, staying out of trouble.

"If it all checks out," he said, "I'm confident I can make this London situation go away now."

"And the reporter at the London paper," I said, "what do you think . . ."

"I'm thinking a call from my attorney to his editor will put an end to that."

"Right."

"And even if they keep publishing that crap," he said, almost to himself, "we can limit the damage."

He must've seen the puzzlement in my look.

"You've heard of SEO, of course, search engine optimization?"

"Of course."

"Well, I'm invested in a start-up that does SEDO, de-optimization. It targets topics or products or news stories and makes it much harder to find them via standard searches."

"Wow, how does it do that?"

"Ha. Beats me. You'd need to ask the Hungarian mathematician who built it. We gave his beta a test run to protect Emma from whatever unpleasant stories might hit after Drummond's car blew."

"So," I said, "That's why it took us so long to find those *Informant* stories about the explosion."

"Pretty slick. Not perfect. Maybe not even legal. But worth an A round of 500K."

"And so . . ."

"I had already tamped down stories in the American rags. Catch-and-kill payments to the publisher. Hawk's old sports agent made the connection. Another 140K. Carolyn doesn't know a thing about all this."

"Hmm," I said, "and so . . ."

"The main thing now," he cut in, "is getting Emma back. Letting her know she's safe."

With the London bombing off the table, I thought, Emma certainly had one less reason to run, but we had to find her before we could tell her the good news.

"Well, I know your private investigator is on it," I said. "Do you think . . ."

"I think Mr. Hawk is doing his best. Although as far as bringing Emma home to safety, there's still the UW thing. Her former FT friends are very unhappy."

This time he lifted his right fist to his chin and pushed hard left then hard right, eliciting two quick cervical cracks.

"Really?" I said.

"In confidence," he said, glancing at the door and then taking his glasses off and looking directly into my eyes, "Mr. Hawk has arranged for us to pay a former FT member for an audio recording, supposedly of Emma planning the UW bombing. Some racy photos, too, apparently. For $250,000, I guess you could call it blackmail, but Hawk calls it a courtesy, an assurance that this FT kid will keep quiet. Says the kid really doesn't want any harm to come to Emma with this incriminating stuff, but evidently he does need quite a bit of cash to continue his schooling. At any rate, the courtesy payment means we'll keep the recording out of the hands of the other FT members, or anyone else who doesn't feel so kindly toward Emma."

I recalled Hawk behind the bar at Dave's place, telling us all to let him handle it.

"You trust Hawk?"

"I know Carolyn doesn't," he said. "They have some history. But I have to trust him. God knows I can't meet with these FT kids directly. Neither can our lawyer. We need a go-between. So, the money went via Hawk. We know nothing about this, you understand."

He studied his elegant shoes. "One more thing, Nathan. Hawk has been watching our Skylandia place. You know, in case Emma shows up there."

"Sure."

"Well," he continued, his eyes floating across the floor to rest on my black Rockports. The corners of his mouth dropped a few millimeters. "Caro goes up there sometimes. Alone." He raised his eyes to meet mine and paused. If we'd been sitting at a bar, he would've taken a gulp of his scotch before what came next. "Hawk tells me she might have a boyfriend over now and then. No big deal. We have an understanding."

"Oh," I said, trying to mask my surprise. "That's very . . ." My mind raced for a way to finish the ill-conceived sentence. Finding none, I started over. "You'll excuse me for asking," I said, "but why are you telling me?"

"Emma found out about her mother's," he paused to consider his words, "friends," he concluded. "She called me about it, very upset. It was the last time I heard from her. I can't tell the police any of this, but you may have the best chance of finding Emma, so I think you should know everything. And as far as I know, that's everything."

He again looked directly at me and we both did the tight-lipped grimace thing men of our generation do to show they understand each other.

"Nathan," Turnstone said, "at some point you need to tell me about your foundation. Carolyn and I are always on the lookout for worthy causes. We love to hike, but we don't seem to have the time these days."

This was my invitation to leave.

* * * * *

Back at the townhouse, my father was napping in the recliner, right where I'd left him. I placed my keys on the table in the darkened entryway and began feeling my way into the kitchen.

"Hey, Nathan," he said, startling me, "which one is channel 13 up here?"

"Thirteen is seven here," I said. "Ten is four. For CBS and ABC, subtract six from the Sacramento dial."

There was silence.

"NBC is tough. You just gotta remember. Five."

"You know, Nathan," he said, still just a voice from the dark corner of the living room, "you really don't want to be alone with those Oba boys."

"No, I don't plan to be," I said, "but thanks."

"Maybe they can work things out for themselves, without you," he said. "I don't think their father can afford any public scandal, given his past."

"Let's hope," I said.

"Well," he said, yanking on the chain of the lamp on the end table beside him and flooding the living room with light. He studied the remote in his hand. "Where's the on button on this thing?"

Chapter 21

MARY BETH DRAKE

October 21

"I do love your massive automobiles," Nigel said as the Dreadnought straddled both southbound lanes of Rainier Boulevard. The driver of a Honda Civic behind us laid on her horn, a pathetic bleating that barely registered in our climate-controlled cabin. Nigel fumbled at the controls on his armrest and the driver's-side window slid majestically downward. He stuck a hand out and waved it noncommittally in the Civic's direction. "One feels positively immune," he said.

I had one eye on the cryptic notes Emma had scrawled on the Cabin Café menu and the other on my phone's navigation app, which was helping me keep track of the street names as we flashed by them. As we'd drifted down the interstate toward Seattle, I'd spent my time searching the internet. I'd discovered a Columbia City bakery that ran an unpaid internship program for what the website said were "Differently privileged Youth, both Gluten-Free and Wheat-Centric, who are dedicated to Principled Food Creation." The place was called Upright and Ethical Baking.

"Oh lord," Nigel moaned as I read the internship application to him. "It will be a monumental moral challenge just to keep myself from slapping someone's upright and ethical face."

I tried not to let Nigel catch me snickering. Whatever else he might be, I had to admit he was entertaining company. "Well, yes, but don't let on when we get there," I said. "And remember, we need to ask for Ron St. Clair."

"It would be much simpler to ask for the man we're looking for, you know."

I rolled my eyes. During the course of our car ride, we seemed to have progressed from flirtation right through the honeymoon stage and into a state of mild irritation that I'd put at about three years along in the typical relationship. "Yes, but Jack must be hiding out with Ron or masquerading as Ron," I explained, not for the first time. "Otherwise why would Emma have written 'Ron St. Clair' on the Cabin Café menu?"

"Oh, of course," he said sarcastically. "Now that you tell me for the fourth time, it suddenly makes perfect sense." One hand on the wheel and the other resting on the window frame, Nigel yawned and goosed the Dreadnought's accelerator as I concentrated on my phone. "OK, South Ferdinand Street," I said. "Turn left here." Nigel piloted the SUV across the northbound lanes, managing to bring traffic in both directions to a halt. There was more honking, followed by increased hand flapping on Nigel's part.

"Yes, I am turning, as I am clearly indicating," Nigel muttered, "and just what are you proposing to do about it, you in your Mini Cooper?"

"All right," I interrupted. "Upright and Ethical Bakery should be right around here. Look for parking."

"It's not even a real Mini, you know," Nigel sniffed as he surveyed the jammed street, trying to spot a patch of empty curb. We cruised slowly down the block. "Here," he said triumphantly, pulling into a space reserved for the disabled.

"Can't, Nigel. It's for people who have mobility issues."

He set both hands on the giant steering wheel and pressed his forehead against them. "Must you always play by the rules?"

"It's for people who can't walk," I explained.

"Yes, I'm not the village idiot," he said, giving me a scornful look. "I understand English quite well, although you Americans have done your best to take all the meaning out of it."

I crossed my arms in front of my chest and glared back at him. "I'm not going to be seen skipping merrily away from this gigantic gift to global warming while it's parked in a handicap space," I said. "People around here are very judgmental."

He exhaled in a rush. "All right, fine. I have a pronounced limp myself, you know."

"Really? Because I haven't seen you limping."

"Comes and goes." He opened his door and swung his legs around so that his feet hung lifelessly toward the sidewalk. "Come on then, get out and help me."

He emitted a small series of impatient sighs as I thought through my next move. That's when I heard the good Samaritan. She stood, a concerned scowl on her face, a few feet away from Nigel's suddenly paralyzed legs.

"Sir, do you need help?" she asked, leaning to the left so she could look around his narrow shoulders and give me the stink eye. He looked over at me. "Do I need help?" he asked. I sat still as a mannequin in the passenger's seat, eyes forward. He turned back to the woman. "It appears I do, thanks."

"Well, it's the least a person can do," said the Samaritan sweetly.

"Maybe not the absolute least," Nigel replied with a toss of his head in my direction.

"OK then, do you have a wheelchair in the back?"

"Ehm," said Nigel. "No, not a wheelchair."

"A walker, then. Or crutches?"

"No. But if you could perhaps just lend me a shoulder."

The Samaritan was taken aback. It was clear that she hadn't counted on having to render such a personal service, one that would require her to touch a stranger. I turned my head to watch and our eyes met just briefly, but it was enough to convince her of the rightness of the cause.

"All right," she said determinedly. She took two tiny, uncertain steps toward Nigel.

"If you could just place your hip up against the seat here," he said, indicating the space between his legs. She hesitated, and he added, "Don't worry, love. Can't feel a thing from the waist down."

For a moment it looked like the Samaritan might bolt, but she was in too deep for that now. "Good, good," Nigel cooed once she was jammed rigidly against the seat. "Now I'll just loop my arm over your shoulders . . . if you could bend down just a little . . . if you could just stoop, like, perhaps, a slightly older person might hunch over . . . there we are!" He flung his left arm around her shoulder and tipped forward into a precarious standing position.

"And now, baby steps! Baby steps!" he instructed. I grabbed my daypack, exited the Dreadnought, and watched from the sidewalk as the two of them minced their way around the front of the SUV.

"If you could just carry on until we get to that seat over there," Nigel said, indicating a bench that sat just up the block from the bakery. The two tiptoed awkwardly across the sidewalk and stood in front of the bench, where Nigel executed a surprisingly graceful pirouette and drifted into a seated position. I sat next to him and fixed my gaze somewhere in the middle distance.

"Thanks, love, we'll take it from here," he told the Samaritan, removing the Dreadnought's keys from his pocket and depressing the button to lock the vehicle. The woman nodded grimly and took off at a fast pace down the block. Nigel and I sat in silence a moment longer. Finally, he said peevishly, "Now that there's no one here who could have seen us exit the vehicle, could we possibly be off to that bakery?" He stood and took off at a surprisingly fast pace, hunched and skittering, as I hurried along behind.

Upright and Ethical Baking was headquartered in a low-slung 1950s store front, the kind of place that probably housed a printing shop when it was built, and then perhaps a beauty school. Next door was a yoga studio (formerly, I bet, a hardware store) and on the other side a custom bicycle builder who served the car-free community from the site of what most likely was once a bingo hall. Nigel and I stood out front and took in the bakery's sky-blue façade and remodeled display windows, where patrons now sat in nooks occupied by polished aluminum café tables, picking at their cruelty-free pastries.

Nigel rolled his eyes. "Let's get it over with," I said, pushing open the door. We approached the counter, where a girl in braids held back by a yellow bandana gave us an eager smile. "Hello!" she said, greeting us like long-lost friends. "Know what you would like?"

"Ehm," said Nigel, eyeing the display case, "what do you have that's gluten free?"

"We have one of the widest selections of baked goods for the gluten-sensitive community in the city," the girl said. "Oh, goody," Nigel muttered under his breath. The girl looked at him, confused, but managed to carry on, "All items on the top two shelves are free of gluten."

"How about vegan?" he asked. The girl indicated the left side of the top shelf with a sweep of her hand. "Good, I'll have one of those," he said, pointing to a muffin the size of a small kitten that sat on the shelf reserved for gluten-tolerant, animal-product inclusive goods. Turning to me, he explained, "I feel as if I've been low on gluten since I left home."

I ignored him and addressed the girl. "I'm still deciding," I said as she reached for Nigel's muffin. "You know, I have a friend who is a baking intern here. I wonder if he made any of today's choices. His name is Ron St. Clair."

The girl straightened and put Nigel's muffin on a bright white plate. She wrinkled her pretty forehead. "I don't know a Ron St. Clair," she said doubtfully.

"Oh, for God's sake," Nigel huffed at me. He turned toward the young woman. "Actually, darling, we know two of the baking interns. Do you know Jack Scanlon?"

"Oh, Jack," she said, dimpling at the mention of his name. "Sure, I know Jack. He baked today." She turned and pointed to a dark, dense loaf on the cooling racks behind her. "The organic locavore 25-grain pumpernickel is his."

Nigel turned to me. "Well, well, Beth," he said. "She knows Jack. Isn't that nice? He made the upright and inedible pumpernickel today."

"In that case, I'll take a loaf," I said between clenched teeth. I took a breath and forced myself to smile at the girl. "I'm so glad to hear Jack is baking. I think this could really be an awesome new start for him, you know?" The girl smiled and nodded. "He wouldn't be around, would he? I'd just like to say hi and give him a little gift for good luck." I began to unzip my daypack.

"Oh," said the girl. "The bakers are here at night. They're never around by the time the shop opens in the morning."

"Of course," I said, trying my best to look disappointed while Nigel accepted the plate that held his mammoth muffin. "Lord," he muttered. "Should warn a man to put on his truss before taking this on."

"Do you know when Jack might be in again?" I asked, then frowned. "Oh, but that would probably be early, before the retail part of the bakery opens, right?" The girl nodded, pouting in sympathy. I sighed sadly, my hand still on the imaginary gift in the backpack. "Well, it's just that I'm not usually out this way, so I don't know how I'll get this to him." The girl and I looked at each other, both of our faces drooping as if I'd just announced that a previously scheduled stint at a very selective yoga retreat would preclude my handing out the Nobel in Stockholm. "Unless," I said, "that is, unless you know where he lives? Maybe I could just drop this by. Leave it on the porch."

"Well, sure," said the girl, smiling in relief at our having solved the problem. "He lives just around the corner. I know because he lives on St. Clair, and I used to live on St. Clair," she laughed happily. "I'm not sure which house, but you just take a right on St. Clair, and he's somewhere in that first or second block."

"Right on St. Clair. Oh, for heaven's sake. Thank you!" I said, accepting my loaf of pumpernickel and retrieving my credit card from the payment dock as Nigel, abandoning his muffin near the milk pitchers, headed through the door. "I'm sure Jack will be happy to see us." I had to run to catch up to Nigel, who had already started the Dreadnought as I pulled open the passenger side door.

"Turn around and get back on Rainier going south," I commanded, consulting my phone. "It's the next right. Damn it, Nigel. It's right on St. Clair, as in *R on* St. Clair, not Ron St. Clair."

Nigel cranked the wheel and executed a six-point turn, all while being closely observed by a young woman on a Peugeot, a brand of ten-speed bike I recognized from my grammar school days. It's so disheartening to discover the items you've grown up with are now hotly sought vintage. The young woman frowned at us, grabbed a phone out of her messenger bag, and took a photo of our SUV.

"Copying our license plate, you reckon?" Nigel said to me. "Won't matter," he yelled at the woman. "It's a rental, my dear."

"I told you people around here are judgmental."

Nigel drove on with a cool indifference to conditions around him, bullying lesser drivers, shocking screen-staring pedestrians, and scattering clumps of cyclists as if he was born to rule the open road. It was a relief to get off the gentrifying main street and into the transitioning residential district a block or two away, where sentient targets for Nigel and the Dreadnought were fewer. We cruised slowly up one side of the street then back down the other side, trying to guess which house was Scanlon's.

"Looks like we're going to have to start knocking on doors," I said glumly. Take it from me, it's no fun to rouse someone from whatever business they're conducting in the back room on a weekday afternoon, all because you want to ask a few questions.

"Hang on," said Nigel. "What's that over there?" He pointed a long finger toward an aging Volvo wagon, another token of my youth that was now coveted for faintly ironic reasons. "On the bumper," he said. "The sticker." He stopped the car, and I descended to the street to get a better look. I bent and stared, then straightened and motioned for him to lower his window. "It's a FreeThinkers sticker, all right," I said. "Look for parking."

The Volvo was parked in front of a Seattle Craftsman bungalow, likely from the 1920s or 30s, that had yet to be remodeled or even maintained with much enthusiasm. The porch sloughed to the south and the clapboard siding, probably once white, was covered in a patina of greenish black mold. I waited as Nigel planted the SUV atop the bungalow's weedy parking strip.

It took a few minutes for anyone to respond to Nigel's insistent pounding on the bungalow's door. Finally, a young man wearing only torn button-fly Levis, fastened half-way, opened the door a crack. His thick black hair was mashed and tangled on the right side, as if he'd slept on it hard. His heavy-lidded eyes were only half open, but even so, I could see they were a startling shade of light blue. Judging by the glimpse I got of his torso just above the undone buttons, he hadn't been at the bakery long enough to develop a carb problem. No wonder Emma might want to look him up when she was in town.

"What the hell is this?" he said.

"Mr. Scanlon?" Nigel asked, "from the Uptight and Indignant Bakery?"

"Upright and Ethical," I corrected as the young man eyed us suspiciously. I caught the pungent odor of pot emanating from inside the house. "Mr. St. Clair . . ."

"Scanlon," Nigel hissed, but I kept on. "My name is Beth Drake and I'm a friend of Carolyn Turnstone, Emma's mom." I flashed Carolyn's creamy calling card with authority, as if it was a search warrant. "She's worried about Emma. No one's heard from her in over a month and, well, we wonder if you might have an idea where she is. We know you and Emma were," I paused for effect, "very close."

"I don't know where Emma is," Jack Scanlon said. He cracked the door open a bit wider and I could see his left arm was arranged in a sling that kept it steady against his chest.

"Look, I'm sorry she's missing and all, but it's like I told that guy Emma's dad sent, I don't know much about what happened after daddy got her off in the UW case and she ditched the rest of us for London."

"Emma's daddy sent a guy?" asked Nigel. Scanlon looked at him doubtfully. "Yeah. The mustache guy. The one driving the dark green Porsche Cayenne. You don't see many of those in this neighborhood." He looked over at the Dreadnought, parked illegally on the yellowing grass between the sidewalk and the street. "Or you didn't used to, anyway."

"Mustache guy," I said. "Would that have been Jason Hawk?" Scanlon looked at me with more interest than he'd previously shown. "Yeah, Hawk," he said. "Used to play football, I guess." He angled his way a few more inches through the door to expose his left shoulder. "Has a hell of a grip, anyway. He about twisted my arm off when I didn't answer fast enough to make him happy. Dude has an anger management problem, if you ask me." Nigel nodded and rubbed his own shoulder in sympathy.

"Well," I said in my softest, most persuasive tones, "I am sorry to ask you to repeat yourself, but if you would tell us what you know about Emma, we'd be most grateful."

"Who's this guy?" Scanlon said, pointing his attractively unshaven chin at Nigel.

"Oh, I'm sorry, I feel as though we've already met," Nigel answered, offering his hand, which Scanlon ignored. "Nigel Turner, London *Informant*. Maybe your mates from FT told you about me."

"They aren't my 'mates.'"

"Yes, that's unfortunate," Nigel said. "But you can understand why they might be upset with you and Emma. First, Emma isn't even charged in the UW operation." He shook his shaggy head sadly. "That must have hurt. And then the Turnstones start paying for your attorney, but not their attorney. Things seem to have turned out much better for you than they did for your compadres. In prison waiting on a faint chance of appeal, after all."

"Yeah, well, the only reason I'm not with them is because I had the recording," Scanlon said defensively. "Daddy Turnstone decided he'd help me after all once he heard about that." The young man reached into the back pocket of his jeans and retrieved a small pipe, lighter, and a tiny bag of herbaceous material that looked more seriously concentrated than the leafy stuff I remembered from high school. He sighed in resignation and came through the door, letting the screen slam behind him. When he sat on the first step of the porch, Nigel and I followed suit, one on either side of the young man.

"OK. What recording?" I asked.

"The recording of Emma talking about how we all were going to burn down the oppressor's concentration camp for primates, the UW lab." He stared numbly out at the sidewalk, where a group of high school-age kids shuffled homeward, the boys and girls mixing it up with playful feints and shrieks. "We were supposed to get the monkeys and chimps out first, though."

"Where's the recording now?"

He gave me a long look, then slipped his arm out of its sling and put a pinch of the weed into his pipe. "I don't have it anymore. I gave it to mustache man. It's not like I was going to use it against her, not really. I just needed to get what I got. Ten grand, that's all, just to help with bakery tuition. And some expenses. Whatever. It's nothing to billionaire Daddy."

He looked up from his pipe. "Now I'm just into this baking thing, all right? No FT. You can tell the Turnstones—all of them—I don't need anything else. From any of them. Ever again. I promised I would delete the audio file from my iPad and I did." He lit his pipe, took a quick puff, and offered it first to me and then to Nigel. I was relieved when we both declined.

Scanlon relaxed into his exhale. "Emma sounds like she's really into FT on that file I gave the investigator dude, talking about how to get into the lab and where to put the bomb and all. But she wasn't really that important to the UW action. Not really. To her, all of us in FT were just something to pass the time. It's better that she got Daddy to pay somebody off." He closed his lips over the pipe stem, then held the lighter over the bowl for another puff. "Or whatever," he said once he'd concluded the next inhalation and exhalation. "Whatever happened, I don't need to know. And I don't miss her. Let her go off with that poor sucker Charlie. See how that works out for him."

"She went off with Charlie, did she?" Nigel asked.

Scanlon let his gaze wander over to Nigel. "So, you're a journalist," he said. "Can't you promise me immunity or something?"

"I can promise you I won't name you as the source of the information," Nigel said. "And Ms. Drake here, she may be the Turnstone's friend, but she's also working as my associate. She promises you the same. Don't you, Beth?" I nodded.

"So, I think she's with Charlie Johnson-Medra," Scanlon said, leaning forward and running his hand over his sleepy face. "I heard he and Emma had a thing going on before he took off on the PCT." He paused. "Charlie," he said. "Seriously? I guess she'd gone through just about everyone else."

"He's thru-hiking the Pacific Crest Trail?" I asked.

"Yeah," said Scanlon. "He was posting about it too. Just search 'Charlie Johnson-Medra' and you can read all the fascinating details." He laughed scornfully. "But the great writer stopped posting a couple weeks back, so who knows what he's up to now."

Nigel already had his phone out. "Is this it?" he asked holding the screen up for Scanlon to see. "Charlie's Facebook page?"

"That's it."

The last entry was an off-center photo of a battered wooden tabletop littered with syrup-smeared plates, sunglasses, and red coffee mugs. Nigel quickly scrolled back over earlier posts, checking for signs of Emma. Finding nothing, he returned to the photo of the tabletop.

Scanlon reignited his pipe and took a long pull. Leaning in to squint at Nigel's phone, he spoke in the tight voice of a person holding a hit. "That picture is new, looks like a Charlie blooper.

Butt dial kind of thing." He tried to suppress a laugh and smoke leaked from his nostrils.

I angled in behind Nigel. "Make that photo bigger, will you?" I moved closer. "That looks like the Lodge at Stehekin. Zoom in on that cup of coffee on the table. Yeah, that's Stehekin. Says so right on the mug."

"What's Stehekin?" Nigel asked.

"Nice little stopping point along the PCT, especially if you're traveling with somebody who's got some cash to spend there," Scanlon said bitterly as he leaned in again to check Nigel's phone. "And, whoa, check out what else Charlie's got on the table."

"A hat?" I asked. "Wait. That's Emma's Fair Isle beanie, isn't it?" Scanlon, putting the lighter to the pipe once more, nodded.

I was excited now and leaned over the young man to face Nigel. "The date on the post is just three days ago." I thought for a minute. "That means they're probably getting close to Harts Pass by now—the last road and resupply before the Canadian border."

"Harts Pass?" said Nigel. I nodded and turned toward Scanlon for confirmation. "Sounds about right," he said.

Nigel's feet slammed against the crumbling porch steps and slapped the sidewalk as he ran toward the SUV.

"Skinny guy's a lot faster than he looks," Scanlon said as I struggled to my feet and took off after Nigel. "Hey!" I yelled, "wait up!" But Nigel already had the Dreadnought barreling north, no doubt headed for Harts Pass.

* * * * *

Nigel Turner @nigelnews
#sweetemma and new boytoy at Harts Pass, running for the border on #pacificcresttrail. The chase is on! #londoninformant

Chapter 22

MURIEL SCHMIDELL

October 21

It was the DeRoux brothers. No mistaking the jeep in the parking lot of my Forest Service office. And now the two lamebrains were coming through my door. Five minutes before closing.

I was pretty sure they wouldn't recognize me. When you're wearing a uniform, even a goofy green one, people tend not to look past the badge.

"Hey, what can I help you with?"

Cody cleared his throat, aimed his gaze over my shoulder at Billy, our stuffed bobcat, and announced, "We need a parking pass thing for the next few days. Or whatever."

He might've been a little stoned.

"Where you going?"

"Up out of Mazama," he snapped as if the answer was obvious, eyes still on the bobcat.

"Well, sounds like you want a Northwest Forest Pass."

"Whatever." He looked at Tommy, who was unavailable to offer an opinion, being lost in contemplation of the inch-thick manual of hunter's guidelines that I've got chained to the counter over by the weather and road conditions bulletin board.

"The Forest Pass," I said. "It's good for a year and lets you park in National Forest lots."

"How much?"

"Fifty bucks."

"It's a rip off, but we don't get a choice, do we?" He turned toward his brother. "Call this the land of the free."

Cody started to reach for his wallet, but he seemed distracted by the array of dead animals we have stuffed and mounted on the wall near the spot his brother stood squinting into the hunting manual. I took the opportunity to check out their jeep. One gun in the rack. A couple of loaded backpacks filling the back seat. And behind the packs—was that the corner of a dog carrier?

"Now, you going into the state park in the Methow?" I asked. "You need a Discover Pass if you do that."

"We're just hiking up, like I said, near Mazama-type thing." Cody brought his gaze down to his brother, still spellbound by the regs. "The forest, you know, the Crest trail. Maybe."

Beth had texted me just an hour ago with a cryptic update from Seattle, which was a surprise since I thought she was snug in her little cabin waiting for Penny to come home. Instead, she was all over my phone with something crazy about needing to catch up with Emma on the Pacific Crest Trail out of Mazama. Funny that these two guys show up right now, headed the same way. I needed time to think and maybe warn Beth. It'd be easy enough to stall them with all the options for parking passes.

"So, I don't know if you might be interested in the Interagency Senior Limited Income Pass, which is good in all types of places. Ten bucks."

"What's limited income?" asked Tommy, torn from his hunting bible by the scent of a good deal.

"I think it's like $40,000 a year," I said.

"That actual income?" he asked, "or like just what you report to the IRS?"

Cody looked at his brother, at me, and then at his massive watch with its camo band. "We look like seniors to you?" he barked. "We'll take the plain old Forest Pass."

"Well, you'd be surprised." I fake-chuckled, which I'm pretty good at after fifteen years in public service. "You only need to be 52 years old for the Off-Season Golden Glow Pass. That one's good on Forest Service lands any time after October 1, so it'd work for you now. It won't work for SnoPark, though, so maybe it's not what you need." I shuffled through some paperwork officiously. "What about the All-Access U.S. Freedom Pass? That's for if you're, um, what they call it here is 'differently abled.' Or, hey, if either of you is a veteran, there's the American Hero Lifetime Pass. It's free if you've got a service-connected disability."

The brothers looked at each other, and Cody, straightening a bit, eyebrows raised, spoke. "Well, my brother here did serve in Iraq and he does have the papers for PTSD."

"That's great," I said. "I mean, not great you have PTSD." Yikes, I thought to myself. Poor Tommy. "But it's great that you can take advantage of this pass, a small thank you for your service."

I squatted down behind the counter, grabbed a brochure, and stood again.

Looking Cody in the eyes—he was definitely stoned—I handed him the brochure. "Here's some info about all the passes." He looked down at the brochure in confusion. "Oopsie!" I said, pretending I heard a phone down the hall. "I've gotta get that phone in the back. I'll get your paperwork for the Veteran's Pass, too. It's an easy three-page form. Have you two on the road in a flash."

I ducked into the hallway, locked the door behind me, and grabbed my binoculars from their usual resting place by the mail slots. I jogged down the hall to the last office on the left and pivoted toward the tinted window. Now I had a good angle on the back of the jeep, and—yes!—the cage in the back. A dog who looked a lot like Penny stood alertly, looking directly my way. I reached for my phone to text Beth.

Muriel   **5:03 PM**

DeRoux bros have dog, maybe Penny, in their jeep, heading to Mazama or PCT.

I sat at the desk and called up the front counter video cam on my computer. The damn camera was pointed out the window, but I could hear the brothers loud and clear.

Tommy: . . . just glad Juni's fat ass is gone. Thinks he can boss us. We do everything. Go to Colville. Cart the bundles to Republic. We run the wax to La Likt. And then we pack the bales. That packing's a skill, man.

Cody: You invented that pack. Should be compensated or something.

Tommy: Then we load the containers. Practically sail the damn boat. All that and we get squat. $500 per bale? C'mon, man. He's rich off the pot *and* the hay.

Cody: Hell, he was born rich. Some of us work for a living.

Tommy: Juni's bustin' our butts, man. I want out.

Cody: We'll just do this one thing, right? Then he's on his own. I'd like to see him carry a bale on his vintage Indian.

Tommy: Yeah, right! Good luck, Juni!

Cody: Where the hell did Little Miss Ranger go? We got to find that girl, get our product back. Remember, we can't have Bella talk. So, like, when we find her, tell her you'll kill all the dogs if she says anything.

Tommy: No!

Cody: Not really, man. Just tell her that. Then we lay low for a while.

On my computer screen, I saw a grainy image of an SUV pulling into the lot. Switching my gaze to the window, I saw the same car jerk to a stop next to the jeep. Porsche Cayenne. British racing green. The brothers resumed their complaints.

Tommy: Man, I just need some quiet time.

Cody: Yeah, get back to our routine. With Vizslas in the Westminster show now, we're going to make some good money.

Out in the lot, a big guy eased himself out of the fancy SUV and limped over to the jeep.

Tommy: That bastard Drake steals our dog and tries to steal our pot. What's up with that, man? See him again, three strikes you're out.

Cody: Or maybe we just come and get you, Nathan Drake. We know where you live, both places. We got Penny. We'll get you.

Tommy: Hey, I'm gonna go back there and get that ranger lady. We got to go, man.

I was leaping up to intercept Tommy when I heard the tinkle of the bell on the front door and a booming voice.

"Well, look at you two boy scouts. Thought that was your jeep."
Hawk.
I double checked the locked door, tiptoed back to the desk, and listened in to their conversation.

Cody: . . . our damn parking pass.

Hawk: Listen, we want the same things, right? Find the girl is job one. You get your wax back. You get the reward. $5,000. Mommy and Daddy get their baby girl. Right?

Cody: I guess. It's $5,000 each, though, right?

Hawk: Right. Then we deal with Junichi. And Drake.

Cody: No thanks.

Hawk: Listen to me, Cody, I have a strong feeling that Junichi's family is going to slap his wrist pretty hard.

Cody: How you know that?

Hawk: Between you and me? I've been helping Junichi's father, a courtesy, to assure that his son's involvement in your whole operation goes away.

Cody: His father? How the hell . . .

Hawk: Listen, will you? Drake knows all about your operation, right? So, I set it up. Poppa will pay if we can shut Drake up. And trust me, Poppa will make Juni go away too.

Cody: Nah, I'm not . . .

Hawk: You and Tommy play your cards right, you can step right in and keep running the whole operation. Send it to Japan or sell it somewhere else. I could help, but only if you want. A courtesy, you know, to keep things cool. You two built a nice little operation here. You deserve a break.

Cody: I don't know. We've been thinking this's too much stress.

Hawk: Hell, Junichi's poppa still needs the hay. You can go straight, just send the hay if you want. I bet he'll give you the RV.

Cody: So . . .

Hawk: So, you and Tommy should get rolling north, don't you think? Like I told you, that Tweet from the English reporter makes me think our girl and her hippie boyfriend are near Harts Pass right about now. Take you boys about three or four hours to get up there, right? You might catch 'em in their camp tomorrow morning.

Cody: Depends on how fast they are. And the weather.

Hawk: Fine. You just bring her back to me. I'll handle Drake myself.

Tommy: That Vet's Pass is gonna be great, man. Hey, ranger girl, what's taking so long?

Chapter 23

NATHAN DRAKE

October 21-22

The phone call from Beth shook me out of a late-afternoon nap. She was talking fast and my end of the call consisted mostly of short, disbelieving questions.

"You're in Columbia City?"

"Nigel drove you over?"

"Emma is on the run to Canada with who?"

"Harts Pass?"

"Tonight?"

My sluggish brain struggled to take in the new information. Beth, it appeared, was suddenly hell-bent on finding Emma before "the Brit twit" caught up with her. I was so confused that I forgot to ask about Penny.

Still shaky on details but with clear marching orders from my wife, I spent the next hour spreading out gear and freeze-dried food on the townhome's carpeted floor as my dad watched silently from his chair. Then I drove downtown to pick up Beth at the light rail station.

There are three options for driving from Seattle over the Cascade mountain range to Harts Pass. From south to north, they are: Snoqualmie Pass at an elevation of 3,000 feet, Stevens Pass at 4,000 feet, or the one-two combination of Rainy Pass at 4,500 feet and, four miles further on the same road, Washington

Pass at 5,500 feet. This highest double pass over the North Cascades Highway was our choice because it also offers the shortest route, about three and a half hours from our place in Seattle if the road is open and clear. It's a spectacular roadway, nearly in Canada, but it gets about 40 feet of snow a year. Most years, the snow closes the high pass from mid-October to mid-May.

A cold drizzle had started outside. Beth was upstairs checking road conditions and weather forecasts as she pulled together her own backpacking gear. Multitasking while packing is never ideal—trips without a toothbrush or favorite hat or worse come to mind—but I kept my mouth shut.

It was after midnight by the time we'd gathered trail staples from the aisles of the dimly lit Safeway—oatmeal, instant coffee, crackers, cheese—and loaded our packs into the Subaru. Lacey had agreed to stay at the house with my father since we had no idea how many days we'd be gone. We stopped to fill the gas tank and headed north on I-5.

The empty interstate gave us a chance to compare notes on the day. I filled Beth in on what I'd learned from Dad about Drummond and the fake bombing. As part of my new effort to be more forthcoming, I even told her about the Oba family, their racehorses, and their penchant for Sahaptin Valley hay, though I did leave out the part about my dad warning me away from Toshi and Junichi. Beth, in turn, told me about her long day with Nigel. When she said Scanlon wanted nothing more from the Turnstones, I let loose a big "hah."

"Oh, that's big of him." I said. "A quarter of a million must be his friends and family rate."

"A quarter million?" Beth asked. "Scanlon got $10,000 from the Turnstones. For his bakery tuition, he said."

"Well, Curtis said he gave Hawk $250,000 for the recording."

"What?" said Beth, slapping her thighs. "You didn't tell me the Turnstones paid a quarter million. No wonder Carolyn said Hawk's expensive. He's probably pocketing all of it except for Jack's ten grand. And he still has the recording."

LUCKY PENNY

"Even if he doesn't," I said, "the beauty is that the Turnstones can't even risk listening to the recording. They can't incriminate themselves."

"Right. They have to trust Hawk when he says that the recording would send Emma to prison."

"So, he's a blackmailer," I said.

Beth shook her head in disbelief.

"Or," I muttered as we exited the interstate, "you could say he's just providing a service."

Moving east on two-lane Highway 530, we turned silent, the distinction between blackmail and fee-for-service lost in the mist along the Stillaguamish River.

* * * * *

The moisture fattened into raindrops as we approached Darrington, where the car's digital dashboard indicated 36 degrees at 2:45 a.m. The logging town, abandoned to sleep, eked out the funding for just one streetlight. It was hanging from a telephone pole at the town's main intersection, so that's where I jumped out and gave the windshield a spray of Rain-X to keep it clear.

The road ahead was empty along the dark stretches of the Sauk and Skagit Rivers, but I drove more carefully than usual because I was anxious about deer and wild turkey jumping out in front of us. Beth was jittering her feet for more speed. She squeezed one last road conditions update from her phone before we lost coverage, but even without it, we both knew it would be snowing on the pass.

"We'll make it," she said, patting the car's dash as if it were a living thing.

More hope than evidence, I thought. But we weren't turning back. Buy the ticket, take the ride.

After we passed through the hamlet of Marblemount, the rain turned to tiny pellets of ice, which scrabbled at the windshield. The progression of weather from this point on was predictable.

197

The only real question: Would we clear the summit before the heavy snow took hold?

Just beyond the power station at Newhalem the hail transitioned to the Northwest's familiar wintry mix of rain, hail, graupel, sleet, snow, and—I swear—mud and pea gravel, which smeared across our windshield and crunched under our tires. Somewhere beyond Seattle City Light's hydropower dam, on the long, straight climb past Ross Lake and up Granite Creek, the mongrel mess of precip turned, in an instant, to a soundless, pure-white field of snowflakes. The weightless flakes danced up, down, and sideways in our headlight beams, a mesmerizing display that forced me to slow even more. A half-inch accumulation already squeaked under the tires.

Just before Rainy Pass, a snowplow rattling its tire chains roared out of the white, its huge blade held up at our neck level as it passed at high speed and disappeared downhill. Almost immediately, the flakes grew to half-dollar size and fell with gravitational urgency.

At Rainy Pass, where the Pacific Crest Trail crosses, about four inches of snow covered the roadway.

"Emma and Charlie were here maybe two days ago," Beth said.

"Harts Pass is, what? Fifteen hundred feet higher than here?" I said. We both knew the Pacific Crest Trail rolled north from Harts Pass at an elevation between 6,000 and 7,000 feet.

"When I checked his Facebook page, it looked like Charlie had a pretty good tent. A newer North Face three-season I think," Beth said, reading my mind. Emma and her boyfriend would need a sturdy tent to make it through this storm.

We were creeping along at 15 miles per hour now, completely alone, through a scene that resembled a muffled, white snow globe. Another couple inches of snow and a passenger car would be high-centering. This is why we drive a boring Subaru, I thought, not for the first time, as our little shoe-shaped tractor plodded faithfully ahead.

As we crested Washington Pass and began the descent, loss of momentum became less of a factor than visibility and braking, so I dropped the Subie into low gear. The road here was straight, but not too far ahead I knew it steepened into a sweeping downhill curve before flattening at the base of the mountains. It was somewhere on that curve that my sin of pride in the Subaru was punished and the steering wheel became useless. Our first 360 spin, as seen in the glow of our low beams, began with an unhurried panning shot of the trackless oncoming lane, followed by a sickening view of the guard rail that fronted the highway's sheer northern drop-off. Next, we gazed back uphill at our own crazy tracks in the snow, and then the merciless black of the rock face on the south side of the highway swept in front of our eyes. The second rudderless spin was much the same as the first, except faster and minus my wild cranking of the useless steering wheel and pumping of the useless brakes. Somewhere in the third or fourth soundless rotation, I remember looking over at my wife—who was covering her eyes—and wishing fiercely that I had left her somewhere safe.

We finally came to a rest in the middle of the road, facing downhill, the left turn signal ticking, just a few flakes now falling on the powdery cushion lit by our headlights. Neither of us had made a sound during the spinout. Now we looked at each other, reached out over the shifter, and squeezed hands.

"I'm sorry," Beth said, her voice shaking.

"Hey, so am I. I'm the one driving."

"No. About this whole thing. About Nigel."

I stared at my wife. Her face was intermittently lit by the ticking turn signal, off and on and off again. She turned away from me and looked out of the window at the white world beyond, and it seemed like I was staring at a stranger. I took my hand from hers and squeezed the steering wheel. "What's Nigel got to do with it?"

"Not very much, really," she said. She rubbed her runny nose slowly on her right sleeve. "Only, I got us into this particular mess because he kind of sweet-talked me, you know? He made me feel important again. Like he understood me. Wanted to be around me. Respected my work." She heaved a hiccupping sigh.

"Yeah, he respected my work so much he sprinted to his SUV so he could beat me to this story. He was like Usain Bolt out there." She sat rigid, gazing straight ahead into the snow now. "After that, I guess I wanted to beat *him* to the story. And so now we're out here spinning around in the snow."

All at once her shoulders sagged and she seemed to grow smaller in her seat. "But that's not all," she said sadly. "What I wanted more was to salvage my ego, show him I'm not the fool he thinks I am. Not the fool you think I am, either."

"What?" I didn't understand the turn this conversation was taking. "I don't think you're a fool."

"Then why didn't you tell me you were at the DeRoux's that second time? After you got bit by the dog and before you picked up the backpack." Her eyes, puffy and bloodshot with crying, met mine in a stare that was more pleading than defiant.

I was surprised. "How did you know about that?"

"So you *were* out there." She resumed staring out of the windshield at the snow, her lips pressed so tightly together they lost color. I was afraid she might start crying again.

"When you came home with a black eye and some cockamamie story about falling over a dead elk, I knew something was up. I figured it involved those two guys who are so fond of hitting you."

"But Beth, the elk part really did happen. I was at the DeRoux's when I fell and scratched my eye, but the dead elk was there, too. I tripped on it. I really did!"

"The elk doesn't matter, Nathan!" Her crying took on more force and I had to lean in and listen hard to understand her. "The part that matters is why you kept your trip to the DeRoux's place a secret at all. Why didn't you trust me enough to tell me? Do you think I'm stupid? Or maybe I'm not important enough to bother with?" She lowered her head and shook it so that her hair made a veil between us. I sat stunned for a moment, then reached out and tucked the soft curtain behind her ear. She flinched at my touch, and I felt my stomach lurch.

"You don't think you're important?" I whispered. "Beth, you're the most important thing in the world to me. That's why I'm here. That's why I'll always be here, I guess, no matter what kind of stupid messes we get into." Her shoulders jerked up and down and she brought her hands up to cover her splotchy face.

"I do keep secrets," I continued, sounding a little desperate even to myself. "You're right. But not because you're not important to me. I always thought I was protecting you, saving you from worries you didn't need."

"You don't think that's a little patronizing," she asked, "to decide for me what I can and can't handle? Let me ask you, Nathan, how am I supposed to make any kind of decision, rational or not, when I don't have information? How do I proceed, whether you like it or not, when I don't know the truth? How is anyone supposed to do that? How does all this silence help us?"

The only sound in the car was the ticking of the turn signal. I reached for the wand and flicked it off. "I should have told you about the DeRoux brothers. I should have let you call the police earlier. I should have treated you like the intelligent adult you are. I was acting like a stupid boy, honoring a promise to a girl I don't even know. If anyone ought to be sorry . . ."

Before I could finish, Beth leaned awkwardly across the shifter and kissed me. I felt her hot tears and maybe a little snot damp upon my cheeks. In the distance, we heard the beep and growl of another plow coming up the grade.

Beth pulled back and made a quick search of the center console for tissues. Finding none, she rubbed her remaining clean sleeve rapidly back and forth across her glistening nose. Finally, she looked up at me, the corners of her mouth beginning to lift just a little.

"Yeah, OK, all true," she said. "Plenty of failures on both sides of this story."

I opened my mouth to respond.

"Maybe just a little more on your side," she snuck in.

"Granted," I said. "But we're on the same side again now, right?"

"And so," she said, perking up a little in her seat, "you still want to find out what happened to Emma, right?"

As my lips parted to issue an answer, she forged ahead: "Because what those DeRoux boys don't know, and what Nigel is about to find out, is nobody kicks us to the curb." She rocked excitedly in her seat and looked at me defiantly. "Nobody slaps us around like a schoolyard bully. And, dammit, nobody steals our dog! Am I right?"

"Well," I began.

"That's the spirit," she said. "Let's go."

I eased the Subaru into low gear and we inched ahead into the snow. The plow approached, ejecting a continuous spray of snow sideways over the guard rail, and then was past us. Finally, as we dropped down alongside Early Winters creek, the snowfall thinned and we were home free on the slushy road to the tiny outpost of Mazama. That's where we'd leave the highway, cross the Methow River, and climb all over again to an even higher elevation on one of the most treacherous unpaved roads in America.

Amazingly, the Mazama Country Store was open at 5 a.m. and ready to sell us a muffin and a cup of steaming-hot Kenyan coffee, not to mention offer us a bathroom equipped with a very well-maintained Swedish low-flow. At that moment, I admired that efficient little store as much as I've admired anything in this world.

We drove to the Lost River crossing and pulled over, waiting for the first bit of light before beginning the ascent to Harts Pass. We put on our hiking boots and snow gaiters and settled into the Subaru's heated seats to enjoy the country store's homemade toasted pumpkin seed muffins with our coffee. A crust of snow, like the brittle sugar topping on a crème brûlée, accumulated on the windshield.

"You could never get this muffin in La Likt," I said. "Bakery wouldn't open till 7 and the toilet is some water guzzler American Standard circa 1975 and . . ."

My mini-rant was interrupted by the crunch of tires on the gravel road. A single wiper swipe revealed a green Porsche Cayenne charging up the road. Two minutes later, still chomping the last of our muffins, we heard the whine of an engine wound tight, and a blue Ford truck towing a rattling horse trailer sped up the rutted road, gravel and dirty snow spraying from beneath its tires.

Beth and I looked at each other.

"No trailers on this road," she said.

Licking our fingers and holstering our coffees in the cup holders, we joined the commute up to Harts Pass. Tracked snow made the first part of the climb fairly easy. As morning light revealed the sheer drop on our left, however, I clutched the wheel and tried to deflect my thoughts from exactly how, if needed, we might escape these deepening tracks in the snow and turn around. We were on the highest road in the state, and even without the snow or our recent close-call on the highway, it would have induced in me a well-founded fear. I gripped the wheel even harder and stared straight ahead. The snowfall slowly slackened, the daylight increased, and the twin grooves led on.

About two-thirds of the way up, just before a sharp switchback, we saw the horse trailer. It was still attached to the truck but tilting precariously with its left wheel dropping off the road's edge. The trailer's rear gate hung open, and if a horse had been in it before, it was gone now. As we inched by the abandoned truck on the right, we could see that its right rear wheel had spun a muddy hole while trying to pull the trailer off the ledge. Fresh boot and hoof prints surrounded the scene, but as we drove on only the hoof prints continued uphill, splitting the Porsche's tracks most of the way to the trailhead.

At last we pulled in to the trailhead parking area. The dark green Porsche, steam rising off its hood, was parked perpendicular to the trailhead along with four other snow-encrusted vehicles. Two we recognized. One was the DeRoux's green Jeep with its Metallica bumper sticker and an empty dog kennel in the back. The other, jammed up against a sign that read "Northwest Forest Recreation Pass Required," was Nigel's massive red Dreadnought.

"The enemy," said Beth. "Let's see how he likes real mountains."

"Those look like government plates," I said, pointing to a white truck with camper shell stashed a few slots away from us. "Maybe Agent Hardy finally stirred his stumps."

We got into our rain gear—Beth's jacket bright red and mine hunter orange—and wondered aloud whether the knobby tire tracks we saw headed toward the trail came from the oversize tires of a fatty bike or—could it be?— a motorcycle. With a bang, the flimsy door of the blue plastic trailhead privy suddenly flew open and a guy dressed like a model from an L.L.Bean catalogue emerged. He wore a retro quilted jacket with leather shoulder pads, thickly insulated snow pants, and heavy-duty Swiss winter boots. A thick Norwegian print wool cap was pulled low over his ears.

As he walked toward us, we recognized the limp first, and then, centered within the 16 square inches of exposed face, the mustache. Hawk. We both shook his hand, though I could tell it cost Beth some effort, and waited for him to speak.

"Hey Nate," he said to me. "Good to see you again."

Beth shot me a curious sideways look and then fired off her first question. "How did you know Emma was near here?"

"From your partner Mr. Turner," he said. Beth flinched at the mention of Nigel. "He posted an update on the *Informant* site last night, as I expect you know. Said Emma is approaching the Canadian border accompanied by," he paused, "I think he called it a 'boytoy.'"

"And he beat us both," said Beth, nodding toward the Dreadnought.

"And so did the DeRouxs," Hawk said, flicking his swaddled head toward the Jeep, his eyes never leaving Beth's.

So, he knows about the brothers, I thought.

"It's like a *Mad, Mad, Mad, Mad World* up here," I said, pointing to all the tracks in the snow leading north. "Maybe Jonathan Winters is up there somewhere."

Hawk's blank look confirmed once again my considerable age and nerdiness. He obviously had never heard of the 1960s movie, beloved by my older brothers, in which every working comedian of the day embarks on a cross-country chase for buried treasure. It was a staple of late-night TV in my formative years. Beth's raised eyebrow added to the rebuke of my comedic timing and made me realize just how sleepy and altitude-addled, or maybe just cold and giddy, I'd become.

"What's your goal, Mr. Hawk?" asked Beth. "Find Emma and bring her back to her parents? Or maybe twist a few more arms and get a little more dirt for leverage against her? That would set you up for an even bigger payday, right? God knows you could use the money."

"I could ask you the same thing, Mrs. Drake," Hawk said. "It's not clear to me what brings you and your husband along on our little camping trip today. Seems to me lots of people might be confused about that. You say I'm digging up dirt." He grunted. "You and that Brit are working together to profit from the poor girl's story. I wonder how Carolyn Turnstone will feel when she finds out what you really are." He glared at Beth, and I found myself moving a few steps closer to her.

"Far as I know," Hawk said, aiming an angry look my way, "no one's hired either of you to help, but my job has always been to find the Turnstone's missing daughter. Whatever it takes. Period." His voice turned cold and sarcastic. "You talk about twisting arms. Mr. Turnstone and I have simply taken steps to assure that fake news about the UW bombing isn't spread by people who don't share your respect for the truth."

"Oh yeah," said Beth, "I guess it's your laudable respect for the truth that explains why you've kept for yourself hundreds of thousands of dollars that Curtis Turnstone thinks went toward payments to protect his daughter."

Hawk's eyes bored into her. Beth returned the stare.

"I get paid for my services, Mrs. Drake," he said nastily. "A flat price for a straight job. And I'm good at what I do. Once I find her, I'm sure I can remove any suspicion that Emma was involved in that little dust-up in London, too. And that's a service that's worth something."

"Well, that shouldn't be difficult, since Drummond's car exploded while recharging," I said. "Pretty clear Emma had nothing to do with that."

This information was news to Hawk.

"It was a bomb," he said.

"We should go," said Beth, hoisting her pack onto her back.

"What proof do you have that it wasn't a bomb?"

"Just a hunch," I said, realizing I'd already said too much.

"Will we see you on the trail, Mr. Hawk?" snapped Beth.

"I'll be there."

We paused at the trailhead to adjust various straps and our hiking poles. The Pacific Crest Trail here showed two sets of newish prints in the snow headed south toward Stehekin. The trail northbound toward the Canadian border showed much more traffic. The fresh snow had recorded a jumble of recent boot prints, tire tracks—and paw prints, quite possibly those of a half-grown dog.

As we set out on the trail, the snow intensified again. In about a quarter mile, the hoof prints of what looked like a large horse joined the parade of tracks headed north.

Maybe Phil Silvers and Ethel Merman were up there with Jonathan Winters after all.

Chapter 24

MARY BETH DRAKE

October 22

Our run-in with Hawk fired me up, so I hit the trail going strong. Plus, I wanted to see the look on that twerp Nigel's face when I passed him on the trail. It's not an attractive admission, but at that moment, in that snowstorm, on that high and wild piece of the Pacific Crest Trail, the thought of Nigel Turner's frozen face kept me warm.

I burned to beat him to the story. Even more than that, I wanted to find Penny, whose rambling paw prints Nathan and I hoped we were following across the wide and snowy ridgetop near Harts Pass.

Yes, I kept telling myself as we marched through the stinging snow, those were the reasons the two of us were out here, finally working together, and they were good reasons, too. But the farther we advanced along the trail and the colder it got, my reasons fell away one by one until I remembered how this all started—meeting Emma—and only one question remained.

I finally said it aloud into the wind: "Where are you, Laura?"

I stopped dead. "Emma," I said loudly. "Not Laura."

Nathan was walking behind me as usual, a position he likes because, he says, that way he can keep an eye on me. Now I could hear that he'd stopped and was waiting behind me. "Did you say something?"

I shook my head, managing a weak smile, opened the arm pit vents on my storm jacket to prevent overheating, and picked up the pace. I finally knew why I was out here: I wanted to prevent another girl from disappearing.

"Hey, Beth, slow down" Nathan said. "It's slippery and we might be out here a long time today." Ice was already turning his short beard a grizzled white. I thought back to our talk in the car and wondered if I should have said anything more about Nigel. Had Nathan detected the spark between us? It seemed unlikely given his inattentiveness to issues beyond hiking, books about Charles Darwin, and sanitation, but maybe I'd never really considered the depth of my preoccupied husband's feelings. After all, he did seem to understand that his secretiveness hurt me. Maybe.

We marched north for a long hour and a half, each alone with our thoughts, even though we probably should have been talking strategy. We had none, of course. Nothing beyond beating whoever else was out there to Emma and her hapless Charlie and pulling them off the trail before the others caught up to us.

The Pacific Crest Trail north from Harts Pass traverses a long, open ridgeline with views of the jagged North Cascades range rising above rolling fields of wildflowers. At least, that's how it looks in high summer. Today, snowfall obscured the peaks and the flowers existed only among the miniature stacks of grass that the pikas had put out to dry along the trail, insurance for the little animals against the hunger of winter. Still, every now and then, the clouds above our heads pulled apart like cotton candy from a paper cone to reveal a tiny patch of hopeful blue. Pacific Northwesterners call these phenomena "sucker holes" because only suckers believe they mean the weather's clearing. After a few encouraging moments, the clouds inevitably knit themselves together again and snow falls harder than ever.

It was while we were under the influence of a sucker hole that I looked ahead and thought I saw color in a flat patch of wind-ravaged white pines downhill from the trail. I stopped, and when Nathan, head down, bumped into me a second later, I grabbed him by the arm and pointed at the trees. He dug beneath his rain jacket, pulled out a compact pair of binoculars, and brought them to his eyes, trying to work the focus with his gloved hands.

"It's some kind of tent, I think," he said. "Maybe just a tarp. Binocs fogged up before I could see."

We stood still, waiting for the snow to close around us again and obscure our approach. "I'll go first," Nathan said. He stowed the binoculars in his jacket and reached for something inside the breast pocket. When he drew his hand out again, it held a gun.

"What the hell is that?" I yelled. I'd never seen Nathan with a gun before. In fact, the only times I've ever been close to guns is when a friend on the Seattle Police force got me into the practice range. The experience cemented my general distaste for firearms. "Where did that come from?" I now demanded.

"Uncle Bob," Nathan said tersely. "Now, let me get ahead of you."

"Wait. Is it loaded? Do you even know how to use it?"

"I have the general idea."

"The general idea? Is that good enough?"

"Beth," he said, passing me by, "it's going to have to be good enough."

Nathan gave me his hiking poles and stuck both hands—the right one holding the gun—in the wide front pockets of his jacket. As we approached the group of trees, I tried to wipe my mind clear of its usual clutter, but I couldn't shake one warning my cop friend endlessly repeated: If you've got a gun, you've got to be willing to use it. I couldn't imagine my mild-mannered husband pulling a trigger, and I wasn't sure if that was a comfort or a worry.

We crept along the trail, coming closer to the flat spot and straining our eyes for movement. I saw none except the tossing of trees in the wind. In fact, I heard the sound of barking before I saw the dog. My first thought was, "Penny," but this was a more threatening sound than Penny ever made, a snarling yawp that called to mind teeth and blood.

"Get back, Beth!" Nathan yelled. I saw a greyish streak shoot across the bright snow ahead of us. Nathan took his hands from his pockets and gripped the gun in both of them. He hesitated a moment, as if he thought the sight of a gun might stop the charging dog. Then there was a flash, and a jolt I felt deep in my chest. The dog gave a high, pitiful yelp and disappeared downslope into the swirling fog. For a moment, we stood still, gaping into the clouds of snowflakes. "I'm just going to make sure it's gone," Nathan said dully, and continued walking ahead.

My legs were shaking so badly that I had trouble picking my feet up and placing them one after another along the slick path. Nathan crept before me, eyes scanning the unmarked snow on either side of our fast-disappearing trail. When I caught up to him, he turned and murmured, "No blood. No dog."

The clouds lifted slightly, and about a hundred paces away I could see a camp of sorts. Someone had strung a blue plastic tarp between the trees to block the wet southwest wind, but the little lean-to had taken on a significant snow load and the right half had collapsed.

When we got about fifty paces away from the tarp, we stopped again. "DeRoux?" Nathan yelled. No answer. He held the gun out in front of him, and I could see that he too was shaking. "Anybody in there?"

We inched forward.

"Do you need help?" Nathan yelled. A gust of wind rattled the white pines, which dropped a load of snow from their branches onto the lean-to. It sagged a few inches farther. As the newly fallen snow settled, Nathan said, "Do you see movement?" I squinted at the tarp, wishing I had my eyeglasses. "Maybe," I said. "Yeah."

"DeRoux?" Nathan called. "Tommy? Cody?"

I saw what I thought was a stick or a branch poking out from behind the tarp. Then a hatless head covered in wild curls appeared.

"Nigel?" I yelled, moving as fast as my shaking legs would go.

It looked like he'd huddled on top of some pine branches placed on the ground beneath the tarp, wrapped in some camouflage-print sleeping bags with what seemed to be two other people—or maybe bodies at this point. Now he sat on a wet log next to a cold campfire ring, shivering hard. He flinched when I touched him, then looked up and attempted a smile. "Joint byline," he said thickly, and I knew he was having trouble moving his jaw to form words. "Still stands."

"Cody?" Nathan repeated, shaking one of the figures on the ground, who slowly shifted to a sitting position. The puppy mill brothers weren't talking, but at least they were still responsive to our touch. We guessed they were somewhere in the first stages of hypothermia. We also knew the third stage ends with full organ failure and death. "You start the stove," Nathan said to me. "I'll get the space blankets." We both turned toward our packs.

We restrung the men's tarp against the falling snow, sat the three of them together and wrapped them in the silver emergency blankets from Nathan's first aid kit. Then we dosed them on cups of sweet, hot tea followed by tiny bites of chocolate. Slowly, they began to come around.

"Have you seen Emma?" I asked Nigel.

"No luck," he managed between his chattering teeth. I held his cup for him and administered small sips of tea. "I tweeted when I left Seattle. Drove like a mad man. Got to the top of that dreadful," his body gave a lurch and he fixed me with a glare. "D...death lane down below." He shook his head. "I'll never understand, Mary Beth, why you call it a 'forest road.' As if we were all setting out on an enchanting little," he shuddered again. "J...jaunt through the wood."

Obviously, Nigel was coming around. I smiled in spite of myself and turned toward the stove so he wouldn't see me laugh. For the first time since he ditched me in Seattle, I thought I might one day miss Nigel after all, but not enough to ever let him beat me to my story. "I thought I'd be all right with my torch," he continued, "but then the bloody snow started. Don't know what would have happened," he gestured to the DeRoux brothers with a shaking elbow, "if I hadn't come across these two."

"We all huddled up here last night," said one of my friends from the Smoke-N-Spit. Cody, I thought. "Got a fire going for a while. Dogs helped us stay warm."

"Yeah," said Nathan. "Look, I'm sorry about your dog. I was sure he was going to tear our throats out."

"Might have," Cody said sadly.

"But I just fired a warning shot, to scare him. I couldn't see very well, so I was just hoping not to . . ." Nathan's voice trailed into silence. "Might have worked," he said after a moment. "Didn't see any blood. Might come back."

"But you said dogs," I said to Cody. "Did you bring more than one?"

Cody nodded. "Penny," he said. "But damn if I didn't lose her again."

* * * * *

Now that I knew Nigel was at least temporarily off the story and Penny was somewhere ahead of us, I was eager to continue up the trail in pursuit of both. We'd lost a good couple of hours tending to Nigel and the DeRoux brothers and I was sure Hawk had passed us by in the storm, even on his bad knees.

"Who else is out here?" Nathan asked once the brothers had warmed up enough to talk at greater length. Nigel answered for them.

"Well, for one, there's some bastard on a bloody motorbike," he said, eyes wide in disbelief. "I thought for a moment I was hallucinating. Entirely possible that I was, but he did leave tracks, didn't he?"

"It wasn't the big Indian, was it?" asked Nathan.

Nigel's face took on the joyful look of a child receiving a cookie.

"You know, now that you ask, that was my first thought exactly!" he exclaimed. "A big Indian. Like a warrior chief in one of your old John Wayne movies."

I saw the brothers exchange glances. "Nah, would've been the Enduro," Cody muttered.

Nathan nodded. "You're sure it wasn't the little one?" he asked Nigel. "Orange color?"

Nigel seemed taken aback. He glanced at me and took a moment to answer. "Well, now. I'm not the sort who'd ever resort to that kind of stereotype. But if I had to, I'd say he was more of a reddish-brown color. A russet. Isn't that it?"

"Had to be the Enduro," Cody quietly repeated.

"No," Nigel insisted. "He was a big Indian. Surely he was." He nudged me with his elbow. "Makes for a very nice detail in the story once we recover Emma and get out of here." He buried his beaky nose in his steaming mug. "I don't think I've ever had a nicer cup of tea, Mary Beth."

"Rather have coffee with a little something in it," said Cody. He met Nathan's eyes. "But thanks, I guess. You didn't have to stop and help, and you did. Maybe I got you wrong."

"Maybe, maybe not," Nathan said evenly. Every so often he tapped the front pocket of his jacket, as if checking to see if the gun was still there. Now, he reached over to his pack and found a leather-covered whiskey flask in the water bottle pocket.

"Just a sec," I said to Nathan. "Give me that. Maybe you and Nigel should go gather some wood, get that fire going strong before we pass out refreshments."

Nathan and Nigel looked at each other, and I looked at them. They shrugged and tromped off together down the trail.

I turned again to the DeRoux brothers. "So, the dude on the motorcycle?"

"Junichi Oba," said Tommy, speaking for the first time. His brother looked at him warily and sighed, pulling the emergency blanket closer around his neck.

"Japanese dude we do a little work for," Cody said. He shook his head. "Only one I know crazy enough to go trail riding on a night with no moon. He's just lucky the PCT is so wide and gentle right here. Bet he laid it down somewhere before Jim Pass, though. He's probably bleeding in some patch of iced-over huckleberry right now."

"What kind of work do you do for him?" I unscrewed the flask's top and handed it to Cody, who took a surprisingly delicate sip and passed it to his brother.

"Work that pays better than selling apples and pears by the side of the highway or scraping weeds at some rich dude's place in Skylandia," Tommy said bitterly. "Work that's almost legal in Washington State, not that I give a rat's ass about their laws."

Tommy passed the flask back to his brother, who held it without drinking. He cocked his head and seemed to come to a decision. "Junichi's an international businessman. We take some of the weed the tribe up in Colville grows and process it into a product that's concentrated for easy shipping. He exports it along with his family's fancy-ass hay to his friends in the land of the rising sun."

"So, your product is some kind of marijuana extract?" I asked. "And that's what Emma—or Bella—stole from you?"

Cody took a quick nip on the flask and nodded.

"We were just minding our own business, trying to get by the way people do—little of this, little of that. Raise some fancy dogs to sell to west siders with more money than sense, process a little pot, rent out a room to a sexy blondie who wants to get away from Mommy and Daddy for the summer. We'll even follow the girl on the trail, like we did last night, as long as Hawk's paying a $5,000 reward for her."

"Five thousand each," Tommy added.

Cody nodded. "Anything to pay the damn taxes and keep the land in the family. Plus, you add to that all we did for that girl Bella—or Emma, whoever the hell she really is—and she takes off with a load of Junichi's product and our favorite little pup, whose gonna be a good breeder someday."

"Junichi's mad at us," Tommy said. "He says we better get back what we owe him. He says we've got a verbal contract."

"Girl would have been lucky if it was us that found her," Cody interrupted. "But Junichi," he shook his head. "Junichi is, what do you call it?" He thought for a moment. "Unpredictable."

Yeah, just ask my tomatoes, I thought. "Listen, I probably don't need to tell you this, but it's best if you don't tell Nigel any of that stuff about your guy Junichi."

"That nosy jerk?" said Cody. "Nah."

The snow had stopped, and a ray of slanting October sunshine lit up the DeRoux's little camp. We all looked up at the sky.

"Clearing?" Nigel asked, advancing toward us and dropping two bushy green branches near the fire circle.

"Not likely," replied Cody.

Nathan followed Nigel and dumped his armful of twigs and branches. He handed Cody a tube of emergency fire starter.

"We're going to go up the trail and see if we can find Emma," he told the three men. "We'll call 911 for you guys if we get a cell signal."

Cody nodded. "Gonna miss that $5,000. Might try to walk out."

Nigel snorted and accepted my offer of a last cup of hot tea. "I'm waiting for the rescue heli, boys," he said. "Better story." He grabbed my arm, "But it's your story now, love. We'll write it together when we get back to civilization."

I shrugged him off to let him know all was not forgiven. Nathan and I shouldered our packs and began following the tracks north: Junichi's motorcycle, and the horse and rider, and yes, there were Hawk's boot prints too. Every so often, under the fresh tracks, I thought I saw the older tracks of a dog. Or maybe it was coyote or fox. The snow started up again, sporadic and lighter this time.

I moved more slowly than I had earlier in the day, my muscles stiff from sitting in the cold. Training my eyes on the few feet of trail directly in front of me, I shuffled my feet one after the other. "Nathan," I said after we had hiked about a half hour, "are we sure these are hoof prints? A horse on top of the tire tracks?"

Nathan bent down for a closer look. "They sure aren't elk or deer," he said, straightening back up. We stood side by side, contemplating the tracks at our feet. I moved my head to the right as if to peek underneath to footprints made by Emma. "Where do you think they are, Nathan?"

"Charlie and Emma? If they were smart, they'd be hiding somewhere off trail right now." He looked up toward the northern horizon. "But I don't think they're smart, Beth. If they were, Emma wouldn't want to risk being seen in Stehekin and Charlie wouldn't accidentally post their location." He exhaled with a sigh. "They're probably doing what most thru-hikers do: grabbing the first flat spot they can squeeze their tent onto at the end of the day."

I nodded. "They might not even suspect anyone's looking for them," Nathan continued, half to himself. "Charlie might not, anyway. So, yeah. I bet we find them right off the trail. If we find them."

We shared an energy bar, then began climbing and descending a series of gentle passes. Cresting one pass, we could see far ahead to rolling hillsides bisected by the long, white ribbon of snow-covered trail. Suddenly, the sound of a two-stroke engine broke our silent world. Nathan grabbed his binoculars and scanned the hillside. "There!" he said, pointing toward the trail climbing the next pass. I could barely make out the orange dot shimmying up the slippery track. After the motorcyclist, maybe a little less than a mile behind, a larger and more sure-footed figure ascended the trail at steady pace.

Nathan took the binoculars from his eyes and squinted into the distance. Then he looked over at me. "It's a horse," he said. "Somebody on a horse. Looks like he's trying to catch the motorcycle."

The motorcycle gained the summit, hesitated briefly, then disappeared over the other side of the pass. The noise disappeared with it. Minutes later, the horse and rider did the same.

Chapter 25

NATHAN DRAKE

October 22

A dogged pace was not unusual for Beth. But this was different. She was clearly burning some of that hyper-amped energy she used to get when working on a big story. At least, I thought as I trudged behind her, it might help keep her warm.

"Hey, Beth, slow down," I said. "It's slippery and we might be out here a long time today."

She glanced back at me and reduced her pace. My pole scraped off a rock and I almost fell forward. She waited and listened to my mumbled curses. In another ten minutes, we were speed walking again through the mushy snow. The path still held traces of overlapping boot prints, tire impressions, hoof prints, and if I wasn't mistaken, dog prints. Not your average day on the trail.

Near the low saddle of Foggy Pass, Beth spotted the blue tarp and I pulled Uncle Bob's old revolver from my jacket. She was instantly worried. My thought was this: I'd just saved her seven miles of worry by not telling her I was packing a gun. But I suppose that was me again, deciding how much my wife could handle. Losing that habit was going to take some work.

I want to say now that I don't regret shooting at the pit bull. The part pit bull. Whatever. On a day like that, so far from the trailhead in bad weather, a serious bite could've been life-threatening. I guess even Cody DeRoux understood that. Or maybe he was just too frozen to complain much. Anyway, maybe the dog would come back.

The brothers and Nigel had spent the night huddled behind the blue tarp, sharing two thin polyester sleeping bags. I recognized, especially in the DeRoux brothers, the signs of impending hypothermia. Their jaws and tongues moved sluggishly, slurring their speech. The muscles in their forearms and hands were so powerless they could barely hold their mugs of tea, much less grip and operate the guns I was certain were inside their packs. Nigel, to judge from his mouth flapping, seemed less physically impaired by the cold.

Even after they all warmed up, it was clear this odd trio's pursuit of Emma was over. The DeRouxs, I sensed, were already mentally distancing themselves from Junichi. They were surprisingly sanguine about dealing with the consequences.

"He'll be gone soon anyway," said Cody. I wondered if he knew something or if it was just the cold talking.

Nigel, meanwhile, was busy recasting his role from scoundrel to big-hearted colleague. He acted like he was handing off the story to his lucky protégé, Beth. Her big break, he made it sound like. Nothing like a dose of bone-chilling cold and wet to alter one's perspective. Beth kept her mouth shut, but I knew she was pleased that Nigel's incapacity would work to her advantage.

* * * * *

We glimpsed the motorcycle, followed by the horse and rider, from about a mile back, getting a look at both as they approached Jim Pass. Judging from the depth of the snow filling the older boot and paw prints, I guessed that Emma and Charlie had come through the previous night, with Penny not far behind. Hawk's big footprints were still sharp and deep.

After we cleared Jim Pass, a large, rocky bowl lay ahead of us. The trail traversed the entire cirque, maintaining the same elevation until it dipped abruptly into a corkscrew of switch backs and disappeared around a corner. I knew that the Devil's Backbone, a short, exposed ridge, was around that bend. Neither motorbike nor horse were visible. We stopped to eat another energy bar and drink some of the warm water we'd poured in our bottles back at camp. We'd just taken our first steps forward when we heard a loud pop echo across the bowl.

"Gun," Beth said.

"Or motorcycle," I added.

Another 20 minutes of fast hiking put us at the top of the descending switchbacks. Stopping to lengthen my poles, I reached an ungloved hand into my rain jacket's chest pocket to double-check the gun. Warm from body heat. Moist from sweat, too. We followed the tracks down the switchbacks. Near the bottom, the trail changed from a series of gentle, back-and-forth ramps to a run of straight-down steps blasted out of solid granite. It was obvious that the motorcyclist had to push his bike down the snow- and ice-covered steps. Long, sliding boot prints with a different tread pattern from Hawk's appeared alongside the tire tracks.

At the bottom of the steps, the trail flattened out, hung a left, and led straight out along the snout of an exposed northeast-facing ridge—the Backbone. The motorcyclist seemed to have ridden again over this wind-scoured snow. The clouds parted, and I could see the expanse of the Pasayten Wilderness rolling all the way to Canada, a deep evergreen backdrop to the black rock and white ice we stood upon. I scanned the trail with my binoculars, but just as suddenly as it presented itself, that ocean of green disappeared behind a curtain of fog, snow, and hail.

Hoods back over our lowered heads, we followed in the tracks of tires, paws, hooves, and feet. They all led over the ridge and around yet another sharp left turn. Beth stopped at the curve. "Whoa," she said. "Looks like somebody went off here."

Catching up to her, I could see that the tire tracks and hoof prints plunged abruptly down the steep slope. Our eyes followed the evidence scrawled on the snow-dusted hillside by the fishtailing bike and side-stepping beast. The tracks led downhill into a wall of green, the beginning of Pasayten's legion of trees.

"There, at the bottom," I said. "The bike."

On its side against the base of the trees lay an orange motorcycle—a KTM 690 Enduro with a fat extra-capacity gas tank. I recognized it from my snooping at the DeRoux Brothers' place. It was steaming slightly. Its handlebars no longer pointed in the same direction as its front wheel, which looked bent out of true.

"Not sure if he crashed or if . . ."

"I can't see," said Beth, "Is that blood next to it, or a red bandana, or something?"

I was wiggling out of my backpack to take a look below when the heavy, wet fog suddenly lifted again. Not a full-on sun break, but a brighter white bubble within the cloud that allowed us a glimpse of our immediate surroundings. We both stopped to scan ahead down the trail, now defined only by the older boot tracks, the paw prints, and Hawk's fresher tread. The trail descended briefly and then punched through a gateway of rock slabs into a pleasing park-like scattering of evergreens within a snow-coated bowl.

Earlier in the season, the lime green tent might've blended in with the hemlock and huckleberry, the grass and the mountain ash, but today the snow acted like a contrast dye on a microscope slide to highlight its position in the bowl. Anybody coming down the trail would've spotted the fluorescent dot nestled in a cluster of trees about two hundred yards above the trail.

"Charlie," I said.

"And Emma," said Beth. "Maybe Penny, too."

We both looked down the slope again at the fallen motorcycle, then back at the tent.

"If Junichi saw the tent, he'd probably be there by now," said Beth.

"He could be hurt," I said.

A sharp crack split the air and echoed in the bowl below us.

Beth had already hoisted her pack and was cinching straps even as she moved down the trail. I hurried behind her. Our vision bubble collapsed, and we were again shrouded in fog.

We entered the wind-protected bowl—I could see why Charlie and Emma decided to spend the night here—and continued on the trail until we reached a creek. Leaving the trail, we crossed and followed the creek uphill toward the tent. Despite the steady exertion, I think we both felt the cold. Perhaps we weren't thinking clearly. At any rate, we had no real strategy to direct our actions over the next several minutes.

The tent was zipped up tight. Crusts of white snow speckled the dome. In front of the entrance, footprints crisscrossed the muddy slush. Two or possibly more sets of fresher tracks led uphill into the trees.

"Hello!" I yelled, standing at the edge of the tree cluster that protected the tent's south side.

"Emma?" yelled Beth. "Charlie? We're your friends. Nathan and Beth? We took Penny from you on the trail?"

A half-inch sheet of snow slid down the side of the nylon tent. The green dome seemed to shake slightly.

"Hello?" I tried again, creeping closer. "Emma? Are you in there?"

More shaking. A muffled moan.

"OK, I'm going to open the fly."

"We've got a gun," Beth warned just before I yanked up the zipper. That's right, I do, a wet gun in my pocket, I thought. I flung back the rainfly.

A young man with full black beard and deep-set eyes stared wildly up at me from under a red wool cap. Charlie, no doubt. He was stuffed inside a sleeping bag and he had a bandana strapped tightly around his mouth. Kneeling into the tent, I reached behind his head to untie the gag. He took a minute to swallow and flex his jaw and said, "He took Emma up the trail to get the bear bags. He's got a gun. He shot at us!"

"Big Asian guy?" Beth asked. "Ponytail?" She leaned over my shoulder to look inside the tent.

"Yeah, that's him. Everything was great until we heard the motorcycle coming. Then we heard a gunshot and Emma pretty much quit thinking about anything else. Seems like she knew who he was. From Fortune Creek. Name's Junky or something."

"What about the horse?" I asked.

"What horse?" he said, confused. "She ran off, Emma did, after the gunshot. Got dressed fast. Took my climbing pants. The Junky dude was pissed off when he got to the tent 'cause she was gone. Fired another shot in the air, tied me up. I think he followed her tracks uphill."

We realized that Charlie, curled in his bag with his neck craned up toward us, was still tied up inside the sleeping bag. I unzipped his bag part way and saw that he was naked, too. I began fiddling with a complex network of knots in the hemp belt that bound his hands behind his bare back. "Does he just want the dope back, or what?"

"He's crazy," Charlie said. "I don't know. Didn't say much. Or, I couldn't understand. I think he's hurt, or frozen from the ride."

I was having trouble getting Charlie free, so I backed out of the tent and touched Beth's arm. "I'll go up and see about Emma. You help out Charlie." I grabbed her arm until she focused her eyes on me. "Stay here, Beth."

I pulled out Bob's gun, released the safety, and held it in my right hand under my half-zipped rain jacket. The tracks led me steeply uphill into the woods behind the camp. As I came to the edge of a small meadow bisected by a narrow, meandering waterway, another gunshot split the still air, this time followed by wild barking very nearby. I ducked behind a tree and saw Emma in the middle of a little clearing, probably less than 20 yards away. She was kneeling in a snow-flecked mud puddle next to the creek. Junichi stood over her, pointing a gun at her head, while Penny pranced side-to-side beside him, barking madly.

"Shut up, dog!" he said, delivering a hard kick to Penny's ribs. The puppy squealed and skittered a few paces toward my hiding spot. I winced, imagining the damage the steel toes in those motorcycle boots could cause.

Junichi's attention returned to Emma. "Why not?" I heard him say. "Why not tell?" I could see Emma begin to answer, and they appeared to argue, though I couldn't hear everything they said over the barking dog. Penny resumed feinting back and forth, just out of boot range.

"I'll kill your little dog," Junichi yelled, pointing his gun at Penny, and then back at Emma's head. "Or maybe I'll kill the dog and you both. Right now." Emma tried to get up and he pushed her roughly back into the mud.

If I was going to make a move, this was the time. "OK," I called out in what seemed like a tiny voice, even to me. "That's enough." Taking a half step from my hiding place behind the trees, I gripped Uncle Bob's revolver in both hands and held it straight out, pointed at the spot where Junichi's eyebrows nearly met.

"Drake! What are you doing here?" Junichi yelped, swinging his gun in my direction. Now that we were aiming at each other, I realized that Junichi probably had more experience shooting people. I gripped the gun tighter, my finger searching for the trigger, and braced myself for whatever came next, either recoil or impact.

Just behind my target, I saw a reddish flash. With a muffled growl, Penny lunged for Junichi, grazing the big man's torso and barely managing to attach her coppery head to the seat of his pants. Once her teeth were set, the puppy held there as if Junichi had suddenly grown a four-legged tail, her hindquarters barely brushing the ground as he turned and swatted at her, left then right. He screamed again, more in anger than pain, and took to pointing his gun in the direction of his rear end. "Run, Emma!" I yelled just as a shot scorched the frigid air.

I dove sideways toward the trees and landed face down in the freezing ooze, lying on top of Uncle Bob's gun and trying to figure out who or what Junichi had been aiming at—Emma? Penny? Me? Slowly, I maneuvered my left hand toward the pain on the side of my head, expecting to feel the warmth of my own blood. As the sound of the gunshot faded from my ringing ears, I became aware of an odd rhythmic bellowing—a heavy mammalian breathing I was pretty sure wasn't me. Carefully I lifted my head.

Emma was running down the hillside toward camp, her arms cartwheeling crazily. In the spot she once knelt stood Junichi, speaking rapidly in Japanese, his hands raised in what looked like a salute to the snorting black horse that pawed the mud before him. On top was a rider dressed in the kind of startling white snowsuit favored by Bond villains on snow sleds.

"*Onii-san*," the rider said, addressing Junichi. "Shame."

Chapter 26

MARY BETH DRAKE

October 22

Poor Charlie, I told myself as I struggled to untie him. Try to have a little sympathy. It was hard, though, when the boy kept whining about whether Emma really loved him. Young love, I thought, who cares?

When Charlie asked whether I thought he and Emma would truly be the first in Washington State to grow teff—"you know," he said, noticing my confusion, "the gluten-free super grain"—I decided to leave him there trussed up like a pork roast. "Listen, Charlie," I said, backing out of the tent, "I've got you loosened up here. Maybe just stay put, since your pants are gone anyway."

I was chugging up the hill, trying to keep my footing in the muddy snow, when I heard a blast of gunfire from above: one shot, maybe two. From the corner of my eye, I saw a flash of bright orange near the edge of the nearest trees, and my legs stopped working. "Nathan!" I shrieked as the echo of the shots subsided. I got no answer except a long string of high-pitched syllables: Junichi. I put my head down and churned forward.

Just as I reached the trees at the lower edge of the clearing, something let out a screech that ended in an unearthly roar, and my whole body went jumpy. I slipped in the slush and fell, then slipped and fell again. It was like one of those nightmares when your ability to put one foot in front of the other suddenly abandons you just when you need it most. Something was crashing through the trees on the other side of the meadow, but I didn't have time to worry about that. I'd finally reached the spot where Nathan lay on his belly, his orange rain coat splayed open like the wings of some windblown tropical bird. Blood oozed near his left ear.

I lay in the muddy snow beside him and put my hand on his back, feeling it rise and fall with each breath. "Nathan?" I croaked.

"I'm OK," he whispered. "Hit my head, though. There a horse here or something?"

"Not shot?"

"Penny," he said. "He might've hit Penny."

I heard more moist snorting and a low moan that wasn't quite human. Junichi resumed shouting, and together Nathan and I looked toward the clearing, both expecting to see Junichi headed for us. Instead, we watched a figure dressed in sparkling white dismount from the biggest horse I'd ever seen, an animal that could have been the model for the heroic statues that dominated the city parks of my childhood. Torrents of steam billowed from its flaring nostrils as the horse danced nervously away from Junichi and its rider. The two figures moved slowly toward one another near the middle of the meadow. Penny, I noted with rising panic, was nowhere in sight.

The rider was speaking in a language I could only guess was Japanese. He—or she—held out a hand expectantly toward Junichi, who stamped his right foot. The gesture seemed oddly juvenile, especially when next Junichi thrust the hand holding the gun high in the air, as if playing keep away. I saw him take a deep breath, but before he could let loose with more invective, a crash came from the trees on the upper end of the meadow, followed by the snap of large branches breaking and the scratchy complaint of huckleberry bushes under assault. The resin scent of macerated pine needles filled the air. The figures in the meadow turned to face the sound, which slowly devolved into a breathy huffing—whoompf, whoompf, whoompf—like a teakettle made sentient and irritable.

Nathan and I looked at each other. That snuffling we'd been hearing wasn't a horse or a dog or even Junichi. "Bear," we said in unison.

"Oh, lord God!" A panicked voice rose from the clump of trees the bear occupied. "Hey there, hey bear!" The voice was familiar to me, but I couldn't quite place it. "Somebody help me!"

"Somebody's in trouble," Nathan said, his voice so measured that I wondered if he could be slipping into shock after the knock on his head. I stared at him as he got to his feet and gallantly offered me a hand up. Once we were both standing, he latched one hand onto my arm and the other onto Uncle Bob's revolver and stepped toward the men in the meadow. I stumbled alongside him reluctantly. "Doesn't seem like a good idea," I muttered. When the black horse emitted a high whinny and shot downhill through the trees, I turned to follow it. Nathan, however, still had a solid grip on my arm. "Come on," he said. "That sounds like Hawk up there."

We didn't have time to take two steps before the bear appeared. She was an impressive female, cinnamon brown, maybe 300 pounds. She stumbled out of the trees and executed a perfect Aikido roll into the clearing, landing on her rump. A white sack coated in saliva hung from her mouth. Shaking her head from side to side and still breathing noisily, she regarded the four of us: Nathan, me, Junichi, and the mysterious equestrian. The bear seemed surprised but not particularly bothered to find us in her meadow, and giving a last, slobber-spraying "woof" in our direction, she set to work gnawing on the bag.

"Somebody over there?" Nathan shouted. "Hawk?"

Hawk emerged on the edge of the trees, cradling his right arm. "Was a damn bear up here," he shouted. "Attacked. Swiped the bag back from me." I could see the long barrel of a rifle sticking up from the top of the pack on his back. As he reached around to grab the gun, he yelped in pain and dropped

227

both arms uselessly to his sides. Bright red drops of blood rolled off the fingertips of his right hand to the snow. For a moment, all of us—bear included—were perfectly still.

Nathan finally broke the silence. "You know," he said, "I think that bear is stoned. We probably ought to back away, real slow."

The bear did seem very much into her own reality, so all of us began a crablike edging toward the downhill side of the meadow while the bear, with a final disgusted snuffle, stuffed half of the sack into her foaming mouth and began sucking on it noisily. Rocking gently back and forth, she stared fixedly at the trunk of a second-growth pine that was no more than two feet in front of her.

"Hey, bear," I quietly repeated as Nathan and I inched away from Junichi. "Just passing through, bear." I was regaining my wits, or at least I thought I was. I'd come up with a plan, after all: Use the bear as cover to propel my injured husband toward the camp below. Once there, I thought, we'd round up Emma and Penny, hot-foot it back home, and bask in the gratitude of the Turnstone family.

It was an unrealistic plan. I see that now.

"Drake, you sad extortionist, stop now!" Faces averted, we edged farther downhill as Junichi continued his tirade. "Stop tiptoeing, you creeping weasel! You spying liar!"

"Tomato killer!" I yelled over my shoulder.

"Stop! I'll shoot! I'll shoot!" A shot zinged past my left side, and it seemed best that Nathan and I stop. "Ha!" Junichi yelled. "Shows you, losers!"

The snow was coming down in fat, wet flakes as the five us met in a ragged circle at the lower end of the clearing. At least the bear hadn't joined us, I thought as I took a quick inventory of firearms. The rider, whose features mirrored Junichi's, held a lethal-looking handgun. Hawk had his semi-automatic rifle, though it seemed useless to him now. Junichi still had control of his pistol, and then there was my husband, who held Uncle Bob's revolver poised at his right hip, like a gunslinger from the golden age of television.

"Toshi," Junichi said, addressing the rider. "They're the ones threatening our family." He pointed his pistol at Nathan and me.

"Me?" Nathan said, turning toward the man Junichi had called Toshi. "Me, threatening? I don't know what you're talking about."

"He's not threatening," I added for good measure. "Really, he's the least threatening person here."

The brothers regarded us silently. "Brother," Toshi said, turning to Junichi. "Our family can't afford scandal. Now, will you please get Mr. Drake's vintage pistol for me?"

"You know what I'm talking about, Drake," Junichi insisted as he tore Uncle Bob's gun from Nathan's hand. He waved the pistol at Nathan, whose innocent gaze seemed only to infuriate the cannabis exporter further. "Yes, you! You dung beetle. You," Junichi paused and searched for better adjective-noun combinations, "crazy crapper digger!" A brief expression of satisfaction crossed his bright red face. "You threaten my family with your pictures of my operation. You're going to expose my business."

Nathan again addressed Toshi. "I was just looking for my dog."

"You are a prying toilet-lover," Junichi yelled. "Spy and extortionist."

"Extortionist?" I said. "You mean like blackmail?"

"Blackmail!" Junichi screamed at us, nodding his head frantically. He placed Uncle Bob's gun in the muck at the rider's feet and pointed his own pistol at me. "Admit it: You work with the British hack. Hawk says you threaten my business with your publication."

"Mr. Hawk says that?" I asked.

"Yes!" Junichi drew the word out into multiple syllables.

"That's funny, because the only blackmailer I know is Mr. Hawk." I pointed in the direction of the private investigator, who, hunched over his injured arm, looked as if he could use Nathan's first aid kit. "And it's the Turnstones he's blackmailing, not you."

The group fell silent. "Unless, that is," I said slowly, "unless Hawk is blackmailing you and your brother, too." I squeezed Nathan's arm. "That's it, Nathan! He's going after the Obas, and we're his cover. The more we poke around the DeRoux's place, looking for Emma, the more it looks like we're gathering evidence on Junichi here." I flapped a hand in the direction of the big man and his pistol, which he still pointed my way. "And that's why he's always so royally pissed off at us."

"Huh," my husband said.

I looked at Toshi next. "I guess to you that doesn't make much sense," I began.

"Yes, it makes some sense, Mrs. Drake." Toshi nodded briefly in my direction, but his eyes were on Junichi. "Junichi," he said, placing his hand atop his brother's pistol and pushing so that it pointed toward the mud. "Hawk is our family's blackmailer."

"What? I'm not blackmailing anybody." Hawk looked up from his bleeding arm and pointed his massive chin toward Nathan and me. "These two aren't as dumb as they seem. They're making it up. Lies is what it is."

"What about the money Curtis Turnstone gave you for Scanlon's silence?" Nathan asked. "Scanlon's not getting that money, but somebody is. And what did you do with Scanlon's recording of Emma's phone calls? You're still holding that over the Turnstones' heads, aren't you?"

"Yeah," I added enthusiastically. "Plus, you've got that dirt on Carolyn, too, right? The hot tub shenanigans."

"The what?" asked Nathan.

"Junichi's right," Hawk interrupted, once more giving both of us the full benefit of his chin. "You're not only a blackmailer, you're nuts. Crazy toilet lovers. Who in their right mind volunteers to spend the summer cleaning pit toilets?" He did have a point, but given our situation I let it pass, and Hawk turned toward Toshi. "If he's not a blackmailer, why's he sneaking around your brother's property, taking pictures? Why does he have his beer pal spy on the loading operation? Why's he got his nosy wife impersonating a German? I'll tell you why:

because they can smell easy money from wealthy families, like the Turnstones *and* the Obas."

Toshi stood silently for a moment, then turned from Hawk toward his brother. "Let go of the gun, Junichi," he said quietly. "Let's settle all of this in a profitable way." With a final stamp of his foot, Junichi reluctantly handed over the pistol. Toshi pocketed it, then turned back toward Hawk, who, his pallor increasing, had taken a seat on a fallen pine. "Yes," Toshi said. "And why does Drake have less than $1 million US in his Fidelity account, and no overseas accounts?" He laughed scornfully. "Water filter royalties worth $50,000 in a good year," he said, shaking his head. "Where did he put the hundreds of thousands he got for his silence? Is there enough space in his tiny cabin to hold such a sum? Maybe he hides it in the rusty Volkswagen?"

"Nathan," I whispered. "How does he know?" My husband elbowed me silent.

"It's really no use, Mr. Hawk," Toshi continued. "Do you think you can fool a family like ours? A family with our own history of bestowing, as you call it, 'courtesies and assurances'? Once you began offering your services, your protection, you thought we wouldn't make some inquiries? We wouldn't watch you, our family's new best friend? We wouldn't notice your luxurious car? The work on your beautiful house?"

"I took your money," Hawk tried again, "but it was only to buy off Drake. I swear. If he exposed the pot business, Junichi was looking at some heavy jail time, US or Japan. You know that, Toshi. American problems require American solutions. You should be thanking me for fixing your family's problems. And while you're at it, you could pay me the second half of my fee for delivering Drake right here to you. Right here," he repeated, "where you could easily bring an end to the problem."

Toshi silently regarded Nathan and me, his own gun still ready. "It is unfortunate how information spreads," he said with genuine sadness. "Perhaps you could be useful still, Mr. Hawk," he added, his eyes lingering on us.

My knees went weak, and I held tight to Nathan, pressing my face into his wet, whiskery neck. "I love you," I whispered. He pressed his mouth to the top of my head, and I heard him take a long sniff of my hair.

Toshi, still watching us, emitted a sudden explosive sigh, and Nathan held me tighter as Junichi's baby brother peeled back the sleeve of his white jacket to check his watch. "I think, Mr. Hawk, you have just enough time to earn the second half of your payment. But first we all walk. Briskly."

"Not yet," Nathan said loudly.

Everyone went quiet. Even the bear seemed to pause in her bag-gumming and tree-staring to look at Nathan.

"You want to settle this profitably, Mr. Oba," said Nathan calmly, "then we need to talk."

"Mr. Drake?"

"At least two million dollars US in profit. In your favored account. In three days."

Two million? Did my husband have yet another secret? Was it a bluff? Or head injury?

Toshi again glanced at his watch. "So intriguing, Mr. Drake. Hard to believe. But, come on then, let's talk. Junichi, please relieve Mr. Hawk of his firearm. And the gun he has in his coat pocket, too."

Nathan let go of me, and he and Toshi stepped into the trees to talk. That's why we're still alive.

* * * * *

At camp, ten minutes later, we found Charlie dressed in a pair of too-short yoga pants, alone and tent-less next to a struggling campfire.

"Emma took off. The dog, too," he said, head down, a catch in his voice. "She took some of the gear, strapped it to that big-ass horse that came out of nowhere"—here he shook his head in disbelief—"not even a goodbye." He sniffled like a six-year-old. "Jack told me she was a user."

Charlie seemed ready to tell us more about the cruelty of love, but he stopped when he raised his head and took in our bedraggled little group—Hawk with his mangled arm, Nathan and me once again holding tight to each other, Junichi wet, unarmed, and glowering. Toshi was the only one who looked comfortable, and why not? He had his pistol in his hand and the other guns bristling from various packs and pockets. Charlie got up and moved closer to Nathan and me.

"This is unfortunate, brother," Toshi said, "It seems our transportation is gone. Your motorcycle. My horse." He shook his head. "We'll have to walk for a while." He turned to Nathan and me and gave us a slight nod.

"Mr. and Mrs. Drake," he said, a sympathetic smile crossing his lips. "You've lost your dog again. I hope you don't lose anything more. I hope you can go on with your quiet life in charming La Likt. Your foundation work, Mr. Drake. Sanitation is so necessary." He turned to me and inclined his head. "Your writing, Mrs. Drake. Perhaps you can tell the Turnstone's story."

"I'd like to do that." My teeth were chattering.

"But not the story of the Oba Family, Mrs. Drake." The smile left Toshi's face, though he remained icily polite. "Our family story is long, and it's very complex. A saga, is that correct? A story that crosses time zones and continents and can reach out and find you wherever you might be, Mr. Drake, Mrs. Drake, Charlie."

He looked at each of us closely. "I think you understand how upset our father would be if the story is told without his approval? Any part of the story? How disappointed the Oba family would be in all of you?"

The three of us stood silently next to the smoky fire, our wet clothes beginning to steam. I could hear a few stray snowflakes sizzle as they fell on the hot stones of the fire ring. Nathan spoke first.

"Mr. Oba, you can be sure we understand. All three of us." Nathan nudged me and I nodded. Charlie did too.

"I hope so, Mr. Drake, Mrs. Drake, young Charlie. I hope you won't disappoint us. Really," Toshi looked down at the gun in his hand, "you must not disappoint us."

He began to turn from us, then stopped. "One more caution." He looked directly at Nathan. "Our fathers, Mr. Drake, are of an age where social media and privacy issues can be confusing. Your father, I think, deserves a new computer and phone, yes? New accounts, passwords, and et cetera? Destruction of his current equipment? One's past should stay in the past. Your father has had such an intriguing life. Many people all over the world still rely on his discretion. He would never purposely betray them."

I had no clear idea what this little speech meant, but Nathan seemed to understand immediately.

"Unfortunate, how information spreads," my husband said coldly, mimicking Toshi.

"He is a good man, yes," Toshi said. "A good father. You must not disappoint him. You must not disappoint us." He nodded ever so slightly.

"We have a long walk now. It's best if we get started." Junichi, still glowering, began to make his way down the stream toward the trail. "You too, please, Mr. Hawk," Toshi said, motioning once more with his pistol.

"I'll stay here," Hawk said quickly, moving sideways to join us at the fire.

"No," said Toshi. "We'd prefer that you come with us, Mr. Hawk. A man with your abilities is always an asset to a family in our business. And you are now part of our family business, Mr. Hawk. You must know that."

The two men studied each other for a moment. Then Hawk smiled. He stuck out his uninjured hand as if he expected Toshi to shake it, but the rider in white only held to his pistol and stared back at the former sheriff. "Well, yes," Hawk said, awkwardly withdrawing his hand and returning it to support his savaged arm. "I'll go with you boys. I'm glad you see the potential in our partnership, Toshi. I might be able to keep an eye on this group for you in the future, for one thing. If they have a future in Sahaptin County, that is." He turned toward Nathan and me and grinned. "So long," he said. "See you around town." Then he ambled toward Junichi and Toshi, who waited just below us.

Junichi smiled at Hawk and then looked toward Nathan. "Yes, Drake," he said, "beware the one-armed man who comes back to kill your wife."

What? I nudged Nathan, who shrugged. Junichi glanced at his brother, dropped his smile, and added in a disbelieving tone, "You know. Like *The Fugitive*. The TV show." He pointed to Hawk, "The one-armed man." We stared back mutely, and Junichi shook his head. "You," he pronounced, "are hopeless."

Toshi clicked his tongue once against his teeth and gazed up at the sky. "The snow is ending, isn't it?" he said. He was right, I realized. The fat flakes were fewer, and to the west we could see a thin band of orange light stretched across the horizon like a smear of marmalade on toast. "It would be best for you to stay the night here and to hike out when the light returns in the morning, don't you agree?"

"Of course," said Nathan. "It would make sense for us to spend the night here."

"It's decided," said Toshi. "Good." He gave us a slight bow and turned toward the trail below. Nathan, Charlie, and I stood by the fire and watched until the three men reached the waterlogged PCT. We were surprised to see them head north. Surprised, but still glad to see them go.

Charlie was the first to speak. "I want to go home," he said. "I want to go home right now."

"Charlie, he told us to stay the night," Nathan said. "It was a warning not to move. He wants a head start."

"I still want to go home," Charlie said. His chest heaved and I understood he was trying not to cry. We were all wet, cold, and dumbfounded by the day's events—Charlie perhaps most of all.

Nathan put his arm around Charlie's shoulders, and I stumbled toward our packs, grateful that Emma hadn't pilfered our gear. Together, the three of us pieced together enough dry clothing to change into something warmer. I thought of Nigel and felt a twinge of fear for him. Could he survive another cold, wet night? Nathan started the stove to boil water, and Charlie and I found a cache of nearly dry wood to stoke our fire. We were putting up the tent when we heard the gunshot.

I'm almost sure it was just one shot, as hard and sharp as a hammer hitting rock, but it echoed around the mountain bowl that held our camp, repeating a half-dozen times and making each of us jump. Instinctively, I moved toward Nathan, who wrapped his arms around me. Charlie dropped to a defensive crouch. We waited for the sound to fade.

"How far away?" Charlie asked. "Who?"

Nathan shook his head. "Not that close to us, I think," he said. "Two miles? Maybe three?"

"Junichi?" I asked. "Hawk?"

Charlie straightened slowly and Nathan loosened his grasp on me. We stared into the fire until we heard the boiling water rattle the pot on our stove. I got out our insulated cups and we all quietly stirred up instant noodle soup. My hands shook so badly I could barely bring my spoon to my mouth.

After we forced the soup down, Nathan filled the pot again and started water for tea. "At least there's good news," he said. "At least the snow really does seem to have stopped." The three of us looked up at the sky, the clouds now streaked apricot and rose by thin rays of early evening sunshine.

We heard the engine before we saw the plane, a steady whine that made us all swivel our heads toward the east. When we caught sight of it, I was surprised at how low the little plane flew.

"Where'd that come from?" I shouted over the plane's twin engines.

"Of course, that's where he was going," Nathan said. "The old map shows an airstrip down the West Fork of the Pasayten. I guess it's still there."

The plane picked up altitude steadily as it headed toward our campsite. It passed directly over us—our heads back, our mouths agape—and the pilot dipped his right wing then his left, as if in salute. We watched as the plane became a speck in the sea of clouds, the sound of its engine becoming fainter and fainter until over the fading hum we could hear the insistent bark of a dog.

"Penny!" Nathan yelled as the puppy leapt toward him.

Chapter 27

Sweet Emma's Ride on the Wild Side

Exclusive: Snowy chase ends in Missing Beauty's desperate gallop to freedom

Informant reporter frees the tech heiress from baddie on bike, mysterious native horseman

By Nigel Turner
Informant Senior Staff

Brewster, Washington State, USA: Blonde and beautiful Emma Turnstone, daughter of tech billionaire Curtis Turnstone, may be on her way to China after an *Informant* reporting team discovered her on a snow-covered mountainside in Washington State. Sweet Emma was last seen riding north toward freedom on a spirited black stallion she nicked from a pair of Native American businessmen who, believing that she had stolen from them, pursued her on motorbike and horseback along the famed Pacific Crest Trail.

Informant reporters discovered the Turnstone Turn-on, missing for more than a month, with bearded boy buddy Charlie Johnson-Medra (pictured). Having learned her whereabouts from exclusive sources, our team began their search for the errant heiress in blizzard conditions and at great risk of personal injury. Aided by respected local mountain guides Cody and Thomas DeRoux and their champion search and rescue pup Penny (pictured), our team soon encountered others searching for the heiress. They included an American Indian duo who appeared to be involved in the marijuana trade, which is legal in Wild West Washington, though not among the less enlightened law enforcement in the nation's capital. The Native Americans reportedly insisted that Sweet Emma had stolen from them a concentrated form of marijuana they called "dab."

In a driving snowstorm, our reporters followed the paw prints of copper-coated canine Penny to the young lovers' bucolic campsite. There, they found that the armed Native Americans had taken Emma and Charlie hostage in an attempt to gain access to the pinched pot. Tensions heightened when an American black bear stumbled into camp, holding in its massive mandible the missing marijuana. During the confusion, daring Emma leapt aboard the Natives' horse and escaped.

Their product thoroughly consumed by the ursine intruder, the Native American businessmen faded into the snowy hills from which their honorable clansmen first emerged some 10,000 years ago. Attempts to identify and contact them are so far unsuccessful. The horse that carried Sweet Emma northward was found tethered to a tree in British Columbia's Waterton Lakes International Peace Park.

The Turnstone Turn-on herself is once again missing. She may be running under the false impression that she is wanted for questioning in an explosion involving her former love, gene tweaker Winston Drummond. However, *Informant* reporters have determined that a faulty battery charger, not a bomb, is responsible for the explosion of an experimental automobile that injured Drummond and killed a teenage boy late last summer. (See: "Plug Ugly: Drummond Car Explosion Caused by Faulty Charge")

Sources tell the *Informant* that Sweet Emma may have made her way to Vancouver, Canada and perhaps on to China—a mysterious beauty who remains unbound by man, riches, or international borders.

Stay with the *Informant Online* for news you can get nowhere else.

--end

"Cheers to you, Nigel!" the Childe Editor messaged, no doubt grudgingly. "Good old-fashioned reporting wins every time."

"Worth every quid of the expense report, darling," I muttered, awaiting the inevitable next ping.

And here it was:

"Video?"

EPILOGUE

MARY BETH DRAKE

May 3

Nathan waited impatiently all winter for fieldwork season as the grant money from the Turnstone Foundation landed in High Country Crapper's account in miraculously regular intervals. "It happened again," he'd gleefully stage-whisper to me on the first of every month, as if saying anything aloud might make the money disappear. "$4,166.66 every month over a five-year period!" Charlie, whom he'd hired as the nonprofit's first employee, would grin shyly from beneath his black beard and the two of them would resume tapping away at their laptops while Penny and I got ready to take another walk, our way of escaping tight quarters and interminable discussions of pit toilet design.

It's been a long wait till spring. The winter snows started early and ended late, with the first big storm hitting that October day we set out in pursuit of Emma. The morning after our encounter with the Oba brothers, Nathan, Charlie, and I, accompanied by Penny, found Nigel and the DeRouxs at their camp, huddled together miserably in front of a smoking fire.

"Beth!" Nigel yelped, as, frozen and exhausted, we trudged toward the meager warmth. "There's no stopping now. We've got to get to the nearest village and file the story." He pointed a long finger at the brothers and announced, "First chopper out is ours." Then he turned back to me. "Ehm, what *is* the story, Beth?"

I did my best to feed him a version that excluded the Obas, whom I portrayed as a couple of local toughs looking for some stolen weed. Scary dudes, but nothing more. Lucky for us Nigel had some fixed ideas about what went down during our snowy standoff, and I didn't feel a need to correct him.

Nathan listened carefully to my story as he squatted near our little stove, which he and Charlie had fired up for one last round of sweet tea before our ragged group took advantage of the break in the snowfall to make a push for the parking lot. As I was describing Emma's fantastic horseback escape, Penny set her head on my knee and sighed, and Nathan looked from our puppy to the pit bull mix, who was tied on a short leash a few feet away from the fire.

"I'm sorry about shooting at your dog, you know," he broke in as I wound up my heavily edited story. He turned toward Cody and opened his mouth as if to say something more—maybe something to justify his actions—but he seemed to think better of it and turned back to the stove.

Cody grunted and we all looked over at the dog, which, tucked into itself for warmth, didn't seem so ferocious now. "Well, yeah," Cody finally said. "Anyway, he came back, didn't he? Been shot at before. These rescue pit bulls. You never know what you're getting. And the Viszlas, too. I'm not sure it's such a good idea anymore. Seems like they're always sick."

"Could be the water in that pond of yours," Nathan said matter-of-factly. "That sample I took showed blue-green algae. Probably fed by the nutrients from the old cow pasture above your place. Produces Anatoxin-A, poison for dogs—elk too—even if they just swim in it. I'd be glad to keep monitoring it. There are a few things you could do to reclaim it. Add some chemicals to the pond."

Cody looked suspicious, but he told Nathan he could do what he damn well pleased since he already acts like their place is his second home anyway, and the two of them have seen a lot of each other ever since. Not just for the pond rehab, but for a beer every now and then and consultation about the latest litter of puppies. Cody even showed up for dinner at the cabin once, though we couldn't get Tommy to come. It's like the woman down at the Smoke-N-Spit said: The DeRouxs haven't had much luck in life. Bad luck or bad decisions, who knows what sends people down a crooked path?

To Nigel's disgust, there were no choppers to the rescue for us that day. Instead, we bundled everybody up the best we could and put one foot in front of the other until we reached our cars. It was an oddly anticlimactic moment. The DeRouxs racked their guns, stowed their shivering dog, and were the first out of the lot, headed, we presumed, back to the old family place. Nigel slumped in the Dreadnought, heater blasting, while Nathan stoically took our ice scraper to the expanse of his SUV windshield. Eventually, the driver's side window inched down and Nigel's beak appeared. "I'm following you down this so-called road, Mary Beth." He made it sound like an accusation. "I'm not letting you out of my sight." Finally, Charlie, Nathan, and I piled into the trusty Subaru, and Penny took up her usual place on my lap. We tried not to meet each other's eyes as we passed Hawk's snow-covered Porsche.

It's Hawk's disappearance that's been this winter's big story, ever since the Turnstones backed off their search for Emma. Nathan and I—and Charlie, for that matter—haven't heard from her. Her father, however, seems satisfied that she's somewhere safe. Maybe China is safe if you're Emma Turnstone and your dad has got some investments over there, but I'll bet she's bored and someday soon we'll all be hearing from her. Anyway, my guess is the Turnstones are pretty eager to keep Emma out of the way of the saga of Jason Hawk.

According to the official narrative, Hawk went missing in a snowstorm while on the search for Emma, a hero to the last. As Nathan and I have told investigators multiple times, we know only four things: We saw him leave with two men whose identities weren't entirely clear to us, he'd been mauled by a bear, we heard a gunshot, and we saw a plane. We have no proof that any of those things are connected, and we have no insight into Hawk's whereabouts—and never will, I might add. Around La Likt, there's plenty of talk about Hawk's drinking, his mortgage, and the lawsuit against him that his most recent girlfriend was just about to file, or so the gossips say. The betting money in town has his body slumped next to his own pistol and a bottle of Jack, probably under six feet of Cascade concrete, which is what they call snow around here.

And Junichi? I suspect he's back home, tending to the racehorses and his relationship with Poppa. But, as with Hawk, we really don't know. Either one of those men, maybe both, could've taken a bullet from Toshi. Either one, maybe both, could be in Japan. Maybe we'll get the answer this summer when the snow finally melts in the high country.

By that time, maybe the Feds will have determined if they care whose dope was in the shredded bear sack found above Emma and Charlie's camp. I suspect they care, all right. They care about burying this investigation as soon as possible. If the choice is between making a case against the missing-and-presumed-dead sports star or the daughter of a tech billionaire philanthropist—all in a state with flexible marijuana laws—they'll take none of the above, thank you very much. The fact that the Fed trackers elected to conduct their search from Harts Pass by going south toward Stehekin instead of north toward the border may be another reason their PR people are not out front on this one.

Nigel's creative efforts have had a happier outcome. As a reward for his heroics in the western wilderness, he got a promotion to an editorship at the *Informant*. He offered me a position as U.S. stringer for the paper, a contract job Nathan urged me to take. "I haven't seen you this happy for a long time," he said. "I think it's because you're writing again."

"I think it's because I'm finally warm again," I replied. But the more I thought about it, the more I figured he might be right. So, against my better judgment, I took the job. As you may have noticed on the Turnstone story, I didn't get the byline. Maybe next time.

Finally, in the slim file labeled "Beth and Nathan: Marital Progress," I suppose I can add one report. As we lay mashed together in our sleeping bags that last cold night on the trail—four creatures in a tent barely big enough for two, heartbroken Charlie already snoring loudly—Nathan told me about his conversation with Toshi. The $2 million he'd promised in exchange for our lives were the profits he estimated that the Oba family would realize if they made two immediate investments: purchasing MetaMorph shares and shorting EvoAg shares. The family completed that business just before the truth about Drummond's car explosion came out. Your basic insider trade, and not a story Nathan would have trusted me with in the recent past. His hush-hush bargaining for our lives didn't exactly sit well with me, but my fingers were finally defrosting, Nathan was alive beside me, and Penny was a warm lump in the downy valley between our feet, so I suppose at times it pays to consider the advantages of selective release of information.

Besides, Nathan assures me things are about to get better for us. This, he says, is the summer we'll finally get hot water and a reliable toilet. He's also set to build our magnificent garage, which will easily accommodate the Subaru, the Volkswagen, all of our gear, and now, the headquarters of High Country Crapper. Nathan even talks of buying a pickup truck, "a small one for Foundation work," as if he's got no recollection of his empty-truck, empty-minds tirades. Meanwhile, as plans for the magnificent garage are discussed and revised, much of our extra stuff is spilling onto the patchy lawn alongside our front porch, where it's on full display to anybody who happens by. Just like everybody else's stuff around La Likt.

I'm skeptical that, with Nathan supervising, any work crew will complete my bathroom and kitchen before the garage is built, but I do see some progress around the cabin. In fact, today Nathan's brother Andy and the increasingly present Cody DeRoux helped Nathan dig a new sewer line from our home to the street. They used the DeRoux's new mini-back hoe. I don't know where the money came from for that piece of pricey equipment, but as is the way of the locals up here, I haven't asked. Not yet, anyway.

All day long the three men played with their new toy, trading turns at driving it along the trench line, spinning it in place, scooping up a shovel load of rocky earth. They seemed impressed with the machine's capabilities as well as with their own skill, and as I watched them through the kitchen window, I grew wistful. In a lonely world, I caught myself thinking, it must be nice to have brothers who are close to you. Or sisters.

At the end of the day, as they were washing their hands under the kitchen's cold-water tap, Cody brought us up to date on his own sometimes problematic brother, whose latest career goal hinges on making the homestead suitable for vacation rental. Cody was skeptical. "I ask him," he said, "how much does he really like strangers on the property, you know? How's that worked out for him before?" Nathan nodded and fingered the side of his head. "Besides," Cody added, "we got another offer."

An import company has asked the DeRouxs if they'd be interested in going to the Port of Seattle to pick up wooden crates containing top-end Yamaha sport motorcycles.

"Which sounds great, right?" said Cody. "I mean, Tommy and me both like the bikes." He dried his hands on the kitchen towel, leaving a dark smear. "Thing is," Cody told us, "the exporter made a big deal about saving the wood from the shipping crates and hauling it to a recycler in West Seattle. Weird, huh? So, I called the recycle guy. He told me the wood is supposed to be rare oak—tight-grained, or something, he said—from some famous forest in Japan. Guy on Vashon Island wants to age his fancy-ass whiskey in it. What you call it. Small batch."

The wooden chair Cody pulled out from the kitchen table scratched across our unfinished floorboards. "Some Japanese forest," he said quietly, "near Hokkaido."

"Hokkaido is home of the Obas," I said as I watched Nathan ferry bottles of beer to the table.

"I know. And now I think maybe those crates are worth more than the bikes, which are pretty sweet rides, like $16,000 each."

"Think they're avoiding taxes?" asked Nathan.

"Or getting around some kind of crazy environmental rules? I don't really care, only why the hell is a company like that calling me?"

"Let's see," I said. "Who do we know with experience using a legal premium export as a cover for contraband?"

"Well, we'll never know," said Nathan, moving swiftly to squash any curiosity I had about Oba family members, dead or alive.

"We'll never know what?" asked Andy as he banged open the front door and reached for an unclaimed beer.

"Who owned this place in the '30s and '40s," said Nathan just before closing his lips firmly around the mouth of his bottle. Well, at least I knew the storyline behind that fib.

The men talked sewer lines and the joys of digging until their beers were empty, their voices melding into a friendly hum as I got up to watch the light leak from the sky outside the kitchen window. Across the road, a flock of black-headed grosbeaks played hide and seek among the aspens and lilac bushes, the new leaves the tender green of heartache. Penny sniffed with intense interest around the mounds of newly exposed earth.

The three men got up from the table and headed outside while I watched them through the window above the sink. Andy had his hand on Nathan's shoulder as they stood over the trench and admired their work. Cody was hosing mud off his shovels before heading home to join Tommy. I reached forward and shoved open the cranky window, which gave way with a sharp chirp.

The memory came upon me so fast I gasped aloud: turned earth and wet blossoms. A girl with a cowboy lunch box standing on a curb, waiting.

Outside, Andy went to cover the back hoe with a blue tarp. Nathan walked to the bright yellow portable toilet that now graces our front yard. The bucket of shame, he calls it.

"Hey Nate, you be careful in there," called Cody as he stopped by the yellow plastic hut on the way to his jeep. He grabbed two corners of the porta potty, set one leg back, and began to tip the tiny toilet back and forth on the soft earth.

Andy joined him, rocking from the other side. "Uh oh, it's an earthquake," he yelled. "Duck and cover. Where's little Natie?"

Sloshing sounds came from within the plastic box. Cody and Andy laughed like boys.

ACKNOWLEDGMENTS

Many thanks to:

- Courageous early readers Lynn Cavanagh, Mary Grey, and Dawn Bass, whose thoughtful comments helped make this book much less incomprehensible.
- Writing group buddies Jen Olson and Vince Bryant, whose fresh ideas greatly improved the story and who cheerfully bought most of the drinks.
- James W. Ziskin, author of the Ellie Stone mysteries and an unfailingly gracious and generous man, who provided encouragement when it was needed most.
- Greg Hollobaugh, talented artist and patient friend, whose cover design is as bright as a new penny.

Made in the USA
Columbia, SC
28 January 2023